FRANCIS DUNCAN

Behold a Fair Woman

VINTAGE

1 3 5 7 9 10 8 6 4 2

Vintage
20 Vauxhall Bridge Road,
London SW1V 2SA

Vintage is part of the Penguin Random House group of companies whose
addresses can be found at global.penguinrandomhouse.com

Penguin
Random House
UK

First published in Vintage in 2016

First published in Great Britain by John Long in 1954

penguin.co.uk/vintage

A CIP catalogue record for this book is available from the British Library

ISBN 9781784704841

Typeset in India by Thomson Digital Pvt Ltd, Noida, Delhi

Printed and bound in Great Britain by Clays Ltd, St Ives plc

Penguin Random House is committed to a sustainable future for our
business, our readers and our planet. This book is made from Forest
Stewardship Council® certified paper.

MIX
Paper from
responsible sources
FSC® C018179

FRANCIS DUNCAN

Francis Duncan is the pseudonym for William Underhill, who was born in 1918. He lived virtually all his life in Bristol and was a 'scholarship boy' boarder at Queen Elizabeth's Hospital school. Due to family circumstances he was unable to go to university and started work in the Housing Department of Bristol City Council. Writing was always important to him and very early on he published articles in newspapers and magazines. His first detective story was published in 1936.

In 1938 he married Sylvia Henly. Although a conscientious objector, he served in the Royal Army Medical Corps in World War II, landing in France shortly after D-Day. After the war he trained as a teacher and spent the rest of his life in education, first as a primary school teacher and then as a lecturer in a college of further education. In the 1950s he studied for an external economics degree from London University. No mean feat with a family to support; his daughter, Kathryn, was born in 1943 and his son, Derek, in 1949.

Throughout much of this time he continued to write detective fiction from 'sheer inner necessity', but also to supplement a modest income. He enjoyed foreign travel, particularly to France, and took up golf on retirement. He died of a heart attack shortly after celebrating his fiftieth wedding anniversary in 1988.

ALSO BY FRANCIS DUNCAN
IN THE MORDECAI TREMAINE SERIES

VINTAGE MURDER MYSTERIES

With the sign of a human skull upon its back and a melancholy shriek emitted when disturbed, the Death's Head Hawkmoth has for centuries been a bringer of doom and an omen of death – which is why we chose it as the emblem for our Vintage Murder Mysteries.

Some say that its appearance in King George III's bedchamber pushed him into madness. Others believe that should its wings extinguish a candle by night, those nearby will be cursed with blindness. Indeed its very name, *Acherontia atropos,* delves into the most sinister realms of Greek mythology: Acheron, the River of Pain in the underworld, and Atropos, the Fate charged with severing the thread of life.

The perfect companion, then, for our Vintage Murder Mysteries sleuths, for whom sinister occurrences are never far away and murder is always just around the corner . . .

This is
a
MORDECAI TREMAINE
Story

CONTENTS

THE MAN IN THE DARK

THE ship's passage through the water had transformed a light breeze into a chilling wind. By the time they were running between the buoys towards the entrance to St. Julian Harbour Mordecai Tremaine was wishing he had changed his mind about enjoying the sea trip and had made the quicker journey by air.

As the vessel brushed gently against the fenders of the jetty he picked up his suitcase and made his way somewhat forlornly along the crowded deck towards the gangway, feeling that it had not been the wisest of voyages for an elderly gentleman to make.

The passengers began to file ashore. Edging his way along he looked up to see Janet smiling and waving at him frantically, her red dress a vivid splash of colour against the blue sky behind her. Mark was with her, a more sober figure in grey flannels but smiling and nodding a welcome no less warm.

He felt a little better. He had met the Belmores in London during the previous winter. When he had accepted their invitation to spend a few weeks with them later in the year at their island home he had been sure that they would do their best to make his stay a pleasant one.

Mark Belmore reached out to take his case as he set foot on the jetty.

'Glad to see you, old man. Good journey?'

Relieved of his burden, Tremaine pushed his pince-nez back into a safer position on the bridge of his nose.

'Chilly towards the end, but the water was calm enough.'

'A cup of tea will soon thaw you out,' Janet said with a smile.

'Car's over here,' Mark put in. 'I couldn't get any closer to the boat. It's always a job finding a place to park in the season when the mail boats are in.'

Here on shore the wind was no more than a breeze again and the sun was beating down warmly upon them. As they walked along the crowded quayside Tremaine's spirits rose with his increasing physical comfort.

He was looking forward to his holiday. Recently he had been jaded and stale, oppressed by thoughts of a world given over to evil. He had deliberately chosen crime detection for his hobby; he knew that the thrill of the pursuit of the murderer would never lose its fascination for him. But it meant, inevitably, facing sometimes a black reaction, when he was overwhelmed by despair for humanity.

It was the penalty he was called upon to pay for his dual personality; for being both the crime investigator, even if an amateur, and the sentimental reader of *Romantic Stories*.

Now, perhaps, he could forget that there were such things as fear, and greed, and a judge putting on a square of black silk in a hushed courtroom.

He looked eagerly about him as Mark Belmore drove the big car from the jetty, past the piled-up tomato baskets outside the packing sheds, and into the narrow streets of the port.

The main street straggled its way from the neighbourhood of the jetty up the slope of the hill against which the town was built. Imposing branches of familiar multiple stores stood on neighbourly terms with more modest but colourful establishments bearing names which would have aroused no comment across the water in Normandy.

There was a continental flavour over its cobbled, winding length; it impressed itself excitingly upon the mind despite the obviously English holiday-makers forming the greater part of the human tide which was creating an ebb and flow of movement on the pavements and between the vehicles attempting the arduous passage from one end to the other.

When they reached the wide road running along the edge of the bay Tremaine transferred his attention to the smaller islands forming the far side of the shipping lane. The tide was full.

'Admiring the view?' Mark commented. 'I'm afraid it isn't so good at low tide. Nothing but rocks and desolation. Most visitors prefer the south and west coasts.'

A hundred yards on they left the bay road and turned inland. Instead of blue water, broken by ships and islands, they looked upon a sea of glass from which the sun was reflected in a shimmering brilliance that dazzled the eyes.

'Tomato houses?' Tremaine asked, and Belmore nodded.

'Yes. Most of the glass on the island is around here. Makes it look a bit untidy but it provides a living for a good many people.'

Open country was confined to an occasional small field; the remaining ground was occupied by houses, some of grey stone, refaced and neatly painted but evidently belonging to the period before the island's prosperity; and some of more modern construction. Nearly all of them, however, possessed an adjoining building of glass in which tomato plants flourished in hundreds.

'It seems to be very much the small man's business,' Tremaine observed.

'In the main that's the case,' Belmore agreed. 'There are one or two companies owning several thousand feet of glass apiece, but most of the growing is done on a moderate scale.'

The bungalow in which the Belmores lived was situated in the north-western part of the island, in the district of Moulin d'Or. The land was generally flat, and apart from one restricted area of cliff the small bays into which the coast was broken were flanked by low sand dunes. The bungalow was built upon a stretch of ground slightly higher than the surrounding area; it had an uninterrupted view of the sea.

'You've an ideal spot here,' Tremaine remarked, as the car turned in through the entrance.

'Well, I wouldn't describe it as ideal,' Belmore said practically. 'The scenery is much better at the other end of the island. But it has its advantages. We're pretty quiet out here and the bathings's good.'

Half an hour later Tremaine had settled himself in his room, pleasantly located on the seaward side of the bungalow, and had cleaned up after his journey. The promised cup of tea had removed the last lingering chill from his bones.

'Janet's getting a meal,' Mark told him. 'Like a stroll while we're waiting?'

They took the road leading to the beach. There was still warmth in the sun's rays and as they neared the dunes Tremaine saw two figures coming from the water, now on the ebb.

'Somebody seems to have taken a late dip.'

'They're regulars, I think,' Belmore said. One of the two figures approaching them raised a hand in recognition and he returned the gesture. 'Yes, it's Valerie and Alan Creed.'

He led the way to the sand. Tremaine, following close at his heels, saw that the two people now slipping into their bathing wraps were not as young as he had at first imagined.

The man, tall and gaunt of frame, his hair short and grizzled, was middle-aged; the woman was a little younger but no longer to be described as a girl. Nor was she good-looking. Her features were pleasant, but her figure was heavy; it was thick at the hips so that what grace she might have possessed was dulled by a hampering sluggishness of movement.

'Still keeping up the habit, I see!' Belmore called.

'Haven't missed a day yet,' the man returned.

He eyed Tremaine curiously. Belmore made the introductions and the four of them walked up the beach together.

'You'll find the island's a grand place for a holiday,' Alan Creed remarked. 'How long are you staying?'

'I haven't decided. It depends upon how long Mark and his wife are prepared to put up with me!' Mark Belmore and the Creeds appeared to be on first-name terms. 'What about you?' Tremaine added. 'Are you a bird of passage too, or have you settled here?'

'Valerie and I are somewhere in between,' Creed returned. 'We've taken a cottage indefinitely, so I suppose we can be classed as semi-permanent.'

Tremaine glanced at Valerie Creed with a frown of concentration. It was true that the name seemed vaguely incongruous; it didn't seem to match her heavy, middle-aged build. But there was something else about her that was eluding him.

She became aware of his scrutiny and he met her glance of enquiry with an apologetic smile.

'I'm sorry, Mrs. Creed. I didn't mean to be rude. I've a feeling I ought to know you. Could we have met somewhere before?'

He thought that briefly her face became taut and somehow watchful.

'No, I don't think so,' she said quickly. 'At least, your name isn't familiar to me.' She turned to her husband. 'We haven't met Mr. Tremaine before, have we, Alan?'

There was no tension in Alan Creed's manner. He shook his head unruffled.

'No, my dear. I'm sure I would have remembered him.' He raised his eyebrows in Tremaine's direction. 'Any idea where it might have been?' he asked.

Tremaine shook his head.

'Probably my memory playing tricks with me. You know how it is. You meet people and they seem to be familiar to you, but it's really because they remind you of somebody else.'

'I dare say that's it. The trouble is that we human beings can be divided too easily into types.'

Something stirred protestingly in Mordecai Tremaine's incurably sentimental soul, but before he could challenge what Creed had said the other had raised his hand to point to a narrow lane running away from the road a few yards ahead.

'Our place is just along here. Dare say we'll be seeing something of you since you're staying with Mark. We're often down on the beach.'

Tremaine watched them until they turned a bend in the lane. Belmore said:

'Nice couple. We rather suspect that they're newly-weds.'

Tremaine looked at him in surprise.

'Newly-weds?'

'I thought that would draw you out.' Belmore chuckled. 'Didn't you notice the looks they gave each other?'

'It did strike me that each of them seemed to be very much wrapped up in the other. But I didn't think of them as recently married. They seem, well, rather too old.'

'Orange blossom doesn't always belong to youth, you know. Anyway, that's what Janet says about them and when it comes to matters of that kind I'm prepared to allow her intuition a clear field.'

'What does Creed do?'

'His job? He seems to be some kind of free-lance artist. I've seen him do a few bits of sketching now and again and he has an artist's drawing-board and various odds and ends that go with that sort of thing in his cottage. I don't think they're particularly well-off. They certainly don't throw money around.'

'Artists seldom can,' Tremaine commented. 'It's little enough of it most of them have.'

They followed the road towards the headland that marked the bay's extremity. Tremaine studied the bizarre agglomeration of grey stone and concrete that straddled the headland itself. It was an architectural hybrid. Originally it had been pseudo-Gothic; now a yellow-painted convexity with tall windows bulged flamboyantly in concrete curves from the grey stone on the seaward side.

'What went wrong?' he asked.

'That's the Rohane hotel,' Belmore explained. 'Bit of an eyesore. Place was derelict for years and then somebody had all those futuristic extras stuck on in the belief that he was modernizing it. I believe he did make quite a respectable job of the inside—put in bathrooms and decent plumbing and so on—but it doesn't do much to help the view stuck up there on the headland like that.'

'Did the alterations attract the guests?'

'No, they didn't. In the end the people who'd taken it gave up the business and left the island. There's a new man running it now. Chap named Latinam. He and his sister have taken it over.'

'It's still a hotel?'

'Oh yes. There are a few people staying there, but not as many as the place can hold. Latinam doesn't seem to be worried, though. I believe he took it over more as a hobby than anything else. He doesn't appear to be concerned about making it pay, so I imagine he isn't in need of money.'

'Quite a rare bird in these days,' Tremaine remarked. 'Do you know him?'

'We nod to each other. But we're really like a village on our own out here. It doesn't take long for everybody to get to know everybody else.'

He seemed reluctant to discuss Latinam further. Tremaine was aware of a sudden restraint in his manner.

'I think we'd better be turning back,' his companion said, looking at his watch, 'or Janet will be waiting for us.'

They reached the bungalow just as Janet was beginning to look anxiously out of the window in search of them.

When the meal was over Tremaine's offer of help in clearing away was firmly turned down.

'If you're sure there isn't anything I can do,' he remarked, 'I think I'll take a stroll along by the beach.'

'Keep the old windmill as a landmark,' Belmore told him, 'and you won't be in any danger of missing your way. We're in a direct line between the windmill and the Rohane hotel.'

They had lingered over the meal and it was growing dark, but it was still possible to see the ruined windmill that had given its name to the district. Tremaine made a mental note of its position relative to the house and strolled towards the beach.

There was very little wind and the sea was sighing gently against the sand somewhere in the gathering darkness beyond the dunes. No other human figure was in sight.

Occasionally a car went past, and once a bus with no more than a handful of passengers caused him to step hastily up to the dunes, but otherwise it was a silent, lonely world.

The darkness intensified. He realized that if he was not to lose his way, or at least have his host and hostess worrying about him, it was time to retrace his footsteps.

He shivered as he turned to face in the opposite direction. There was a chill in the air now that the sun had gone down.

Ahead of him he could see two or three lights. They were close together and seemingly poised in the darkness. They puzzled him for a few moments and then he realized that they must belong to the Rohane hotel.

They appeared to be aloof, having no contact with the world; they were unfriendly to an extent that was almost sinister. The fancy was plainly absurd and he dismissed it from his mind.

He almost went past the road that led to the bungalow. Becoming suddenly aware of it he turned abruptly, and as he did so a man's figure loomed up unexpectedly in front of him so that he was only just able to avoid a collision.

'I beg your pardon!' he ejaculated, startled.

With a growl in reply the other brushed roughly past him, a vague indistinct shape against the shadow of the wall that bordered the road at this point. The sound of his footsteps moved towards the beach and then stopped, as though he had stepped on to the grass verge.

Not a particularly friendly individual. Unless, of course, he had been too startled to collect his thoughts.

Standing there peering into the darkness Tremaine was suddenly aware of a sense of foreboding. The atmosphere had become charged with evil; malign powers were abroad.

He turned and set his face determinedly towards the bungalow. It had been somebody with a grudge against the world, that was all. No need to let his imagination get out of hand just because it was dark and lonely and he was in need of a holiday.

Mark and Janet were waiting for him in the lounge when he got back and talking to them he forgot the brief incident in the gloomy lane.

It did not, in fact, recur to him again that night. But as he was undressing later something else did come back to his mind.

He found himself recalling his meeting with Alan Creed and his wife, and before he fell asleep he wondered why Valerie Creed's face had seemed familiar and where it was he had seen her before.

2

DISAPPOINTMENT FOR THE MAJOR

THE following morning, whilst Mark and Janet were occupied with the daily routine of the bungalow, Tremaine took the morning newspaper down to the beach and found a seat amongst the rocks.

There were few people about, although it was a sunny morning with only the lightest of breezes to fan the rock pools. Two small boys were working with determination on a sand castle that was sufficiently mediaeval in design to reflect a recent school lesson on historic fortifications. A middle-aged couple were settling down with the obvious intention of enjoying a placid holiday, the man with a paper-backed novel and the woman with her knitting. A stray dog was dashing in and out of the water.

Tremaine was returning to his newspaper, disappointed with the lack of any human material upon which to practise his hobby of fitting backgrounds to faces, when he heard voices behind him. He glanced around and saw that four people had appeared on the dunes and were clambering towards the rocks.

They chose a place not many yards away; bathing wraps were discarded and they stretched out in the sun.

It did not take him many moments to pair them off. The fair-haired girl was the complement of the wiry young man with the somewhat sharp features who was sprawling face downwards on the towel at her side; the girl with the dark hair was clearly much more interested in the fourth member of the party, the young man who seemed to be preoccupied and who was sitting with his hands clasped around his knees.

He was near enough to overhear what they were saying without consciously eavesdropping. The dark girl, he learned, was Ruth, and the fair one Nicola. He watched the four of them a few minutes later as they clambered over the rocks and dived in where the water was now quite deep.

Supple and hard young masculine bodies, the wet gleaming on bronzed skin; the curve of an arm where feminine beauty of form moved smoothly and cleanly against the water and the sky—Tremaine openly laid aside his newspaper to watch the better.

When they came back Nicola pulled off her bathing cap, shaking her hair free. The sharp-featured young man, whom she had addressed as Geoffrey, picked up a beach-ring and tossed it to her. An energetic game developed as Ruth and her companion joined in.

A fifth player made an uninvited appearance. The stray dog, after circling disconsolately in the neighbourhood of the two small boys, who showed no desire to welcome him, realized that a fine new opportunity had been opened up. He came bounding hopefully along the beach.

Nicola, leaping for the ring, missed it by several inches. The dog pounced upon it triumphantly.

Evading the girl's outstretched hand he headed for the rocks. Tremaine found himself facing gleaming brown eyes and menacing looking jaws. He leaned forward coaxingly.

'Good dog—here, then!'

Under the impression that he had found a sympathetic spirit the dog dropped the ring. With a quick movement Tremaine snatched it away and tossed it back to the fair-haired girl.

'Thank you,' she called. 'I think he wants to join in.'

'Dogs can't resist a game on the beach,' he returned. 'But they're rather a nuisance sometimes.'

Aware that his intervention was unwelcome, the dog did not try to carry off the ring again, but remained careering happily on the fringe of the game until the sight of a canine acquaintance scampering along at the far end of the beach caused him to bark joyously in recognition and rush off to join forces.

The four young people came back to the rocks to collect their wraps, nodding to Tremaine as they went off.

A cheerful, pleasant little crowd, he reflected as he watched them go. Clearly on good terms with each other and making the most of their holiday. He hoped he would see more of them.

In the afternoon Janet and Mark took him for a drive around the island, but he was on the beach again shortly after breakfast on the following morning.

A spell of fine weather seemed to have settled in and it was very pleasant on the rocks with the sound of the sea as a lazy background. Later in the day it would probably be too hot for comfort, but at this hour the sun was soothing without being scorching.

The same middle-aged couple made their appearance together with the two small boys, and then the fair-haired girl and her companions came down from the dunes.

She recognized Tremaine and smiled.

'Good morning.'

Tremaine adjusted his pince-nez in the habitual gesture that invariably made him seem a good deal more helpless than he was.

'Good morning. Are you going in again today?'

She nodded, her hands deftly fitting her bathing cap into position.

'Yes. It looks inviting, doesn't it?'

She was not as young as he had thought. At close quarters he could see a maturity in her face that added several years to her age. With a sense of shock he glimpsed a plain gold ring on the third finger of her left hand.

All four of them, indeed, were older than his first impression had suggested. Their light-heartedness, no doubt born of the holiday atmosphere, had given them a youthfulness which had been deceptive.

Geoffrey appeared to be the senior member of the party. There was a restraint in his enjoyment, as though he felt that to be too exuberant would occasion a loss of dignity.

He wondered whether it was Geoffrey who was the husband. Somehow he did not think so. The intimacy between Geoffrey and Nicola did not seem to be that of the married state.

On the other hand the other young man, whom he had heard them call Ivan, was quite evidently far more concerned with the dark-haired Ruth than with the fair-haired Nicola. It posed an intriguing problem.

More than that, it was challenging. He disliked being unable to put people into their correct compartments. The incident of the dog on the previous day had effected an introduction, but it was difficult to pose the right questions without being so obviously after information as to warrant a snub.

But fate came to his aid, as it often did, having apparently a warm corner for Mordecai Tremaine and his insatiable curiosity. Mark came unexpectedly down to the beach.

'Thought I might find you here,' he remarked, as he made his way over the rocks, 'sunning yourself like an old lizard.'

'I thought Janet intended to keep you running around until lunch-time.'

'She relented,' Mark said, stretching himself. 'Thought you might be feeling lonely and sent me off to console you.' He glanced around. 'Beach is pretty empty. It usually is, though, except at week-ends.'

The dark, serious-faced Ivan came running for the beach-ring in their direction. Mark waved a hand in greeting. Tremaine straightened his pince-nez hopefully.

'You know these young people, Mark?'

'They're from the Rohane hotel. They're often down here.'

'Do they live on the island?'

'Not all of them, but they seem to be spending quite a long while here this summer.'

Tremaine sat regarding the lithe figures at the water's edge.

'Who's the girl with the blonde hair? The one in the blue swim suit.'

'That's Nicola Paston.'

'She's married, isn't she?'

'She was. She's a widow. Her husband was killed a couple of years ago. His 'plane crashed on the way home from the Middle East.'

'A widow?' Tremaine pursed his lips. 'That's bad. She looks too young to have known that much tragedy.'

'In this current world,' Belmore observed, 'tragedy isn't any respecter of age, let alone persons.'

'I suppose you're right. It doesn't seem to have left a permanent scar on her, though. Being young has its compensations. It isn't too late to start again.'

'You mean Geoffrey Bendall?'

'Is that his name? I've only heard him called Geoffrey. I've been trying to make out their exact relationship. At first I thought they might be engaged and then I saw her wedding ring and couldn't fit him into the picture. Her being a widow explains it, of course.'

'Does it?' Belmore remarked, amused. 'You make it sound highly intriguing. I suppose your detective instincts just can't help coming out.'

Tremaine made no comment. The truth was that it was not so much his detective instincts as his sentimental leanings that were responsible.

He was not anxious to admit as much. He had refrained from bringing any copies of *Romantic Stories* to the island; he had not wanted Janet and Mark to discover his weakness for that particular brand of literature.

'What about Ruth?' he asked. 'The dark-haired one.'

'She's Ruth Latinam. Sister of the chap who's running the Rohane hotel. I mentioned him yesterday.'

'She isn't married, is she? I haven't noticed her wearing a ring.'

'No, she isn't married. Nor is Latinam. At least,' Belmore added, 'I suppose he isn't. He certainly hasn't a wife living with him at the hotel and I've never heard any mention of his having one anywhere else.'

The beach game broke up. The little party came back to collect bathing wraps and towels.

'You believe in taking your pleasures energetically,' Belmore remarked.

'Nothing like it,' Geoffrey Bendall said. 'Strength through joy, or the English taking their ease.'

'Stop talking like the country's oldest humorous magazine, Geoff,' Nicola Paston said. 'You know quite well we know you're not the cynic you're always trying to make yourself out to be.'

'I resent that,' Bendall said, grinning. 'You're trying to rob me of the only thing I have left—my reputation for threadbare wit!'

Belmore made the casual introductions of the beach. The fourth young man, Tremaine discovered, was Ivan Holt. It was very obvious that he was in love with Ruth Latinam; his eyes rarely left her.

'I hear that you and your brother are at the Rohane hotel, Miss Latinam,' Tremaine remarked.

'I hope you aren't going to hold it against us,' she returned with a smile. 'I'm afraid it's a terribly ugly place in some ways, but Hedley—my brother—just couldn't resist buying it.'

'Miss Latinam's brother is an irresistible character,' Geoffrey Bendall said. 'Once he makes up his mind to go after something the opposition reacts like the walls of Jericho.'

'I sometimes think it's a pity the walls of the Rohane hotel didn't fall down flat before we had an opportunity of moving in,' Ruth Latinam said lightly.

'That would have meant that we shouldn't have been able to come to it for a holiday,' Ivan Holt put in, 'and we might not have met. I'm all for your brother.'

'You don't know what you're saying, Ivan,' the girl returned, a little hesitantly.

'Look here,' Geoffrey Bendall suggested, 'why don't you two come along up to the hotel with us and have a drink? That's if you aren't doing anything.'

'Oh no,' Tremaine responded hastily, before Mark Belmore could reject the invitation, 'we aren't doing anything.'

The six of them left the beach and strolled up the road towards the unprepossessing profile of the Rohane hotel. There was a great deal of friendly banter but no serious conversation; Tremaine learned nothing more of his companions beyond the fact that none of them seemed to be troubled by cares of any kind.

It must, of course, be an illusion. It wasn't the kind of world in which anybody could be completely carefree. Not, at least, anybody with the usual thinking mechanism; and they were obviously all intelligent people.

What did they do when they were not on holiday? How did they spend their time when they were removed from this disembodied existence in which there were no backgrounds and in which they were apart from the stresses and strains besetting the ordinary business of keeping alive?

Ruth Latinam was fairly easily explained. No doubt her chief occupation—at present, anyway—was helping her brother to run the Rohane hotel.

Evidently she was finding this part of her duties to her liking; a morning on the beach in pleasant company was clearly an enviable way of earning a living.

At close quarters the hotel seemed less repulsive; the full effect of its ill-assorted exteriors could not be seen.

The lounge to which Bendall led them already possessed one occupant, an elderly man with a military air, rather threadbare now, as though it was a long while since he had wielded any actual authority and he was finding it increasingly difficult to keep his head above water.

Tremaine had met his like in the once-fashionable spas, trying pathetically, despite their brusque manner, to retain the shreds of a vanishing social standing with neither an official position nor the necessary financial means to keep up the masquerade effectively.

' 'Morning, Major,' Bendall said with a nod. 'Care to join us in a drink?'

There was a faint trace of condescension in his tone, but the military-looking man did not appear to notice it. He reacted with a speed which was all the more embarrassing because he tried so patently to hide it.

'Why, yes, my boy. Be delighted.' He crossed towards them from the seat he had been occupying at the window in the big bay overlooking the sea. 'Been down to the beach again, eh?'

'The passion of the English for cleanliness, you know, Major,' Bendall returned. 'Dinner-jacket in the jungle and all that.'

'Hrrm.' The major cleared his throat. 'Quite so. Wish I could join you.'

He seemed unaware of the irony which had been in Bendall's manner. He glanced at Belmore and Tremaine. His grey eyebrows, smoothed down over pale eyes from which the colour seemed to have been bleached by the tropical service that had wrinkled and tanned his face, rose in enquiry.

'You know Belmore, of course,' Bendall said. 'This is Mr. Tremaine, a friend of his. Mr. Tremaine, meet Major Ayres, one of our fellow residents.'

'How d'ye do.' The major held out his hand. 'Trying the island for a holiday, eh? Couldn't do better. Good climate, good food, no confounded trippers. Not much more to ask for, what?'

'No, I suppose not,' Tremaine said. He took the major's hand, wincing at the other's unexpectedly vigorous grip. 'You holidaying, too, Major?'

'Dare say you might call it that. Finished with the service now. Just settling down where I want and for as long as I feel like it. Not married. No ties. No one to bother about. Besides, makes a change after a lifetime of soldiering all over the world.'

'I imagine it does. Being able to choose where you're going instead of having the War Office do it for you must have an appeal for an old soldier, Major.'

Bendall had obtained the drinks—an elderly man who was evidently a waiter had appeared in response to his ring—and they drifted to the chairs placed in the bay. The door was pushed open and another man came in. He was much younger than the major, and whereas the major was tall, spare, and grizzled, with a vague suggestion of an old tree past its prime and toppling to destruction, the newcomer was short, round of body and face and with a jovial boisterousness born of a sense of well-being and satisfaction with the world.

'Back already, Bendall?'

The voice fitted the face. It was rich and full of a hearty approval of the way in which the universe was being conducted. Evidently, Tremaine diagnozed, a fortunate being whose own private universe was doing very nicely.

'Your sister told us you might need her later in the morning,' Bendall was saying. 'We didn't want her to incur any brotherly displeasure on our behalf.'

Once again there was that faint undercurrent of irony. Major Ayres had made rather too obvious a point of letting it be seen that he hadn't noticed it; the newcomer simply took it in his stride and metaphorically trampled it underfoot.

'You will have your little joke! The place is going to seem flat when you leave us. You're fixed up with drinks, I see. Anything else I can do for you?'

'I think you've already done enough,' Nicola Paston said.

Tremaine gave her a curious glance. Did she really have the air of one who concealed a barb, or was he up to his old tricks again?

Ruth Latinam touched her brother's arm.

'This is Mr. Tremaine, Hedley. A friend of Mr. Belmore's.'

'Is that so?' Latinam turned on his heel, rather like a well-balanced top. 'Glad to know you, Mr. Tremaine. Welcome to our little island. I take it you haven't been over here long?'

'No, I only arrived yesterday.'

'Haven't had time to get your bearings yet, then. Well, any friend of Mr. Belmore's is welcome here. Drop in any time.'

'That's very kind of you, Mr. Latinam.'

'Not at all. Moulin d'Or's a pretty compact little place when all's said and done, and we're a happy family up here at the Rohane, eh, Ruth?'

'We like our guests to be happy,' Ruth Latinam said quietly.

Tremaine pushed up his pince-nez. He studied Hedley Latinam, aware that he had never met the man before and yet conscious of some vaguely familiar atmosphere about him. He belonged in some other setting.

Mark Belmore was sitting next to Ivan Holt.

'Are you going to the sand racing?'

Holt looked uncertain. His glance flickered towards Ruth Latinam.

'I haven't made up my mind,' he said doubtfully. 'It rather—depends.'

Latinam overheard him. The hotel proprietor's jovial face took on a knowing expression, significant but good-humoured.

'Maybe we can make one or two guesses about that!'

Ivan Holt looked uncomfortable. His sensitive face became shadowed with a sudden tenseness.

'Maybe,' he said shortly.

'Women!' Latinam announced, his smile wide. 'Never can made up their minds! What about it, Ruth? Are you going to put him out of his misery?'

Ruth Latinam's dark eyes were troubled. Tremaine saw the flush creep up from her graceful throat.

'I don't know what you mean, Hedley.'

He held up his hands in mock defence.

'All right, all right. I'm sorry. Didn't mean to put my foot in it. Just taking a friendly interest in my sister's welfare, that's all. Why don't we make up a party and all go?'

'Fine,' Geoffrey Bendall said. 'Transport on the house and seats overlooking the hairpin bend. I'm all for it. Any other takers? You, Nicola?'

'Just what is this sand racing?' she asked.

'The local motor-car and motor-cycle clubs are holding a race meeting at Firon Bay,' Ivan Holt said. 'There aren't any suitable roads on the island so they're marking out a track on the sands.'

'But won't the sand be too soft?'

'It'll firm up well enough once the tide's gone back, and they'll arrange to finish the programme before it's due to come in again. There've been several quite successful meetings.'

'Sounds like a thrill,' Nicola Paston said.

'Don't expect too much. There won't be any speed records broken. But it should make an interesting afternoon. There are several really good drivers in the local clubs.'

Mark Belmore glanced enquiringly at Tremaine.

'Does it appeal to you? Janet was wondering this morning whether you'd like to go to the meeting.'

'It sounds rather promising.'

'Capital,' Hedley Latinam interposed. 'Why not come with us?'

'We don't want to butt in on your arrangements,' Belmore said diffidently.

'Don't let that bother you. I like a crowd around me. The vulgar streak, I suppose!' Latinam chuckled at himself. 'Come on, let's make a date of it. Your friend's on holiday and I dare say your wife will appreciate a little extra company. The ladies do, you know.'

'That's true enough.'

'It's settled, then. We'll leave just after lunch. Round about two o'clock. The meeting's due to start at half-past so there'll be ample time.'

Latinam's enthusiasm had stirred the others. Even Geoffrey Bendall was revealing more interest. Major Ayres, who had been hovering indeterminately on the fringe of the group, edged nearer the centre of things.

'Should be a jolly good show, what? Must be years since I saw any car racing.'

Hedley Latinam turned very slowly. Something of the joviality seemed to have gone out of his face although he was still smiling.

'I'm sorry you won't be able to join us, Major. It's just too bad.'

The major's expression changed.

'Too—too bad?' he echoed hesitantly.

'I remember your telling me that you'd be going into St. Julian Harbour tomorrow on some business or other. Pity that. It means that you won't be able to get back in time to come along with the rest of us.'

'Business?' The major seemed disconcerted. He cleared his throat. 'Hrrm. Yes. Of course. Stupid of me to have overlooked it.' He finished his drink with a good deal more haste than he had so far shown and set down his glass on the bar at one side of the room. 'Got to be off now. Promised to call on a fellow in the village this morning about a fishing trip.'

'Don't let us keep you, Major,' Latinam said. 'You'll be in to lunch, of course?'

'Hrrm. Yes, be in to lunch,' the major returned.

He went out. His face had the expression of a small boy who had just been robbed of a treat upon which he had set his heart.

3

CONFIDENTIAL BUSINESS

MARK BELMORE looked at his watch.

'I think we ought to be making a move as well,' he observed to Tremaine. 'Janet wants us back in good time so that we can make an early start this afternoon.'

'Something laid on?' Latinam asked breezily, and Belmore nodded.

'We thought about running down to the other end of the island. For the scenery.'

They made their farewells and took the road that led towards the bungalow.

'Mr. Latinam seems to be on good terms with his guests,' Tremaine commented.

'I suppose it's part of his business.'

There was a touch of dryness of dryness in Mark's manner and Tremaine regarded him shrewdly. Although his friend had not said so in words his manner left little doubt that his opinion of Hedley Latinam was not high.

'His sister seems a very charming woman.'

'It amazes me,' Mark said, 'to think that Ruth and Hedley Latinam are brother and sister. They seem so unlike, not only in looks but in temperament as well.'

'I suppose that isn't so very unusual. You find striking divergencies of character even in members of the same family.'

'Well, *you* should know. I dare say you've made a study of that kind of thing in the course of your criminal investigations.'

Tremaine straightened his pince-nez with a gesture of embarrassment.

'You're making it sound too grand, Mark. Any investigation I've been mixed up with has been mainly carried out by the police. I'm just an amateur who's had a certain amount of luck once or twice.'

Belmore grinned.

'That isn't what *I've* heard.'

Ahead of them down the road they could see Major Ayres. He was carrying a stick, but he was stepping out briskly for all his greyness and his years. In the hotel lounge Tremaine had had the impression of a man past his prime but now the major's spare figure was erect and he was walking with a purposeful stride.

'I was puzzled just now, Mark,' he said, probing. 'Apart from Miss Latinam and her brother all the people we met are guests at the hotel, aren't they?'

'Yes, that's right.'

'I couldn't make out the relationships. Between Mr. Latinam and the others, for instance. He seemed much more familiar towards them than I would have expected—more like another member of the party.'

'That was just his way. Latinam's always like that. He isn't in the place to make money and he doesn't have to keep a guard on his tongue for fear he'll say something to upset one of his guests. I dare say that helps to make sure that nothing does go wrong. After all, it's one of the laws of economics that the more money you have the more you can borrow; and I imagine it works out on much the same lines where the hotel business is concerned! Besides, they've all been there for some while now. The Rohane doesn't appear to do anything with the ordinary fortnight's holiday visitors.'

'You mean they've had time to get used to each other? I suppose that does explain it. What about Major Ayres? Has *he* been staying there long?'

'He's the oldest inhabitant. Apart from Mrs. Burres. She was probably still in her room. Sometimes she doesn't appear before lunch-time.'

'The major and Mrs. Burres are more or less permanent?'

'Latinam took them over with the hotel. Part of his agreement I shouldn't wonder. I feel rather sorry for the major and the old lady. Neither of them seem to have any relatives to speak of—none who have much of an interest in them, anyway. They came to the island because they wanted a reasonably warm spot to settle in and couldn't afford to pay too high a price for it.'

They reached the bungalow in good time for lunch and when their meal was over and Tremaine had insisted on helping to clear it away they set out on their excursion.

That part of the island where the Belmores lived was the lower end of it; the land sloped, gently at first and then quite steeply, up to the south-western end, which was visible as a tree-clad plateau rising out of the plain. Mark drove towards this high ground, taking a route through the centre of the island which passed near the ruined windmill that was the reason for the name of the surrounding district.

At close quarters it was plain that it was in a dilapidated condition; its sails, broken and split, hung dejectedly, and the body of the windmill was open to the sky in several places.

'So that's Moulin d'Or.' Tremaine turned to keep it within view as the car threaded its way down the narrow lane through which they were travelling. 'Why golden windmill? It looks anything but that!'

'It used to belong to the wealthiest man in the district,' Janet told him. 'I'm going back a hundred years now, long before the island knew anything about making money out of tomatoes and tourists. He used to grind all the corn that was grown on this side of St. Julian Harbour and he used to charge a high price for doing it. He was supposed to have a hoard of golden coins hidden in the mill and that's how it came to be called Moulin d'Or.'

'And *did* he have a hoard of gold?'

'Nobody seems to know. Some people said that he did and others that it was all rumour and that there was no gold at all. Whatever was the truth, either the gold or the rumour of it killed the miller in the end. He was found one morning lying outside his mill with his throat cut. Nobody ever found out who did it, and nobody—not to talk about it, anyway—ever discovered about the gold.'

'I suppose plenty of people have tried to find it?'

'Well, they did at first, and then the story grew up that the mill was haunted. There were all sorts of tales about the miller's ghost having been seen—guarding his treasure, I suppose—and the islanders have always kept well away from it. That's why it looks so dilapidated. It's a wonder it hasn't tumbled down long ago.'

'It's an interesting story, anyway,' Tremaine remarked. 'I must go across sometime and have a closer look at it.'

'Better watch out for the miller then!' Mark told him with a chuckle. 'Ghosts can be awkward customers to deal with!'

The island scenery had already grown more attractive than that to be found in the flat and rather untidy-looking area of the bungalow with its low, stone walls and light, sandy soil. They were climbing the slope leading to the plateau now, and when he glanced back Tremaine saw that blue water was visible on either hand; the entire stretch of coastline to the west was clearly outlined. The grey pointed tower of the church at Moulin d'Or rose out of the plain; the sun's rays shimmered upon the glass of the greenhouses clustered thickly around it.

'You're looking at the workshop,' Mark commented. 'It hasn't much beauty but it helps to keep the island solvent.'

They drove on through a green countryside of scattered houses and small farms to reach the coast at the island's other extremity. To gain the bay which was their objective they had to descend a long, winding lane, bordered by tall hedgerows. At intervals during their descent a turn in the path or a gap in the hedges gave them a glimpse of the beach with its surrounding cliffs.

They passed a number of holiday-makers, laden with bathing wraps, towels, and hold-alls, plodding steadily in the opposite direction. Despite the perspiration glistening on his forehead, for they had had to leave the car at the head of the lane, Tremaine's sentimental soul was expanding.

'I like a scene like this. It makes you forget about the unpleasant things like war, and murder, and treachery, you have to read about in the newspapers every day.'

'Wars, and murders, and treachery need human beings to bring them about,' Mark Belmore said soberly. 'All the raw material's here, you know, just as it is anywhere else. How do we know what's going on inside the minds of the men and women we meet? They may look as though they're perfectly happy, without an evil thought in their minds, but we can't be certain of it.'

Tremaine stopped for a moment or two at the bend in the path at which they had just arrived and regarded his friend curiously.

'What's on your mind, Mark?' he asked quietly.

'Nothing,' Belmore returned quickly. 'Nothing at all. Come over here,' he added, moving towards the hedge. 'You can just see Mortelet lighthouse from this point. It's a dangerous coast for shipping hereabouts, but the mail boats keep well clear of this side of the island.'

It was clear that he wanted to change the conversation. Dutifully Tremaine noted the slender lighthouse perched precariously, it seemed, upon the vicious outcrop of rocks, and they went on down the path.

Deck-chairs dotted the beach. The tide was almost full and gay figures fringed the water, flanked by a screen of brightly coloured floats. They walked awkwardly over the loose pebbles almost to the water's edge.

'I'm going to enjoy my afternoon,' Tremaine said enthusiastically.

'So am I,' Mark said significantly. 'But not by watching all these energetic people. They wouldn't dream of working as hard anywhere else.'

They settled down in deck-chairs. All three of them had brought newspapers, but Tremaine had already looked through them during the morning and he was in any case far more interested in what was going on around him.

He watched the swimmers and the occupants of the floats. It was a pleasant, soothing scene, and he allowed his mind to be lulled by it.

He glanced at his companions. Mark was immersed in his newspaper; Janet had allowed hers to fall to her lap and she was lying back with her eyes closed.

'The tide's going back pretty quickly,' he observed to Mark. 'I think I'll take a stroll along the beach.'

'Go ahead. Like me to come with you?'

'No, you stay where you are. You look far too comfortable to be moved and I'm sure Janet won't want to do any more walking just yet.'

'I can't say I'm keen on the idea myself,' Mark admitted. 'All right, old man. You'll find us here when you get back.'

Tremaine picked his way over the pebbles and the soft patches of wet sand left by the retreating tide. The cliffs flanking one side of the bay looked promising, as though they might contain caves; he could never resist the lure of a cave.

He climbed blithely over a mass of tumbled rocks barring his path, oblivious to the damage he was doing to his shoes when he slithered on the treacherous seaweed or momentarily found his foot wedged between the sharp ridges where the hard stone had been worn away unevenly.

The first cave was disappointing. From a distance it had appeared to be of impressive size but a closer inspection proved it to possess very little depth.

Now, however, he could see that it was possible to climb for a considerable distance around the foot of the main cliff. At high water the approaches by way of the main beach to the various bays and inlets were cut off, but at this state of the tide there was no danger in choosing a route over the rocks although a certain amount of clambering was involved.

He scrambled over the fallen and partially eroded boulders. His pince-nez had begun to slip and several times he was only just in time to save them from disappearing into a rock pool. But the spirit of exploration was aroused in him now.

He found himself eventually on a wide ledge overlooking a sheltered inlet. At the back of the inlet was a cave which had the appearance of running some distance into the cliff.

He was on the point of sliding down to the pebbles when he realized that there were two men sitting on the rocks near the cave entrance.

There were plenty of people in the neighbourhood, some of whom—although they were mainly children—were also scrambling over the rocks; he could hardly have expected to find the inlet unoccupied. His hesitation was due to the fact that one of the men was Hedley Latinam and the other was Alan Creed.

Latinam's dumpy figure there could be no mistaking, and although Creed was now wearing sports jacket and flannels instead of the bathing wrap in which he had last seen him he was sure that this was the gaunt man whom he had encountered with his wife on the night of his arrival.

There was nothing to prevent him going down to make himself known. But somehow he did not do so.

It was the expression on Alan Creed's face that held him back. The man's features, rendered unnaturally prominent by his sunken cheeks, with eyes that stared fixedly from beneath grizzled brows, had had a slightly forbidding air even at that first meeting; and now they were grim and set.

Latinam he could not see, for the other's back was towards him; but he could imagine the pudgy joviality still there in spite of any opposition; he was the kind of man who persisted in being hearty under any circumstances.

Deep in conversation they did not notice him. Carefully he began to withdraw, but nevertheless he could not avoid hearing something of what was being said.

It was Creed's voice that came first, a harsh note in it.

'How can I be sure of that?'

'My dear fellow!' Latinam's tones, on a higher note, vibrated with a mixture of good feeling and distress at being misunderstood. 'I won't let you down. You know you can trust me!'

'I know I've got to,' Creed returned.

That was all. As Tremaine slipped back out of sight the rocks blanketed the rest.

He felt a twinge of disappointment and frowned at himself. To what base levels was he descending? Listening to other people's private conversations was no way to behave, even if he *was* more than a little interested in the study of humanity.

Still, it would have been intriguing to have heard more of what Creed and Latinam had been discussing. From the look on Creed's face it had not been an ordinary conversation; whatever had been the subject it had been something that touched him deeply.

Why had they chosen that secluded inlet for their meeting? It had meant a climb over the rocks, all very enjoyable for an elderly bachelor who still retained his boyish enthusiasms but hardly what one would have connected with two people such as Creed and Latinam. Creed did not have the air of a man who went climbing over rocks for the fun of it, and Latinam, for all his jovial appearance, was unlikely to be any more given to such a hobby.

It was all very odd.

When he got back to the beach he found that someone else had joined Mark and Janet since his departure. There was another chair placed on the far side of Janet's and a man was sitting there.

His age was indeterminate. His face was alert and intelligent, but his hands were wrinkled, betraying that he was older than his features suggested.

He was clean-shaven but his chin had the dark, stubborn look that goes with a constant struggle to keep down a beard. Blue eyes twinkled behind thick-rimmed spectacles as he glanced up at Tremaine.

'This is another of our neighbours,' Mark explained. 'Ralph Exenley. Ralph, this is Mordecai Tremaine.'

They shook hands. Exenley's grip was firm and friendly, and Tremaine felt an instinctive liking for him.

'I'm afraid you won't find much excitement here,' Exenley said. 'We're a disgustingly law-abiding community.'

Tremaine looked enquiringly at Mark and that gentleman grinned.

'I've been giving the game away. Telling Ralph all about your excursions into crime.'

'I hope he hasn't been spinning too many fairy tales,' Tremaine remarked to the newcomer. 'It makes people expect to see a lean and hungry man-hunter, and when *I* come along it takes them a long time to get over their disappointment.'

'He's been very complimentary. Anyway, I've read about your exploits already.'

'You're interested in crime?'

'Well, I like reading criminology when I get bored with looking at tomatoes.'

'Ralph's a grower,' Mark elucidated.

'You must come over to my place,' Exenley said, 'and I'll take you through the greenhouses.'

'Be careful!' Janet put in, smiling. 'Ralph's an enthusiast. Especially where tomatoes are concerned!'

'I like meeting enthusiasts,' Tremaine said. 'After all, there are so many people in these days who don't seem to be able to raise any feeling about anything.'

'You've been warned, anyway,' Exenley remarked. 'If you'd like to take the risk, what about tomorrow? After lunch, though, if you don't mind. I'm usually busy in the mornings although the peak of the season's over now.'

Belmore made a gesture of regret.

'I'm afraid it can't be tomorrow, old man. We've arranged to go to the sand racing over at Firon. We're joining a party Latinam's taking from the Rohane.'

'I'd forgotten about the sand racing,' Exenley returned. 'Might look over myself. Let's make it the day after. Any time after lunch will do.'

'I'd certainly like to take advantage of your offer,' Tremaine said. He glanced enquiringly at Exenley. 'You know Mr. Latinam, of course?'

'By name. And I think everybody on the island must know the Rohane hotel. But I've never actually met Latinam. I must be the only person in Moulin d'Or who hasn't as far as I can make out! Just happened that way, I suppose.'

'And Mr. Creed?' Tremaine said, unable to resist the search for information.

Ralph Exenley's eyes were twinkling behind his prominent spectacles.

'Yes, I know Alan. His wife, too. Nice couple. They've been over to my place a couple of times. Trouble is that as a bachelor I'm not too well placed to offer hospitality. My entertaining is strictly limited.'

Exenley was a pleasant companion and Tremaine was sorry when the other rose from his deck-chair.

'Time I went back to croon over my tomatoes. They provide my daily bread and if I don't water them they'll be taking their revenge by dying on my hands.'

'You two ought to get on together,' Belmore said, as Exenley went off up the beach, towards the path leading up the cliff. 'You certainly start with the advantage of a mutual set of interests. Tomatoes and crime! They make an odd pair.'

'Anything goes with crime,' Tremaine said, a little sententiously. 'Crime is universal.'

'I was saying to Ralph,' Mark went on, 'that there's something right in your line of country in today's newspapers.'

'What do you mean?'

'The prison break from Parkhurst. Surely you saw it? Fellow called Marfield, doing ten years for forgery.'

'Yes, I did see the account.'

'Needed a cool nerve. Squeezing through a ventilator shaft in the dark isn't my idea of a pleasant occupation.'

'There was freedom on the end of it.'

'For how long? I know something about living on an island. You can bet that the moment the escape was discovered every exit was put under guard.'

'A man desperate enough to make that kind of getaway isn't going to give up easily,' Tremaine said. 'And they don't seem to have caught him yet.'

Belmore stared thoughtfully out to sea.

'I wonder what's in his mind? This is one occasion when I can understand what made you take up crime detection. It must be fascinating to find out the reasoning of people like Marfield, really desperate criminals who know that the odds are all against them. Is the desire for freedom alone strong enough to drive them to take the risk of trying to escape? Surely they must know that if they're caught freedom will be further off than ever!'

'They don't think of that when they're eating their hearts out behind walls,' Tremaine observed soberly. 'They only see the prize and don't look at the penalty. Besides, they delude themselves that once they're out they'll stay out. They don't appreciate the odds against them. And it may not be the prospect of freedom that attracts them as much as the thought of revenge.'

'Revenge? Meaning Marfield in particular?'

'Meaning Marfield in particular,' Tremaine agreed. 'I read a good deal about the Armitage case at the time and I can imagine that with Marfield walking about somewhere a free man, even though the police are after him, one or two people are going to feel very nervous.'

'But it won't be as simple as that,' Belmore objected. 'Surely the police will be aware that Marfield's likely to try and get his revenge? They'll have warned Armitage and they'll be watching everybody who goes near him until Marfield's safely back in jail.'

'Perhaps. If they know where to find him. This morning's report said that Armitage disappeared shortly after he was released. It doesn't necessarily follow, of course, that he's disappeared as far as the police are concerned, but they aren't going to be able to do much protecting until they've located him.'

Janet looked at them both in mock irritation.

'Will you two stop talking in riddles? What *is* all this about someone breaking out of prison and wanting revenge on a man called Armitage?'

'It's connected with a case that was in the news a couple of years ago, my dear,' her husband told her. 'A big forgery gang was rounded up by the police and this chap Marfield who's just escaped—he seems to have been the ringleader and a pretty desperate character—was given a sentence of ten years. He might have got away with it if another member of the gang hadn't given evidence against him. Naturally enough Marfield took a poor view of it and threatened from the dock that some day he'd get his revenge.'

'It was Armitage who gave him away?'

'That's right.'

'But why? I thought there was supposed to be honour among thieves.'

'Only in books,' Tremaine said. 'You need only read the reports of trials like that of Browne and Kennedy, who were responsible for the murder of a policeman, to see what happens in reality. Once the police have caught up with them these fellows try to put all the blame on their accomplices. Not a very edifying spectacle, I'm afraid.'

'When it comes to murder,' Mark observed, 'it's a case of each trying to save his neck at the other's expense. In lesser crimes I suppose they do it to get off with a lighter sentence. The police do make certain allowances, don't they?'

'Well, it's taken into account. Armitage, the chap in this instance, was given something like twelve or eighteen months. But in his case I think there were other extenuating circumstances. He didn't realize what was going on at first and when he did find out he was in too deep to draw back.'

'We'll hope for his sake that Marfield doesn't catch up with him.'

'I don't suppose he will,' Tremaine said. 'The police don't let much slip past them. They'll have Marfield back in his cell before long.'

He wasn't especially interested in the Armitage case or in Marfield, either. Not on this pleasant, sunlit beach.

He was on holiday and he wanted to forget that such a thing as crime existed. He should have been wiser, of course. He should have known that he was attempting the impossible.

4

PLAN FOR EASY LIVING

SAND flurried from racing wheels; noise boomed wavelike across the beach. Sitting on the pebbles, a few yards from the limits of the track, Tremaine found both the noise and the movement stimulating.

The young men who were providing the afternoon's excitement had obviously—in most cases at least—built their own cars from a miscellaneous collection of parts. But interest had been sharpened by the fact that the two motor-cycle and light-car clubs the island possessed were competing against each other in all the events.

So far North and South appeared evenly matched. South had produced some skilful cornering in the motor-cycle events, bringing them useful points; whilst North had retaliated by gaining two firsts, a second, and two thirds in the light-car section. Their outstanding performer was a helmeted and goggled young man in a blue machine which was higher in the body than those of his competitors and which bore the number 42.

Nicola Paston gave a gasp of excitement as the blue car shot once more past the finishing flag. She was sitting close to Tremaine and he could see the flush in her eager features.

She turned to Ivan Holt, just behind her.

'Who *is* Number 42, Ivan? You know most of them, don't you?'

'Well, I know Number 42,' he told her. 'That's Descamps, the club secretary. He spends practically all his spare time on that car.'

'Foolish young man,' observed Hedley Latinam.

They were all sitting so close together on the shingle that edged the sand upon which the track had been marked out that the conversation was general.

'Why so?' Holt asked.

'Why lavish so much affection on a mere piece of machinery when there's so much beauty to be appreciated on the island!' Latinam glanced at his sister. 'A very short-sighted policy. Don't you agree, Ruth?'

'If it satisfies Mr. Descamps,' she returned calmly, 'that's the important thing. After all, he may not be interested in the island's—beauty.'

'A man who can give so much to machinery should be capable of great things in other directions—when the right moment comes,' said Geoffrey Bendall's cynical voice. 'I think Mr. Descamps has something. If he can put up with the vagaries of the internal combusion engine he'll be able to take the vagaries of the feminine temperament in his stride.'

Mordecai Tremaine's antagonism was instinctively aroused. His bruised idealism prepared to leap metaphorically into the breach.

But he restrained himself. It was only Bendall's manner. He didn't really mean it. He only said things like that in order to create an impression.

'You're not a racing-car enthusiast, Mr. Bendall?'

'Did I sound so plain?' Bendall said, faintly amused. 'Well, it seems a silly business to me to go tearing around a race-track risking one's neck.'

'There's money in racing,' Latinam said.

Bendall grinned at him lazily.

'I'll take your word for it. You've obviously got the Midas touch so you can speak with authority.'

Tremaine looked at him. Bendall's smile had robbed the words of any direct offence but he did not think that Latinam was altogether pleased. There was a fixed quality in the plump man's jovial expression, and his voice seemed to hold a questioning note that was more in earnest than the conversation merited.

'Are you looking for an easy way of striking it rich?'

'Gold is where you find it,' Bendall said. 'I'm looking for a rich old man without too many troublesome relatives who doesn't know where to leave his money.'

Nicola Paston drew in her breath as though she had been startled. The flush had left her face; she was sitting quite still, staring intently at Geoffrey Bendall.

Latinam took out a cigarette and lit it with an ornate silver lighter. It possessed an elaborate cap shaped like a lion. It was, Tremaine thought, somewhat pretentious, rather like the man himself.

'It sounds original. How do you propose to set about it?'

'I haven't got down to the details yet.' Bendall shrugged amiably. 'The ideas come easily enough, but I never could care much for the donkey work of planning.'

Latinam shook his head deprecatingly.

'That's a pity. Can't get along without planning. What line were you thinking of following with this rich old man with no relatives to come asking awkward questions?'

'Oh, I thought about striking up an acquaintance with him somehow—after I'd watched him for a while without his suspecting me so that I'd know his habits. I could save him from drowning, or haul him from underneath the wheel of a bus in the nick of time. There are plenty of possibilities; it's just a matter of deciding on the right one and preparing the setting.'

Latinam gave a burst of laughter and brought a podgy palm down upon his thigh.

'Capital! All you've got to do now is to find a rich old man and persuade him to go for a swim or take a bus ride. Of course, after that you'll have to get him to make a will leaving you all his money and then see that he dies, but that ought to be simple enough for anybody with your imagination.'

Bendall's face was perfectly sober.

'Yes, I think so,' he returned gravely. 'A rich old man who'd been living on his own for years would probably have some kind of bee in his bonnet and he'd fall for the right story. If I made sure beforehand that he had a weak heart it might not even be necessary for me to help him into the next life after he'd made his will.'

Nicola Paston's blue eyes were wide and there was an expression in them Tremaine could not read. He could not believe that it was fear, and yet it was fear of which it reminded him.

'Don't take any notice of Geoffrey,' she said hastily. 'When he's in one of these moods he says all kinds of ridiculous things.'

'My dear Mrs. Paston,' Latinam said, a chuckle rumbling up from his plump being, 'please let him go on. He's amusing me and I like to be amused. I know he doesn't mean a word he says but it's still entertaining.'

'Hang it all,' Bendall said, aggrieved, 'I *do* mean it.' He raised his eyes in an imploring manner. 'Will no one take the jester seriously?'

'They certainly won't,' Nicola Paston said firmly. 'If you keep on like this, Geoffrey, people will expect to see you going about wearing a cap and bells!'

'And why not?' Bendall demanded. 'It would bring a little colour into this drab mechanical age if we appointed a few official jesters to cheer us all up. If we don't treat life as a comedy we're compelled to admit what a damned tragic mess it all is.'

'Come now, you're exaggerating,' Tremaine said protestingly. 'Unpleasant things do go on in the world, but there are plenty of pleasant ones, too. We've moved forward, even if not as much as we'd like.'

'True enough,' Bendall said, momentarily without cynicism. 'The Middle Ages had jesters and colour, but they had other things as well. Poor drains, for instance,' he added, with a return to his former manner. 'Although I dare say we could uncover a few smells just as bad if we started digging in the right places. Don't you agree?' he finished, turning to Latinam.

'*You're* doing the talking,' Latinam countered, his broad face still crinkled good-humouredly. 'But let's get back to this rich old man who's going to keep you in luxury by dying so conveniently. You said something about choosing one with a bee in his bonnet. Have you any particular preference in bees?'

'My goodness, yes!' Bendall returned. 'I've given a lot of thought to that. I'm going to pick a woman-hater.'

To Tremaine's disappointment, his romanticism badly ruffled by this further display of cynicism, no reply came from Latinam. It was Nicola Paston who spoke, a faint shrillness in her voice.

'I think the next race is going to start. What is it this time, Ivan?'

Ivan Holt flicked over the pages of his programme.

'Five-lap Scratch race for motor-cycles. 351 c.c. to 500 c.c. Half-a-dozen riders from each club.'

'Oh, dear,' came Janet's voice from somewhere on the fringe of the gathering. 'I wish I'd brought some cotton wool with me. They're such noisy things.'

'They do rather let people know they're coming,' Holt admitted. 'But they're not as dangerous as they sound. It isn't often a good rider does himself any damage whereas it's fairly easy to overturn a car on the bends.'

'I love to hear them all coming round together,' Nicola said quickly.

She sounded a little feverish, as though she was talking not because she really wanted to say anything but because she wanted to keep the conversation going somehow.

Geoffrey Bendall leaned towards her.

'It's all right, Nicola,' he said softly. 'I'll be a good boy.'

The line of motor-cycles roared forward as the starter's flag went down, held together for a few seconds, and then began to thin out as the leaders went ahead. The conversation died away as all eyes began to concentrate on the race.

No time was lost between events. The tide was creeping in now, a line of silver, menacing the seaward part of the track.

Following the motor-cycle race, in which South gained a narrow victory, a line of cars assembled quickly. Among them was Number 42, the high-built blue car. It rushed into the lead and held it determinedly, despite the forcing tactics of its nearest rivals.

'Your friend Descamps means to win, Ivan,' Ruth Latinam said.

She was sitting at Holt's side, but until now she had made no attempt to open a conversation.

Holt smiled at her. It was a very betraying smile. Mordecai Tremaine thought that it was pleasant to see young people so obviously in love with each other.

'I think he'll do it,' Holt returned. 'There's only the chap in the yellow car to touch him.'

By the time the final lap was reached the race had resolved itself into a struggle between the blue car and its yellow rival;

the points totals of the teams were almost level and excitement among the watching crowd steadily mounted.

At the first bend the blue car held its lead, sand scattering from its wheels as it scraped around as though glued to the ropes. At the second, the last before the straight run to the finishing line, the yellow car edged forward in an attempt to overtake.

The wheels of both cars seemed to touch. They skidded together across the sand.

Nicola Paston cried out. Ivan Holt leaned forward, and Tremaine realized afterwards that he had been protecting Ruth Latinam with his own body.

It was a bad moment. But both drivers managed to keep to the track. The flag went down with the blue car still a few yards ahead.

There was a burst of applause, both for the victor and for the skill each driver had shown in averting what might have been a serious accident.

The cars had run off the track beyond the finishing line and were slowing down. The blue car seemed to be in trouble. It was travelling erratically; when it finally came to a standstill after spinning round in an ungainly circle, the driver did not attempt to leave his seat.

'Hullo,' Holt said. 'Looks as though something's wrong.'

Ambulance men from the cluster of officials gathered in the space inside the ropes were racing forward. They reached the driver and helped him clear of the car. He was clutching his right wrist and seemed to be in pain.

'I'll go across and see how things are,' Holt remarked, climbing to his feet.

Tremaine turned to Ruth Latinam as Holt moved away.

'Mr. Holt knows some of the club members?'

She seemed glad of the opportunity to talk to him.

'Yes, he's stayed in the island before. He was working over here at one time and I believe he used to be a member of one of the clubs himself.'

'I noticed that he seemed to know a good deal about what was going on. He seems rather a reliable type of young man,' he added, adopting the role of the elderly gentleman who was taking a fatherly interest in the coming generation. 'I like the look of him.'

'Yes,' she said quietly, 'Ivan's a very reliable person.' She leaned forward to touch Nicola Paston on the shoulder. 'Can you see what's going on, Nicola?'

'I don't think the driver can have been badly hurt, but I dare say Ivan will bring us the news in a moment or two.'

They did not have to wait for Holt's return. It was announced over the loud-speaker system that the driver of the blue car had sustained a badly sprained wrist; he would be unable to compete in the final race which was now due to be run.

'Too bad,' Belmore said. 'I make the scoring just about level. This last event would have been a real needle effort if Descamps had been driving.'

Latinam shaded his eyes, peering towards the group of cars and officials.

'What's happening to Holt? Can you see him, Ruth?'

'No,' she returned. 'I wasn't watching him very closely and I didn't see where he went.'

In a few moments there was a further announcement. In view of the accident to Mr. Descamps and as the final race would decide the winning team, it had been agreed that Mr. Ivan Holt, a former member of North club, should take over car Number 42. The announcer asked the crowd to show their appreciation of Mr. Holt's sporting gesture.

Hedley Latinam beamed. He seemed to accept the rattle of applause almost as a personal ovation.

'This should be worth watching! What about it, Ruth? Are you going to give the young man a favour to wear on his radiator?'

'Don't be silly, Hedley,' she said in a low tone.

'It's what the knights of old did, isn't it? They wore their lady's emblem when they went to the jousting. That's the word, isn't it, Bendall?'

'I wouldn't know,' Bendall said. 'I'm no knight.'

By now the tide was encroaching upon the far side of the course. There was clearly no time to be lost if the final race was to be completed.

The cars manoeuvred into position, the blue car in the centre of the line. They recognized Holt at the wheel; he was taller than Descamps and could easily be distinguished among the other competitors.

'The fellow in the yellow car's there again,' Belmore remarked. 'Looks as though it's going to be another ding-dong tussle.'

Janet spoke seriously.

'I do hope there isn't another collision. Mr. Holt hasn't driven the car before—at least, I don't suppose he has.'

'He's driven it once,' Ruth Latinam told her. 'A day or two ago. He went out with Mr. Descamps on a practice run. But of course he isn't really familiar with it.'

It was noticeable how the emergence of a joint personal interest in what was going on had broken down all restraint between them.

Not that there had in any case been a great deal; it was true that Ruth Latinam had spoken very little, but on the other hand she had responded readily enough to any remark that had been made to her. But now she seemed just a little more ready to take the initiative, a shade more eager to join in what was being said.

The far side of the track had now been considerably narrowed by the steadily approaching tide. The first few laps saw the blue car lying third; Holt was clearly holding back, making sure of the feel of the controls before attempting a bid for the lead.

Ruth Latinam's eyes were fixed upon the circuit; her hands were clenched and there was a look of strain upon her face. Once Tremaine saw her turn away to glance at her brother and then at Geoffrey Bendall, as if to see whether they had noticed any sign of agitation in her.

What if they had! Tremaine wanted to get up and tell her what was in his mind.

Look here, if you're in love with that young man you *ought* to be feeling anxious about him. What does it matter about letting people see what you think!

But, of course, it wouldn't be any good doing anything of the kind. She would only look upon him as an interfering old busybody, and she'd be quite right.

The blue car moved up into second place. Holt was driving confidently. Perhaps over-confidently. He took the next bend rather wide; the car swerved and went into a skid.

Ruth Latinam's hand flew to her mouth. She gasped. Her brother gave her a sudden, intent look.

The blue car had skidded off the track into the advancing sea, sending up a spray of water. But the danger was not as great as it seemed, for Holt had managed to regain control. In another moment or two he had cut back to the track and was speeding over the sand towards the next bend.

Ruth Latinam relaxed, and her brother chuckled.

'It's all right, my dear. You aren't going to lose that young man of yours—not yet!'

Brief though the incident had been, it had robbed Holt of any chance of winning. He made a desperate effort that brought him back into second place, but before he could close the twenty-yard gap still separating him from the yellow car the finishing flag had swept down.

'Bad luck,' Bendall commented. 'Another lap and he might have done it.'

'He recovered from that skid very well,' Belmore agreed. 'Pity it happened so near the end of the race.'

A few moments later Holt came towards the stretch of shingle upon which they were sitting. There was a smear of oil on his face and he was still wearing overalls.

Latinam climbed to his feet and held out his hand.

'Well done. You had us worried when you went into the water, though. Especially Ruth. I think she was afraid we'd seen the last of you!'

'Sorry about the skid,' Holt returned. 'Descamps warned me that she needed holding on the bends, but I suppose I was a bit careless. Thought I knew all the answers.'

'Are you all right, Ivan?' Ruth Latinam asked.

'Sound as a bell. Gave myself a fright, but that's all.' Holt indicated his overalls. 'I'll go and get out of these. Just thought I'd show you I was all in one piece!'

He sounded casual, but the expression in his eyes as he looked at Ruth Latinam gave him away.

Tremaine pushed up his pince-nez and gazed upon the two of them benevolently. They made an attractive pair.

It was a pity about that hint of frigidity in Ruth Latinam's manner, as though she was trying to repress her feelings all the time. It made her appear unresponsive and he did not think she was really like that underneath.

But probably it wasn't very important. Everything would come right in the end.

It always did in *Romantic Stories* and he liked to think that the same kind of thing happened in real life.

5

UNEASY ENCOUNTER

RALPH EXENLEY's bungalow was similar in design to that occupied by the Belmores.

'Sorry about the mess everywhere,' he remarked, moving a pile of periodicals to enable Tremaine to sit down on an easy chair in the lounge. 'As long as I can find a chair and a pipe—and an occasional clean plate—I'm afraid I don't bother about how things look.'

'I'm a bachelor myself,' Tremaine said, understandingly. 'You look after yourself, then?'

'Well, I've a woman who comes in now and again—just to straighten things out when they look as though they're getting out of hand—but apart from that I'm my own housekeeper. I prefer it that way. I can please myself about meals, and if I want to go on working for an hour or two extra there's nobody to consult but myself.'

'Doesn't it make life rather lonely for you?'

'I find plenty to keep me going with a few hundred feet of glass to look after,' Exenley rejoined cheerfully. 'Anyway, I'm not much of a fellow for company. Give me my pipe and a book and I'm happy enough.'

'Isn't it sometimes rather dreary in the winter?'

'I'm not sure I don't prefer the winter months. Not so many visitors to clutter up St. Julian Harbour and the rest of the island. Saving your presence!' Exenley added with a chuckle. 'What with getting the place in order for the next growing season and spending an occasional evening with Janet and Mark I don't give way to boredom. Anyway, I prefer my quiet retreat to *your* kind of excitement. I dare say you find things a shade *too* exciting sometimes!'

'Exciting?' Tremaine adjusted his pince-nez with an air of innocence. 'Me?'

'I mean this crime detecting of yours. Don't you end up in an awkward situation now and again?'

'Everybody seems to be taking me a great deal too seriously,' Tremaine returned. 'I can assure you that I go months at a time without any more contact with crime than I get from reading the newspapers.'

'You disappoint me! I thought you'd be full of all kinds of tit-bits of information about criminals and their ways!'

As they went out into the garden Tremaine compared Ralph Exenley's particular brand of cheerfulness with Hedley Latinam's. It was unforced and quite unselfconscious, whereas with the plump man he sometimes had the feeling that it wasn't altogether sincere; that Latinam was trying to appear more jovial than he really was.

He indicated the big greenhouses at the end of the garden towards which they were walking.

'When you said you had several hundred feet of glass you meant these greenhouses?'

'We talk in so many feet of glass,' Exenley explained. 'As you can see, I've four houses. Each of them is a hundred and fifty feet long. Some people have more, of course, but quite a few make do with a good deal less. On the other hand I don't supplement my income by taking in visitors. Another disadvantage of being a bachelor!'

In front of the greenhouses was a tall framework of timber, on the top of which was a large tank. A pipe rose over one side and a wooden ladder was fixed permanently against it.

'Your water tank?' Tremaine enquired.

'Tomatoes are thirsty creatures,' Exenley nodded, 'and watering's very important. If you don't keep it up you soon see the results in the plants.'

'I notice you don't use a wind pump although there are a good many in the district.'

'I've a motor in the shed over there. It's cheap enough to run and it fills the tank quickly. I usually run the motor when I start watering and leave the tank full so that it's ready for the next time. No danger of being caught with an empty tank, then.'

They walked past the solid beams of the water tower and approached the greenhouses. Away to the left Tremaine saw a brick-lined pit with a boiler built into it. A stack of coal near at hand revealed its purpose.

'There are warm pipes running into each greenhouse?'

'That's right. They aren't needed when the weather's really hot, of course, but early in the season you need to keep the fire going if you want to make sure of your crop.'

They went through the open door into the nearest of the houses. The air was warm and heavy. Exenley led the way between the rows of tomato plants supported by cords.

'Not very bracing, is it! After an hour or two of picking I'm glad to get into the open again.'

Tremaine could imagine the discomfort of physical exertion beneath the glass roof with the sun beating down upon it. Already he was uncomfortably warm.

'You pick from the bottom?' he asked, looking about him.

'Allows the fruit to come on, then,' Exenley said. 'Picking, stripping, and watering keep me on the go during the main cropping time. Fortunately I don't do any packing. I've a contract with a local packing firm who handle that side of the business.'

'The soil looks quite hard,' Tremaine observed. 'I would have expected it to be much looser.'

'Hard? Not on your life.' Stooping, Exenley plunged his fingers into the ground around one of the plants. 'See?' He allowed the fine grains to run back to the earth. 'They've plenty of room to breathe.'

Tremaine bent down to make his own test, feeling the soft, moist soil.

'What made you decide to go in for growing tomatoes?'

'The need to earn a living, I suppose! I lived on the island for a short while a good few years ago and thought I'd come back and settle down here. Besides, I like watching things grow. Does me good to watch them develop.'

There was a passionate note of sincerity in his voice. His stocky figure seemed to have acquired a new virility.

They retraced their steps slowly through the greenhouse.

'I'm glad to be outside again,' Tremaine remarked. 'I don't envy you having to work in that heat.'

'You get used to it,' Exenley told him. 'You're always in the dry, anyway. Better come up to the bungalow,' he added, 'and have a swill. Surprising how much dirt there is attached to tomatoes.'

When, an hour or two later, Tremaine took his leave, it was with the feeling that he had known the grower a long time. Exenley was easy to get on with. He had replied good-humouredly to the host of questions with which he had been plied; he had no awkwardness of manner, despite the restricted life he was now leading.

'Look in again,' he said, as Tremaine went through the gateway to the road. 'I'll be glad of someone to talk to, and if you do happen to come when I'm busy there's no reason why you shouldn't watch me on the job. That's if you don't mind my disreputable appearance.'

Tremaine felt very satisfied with life as he walked down the road. The weather was fine and warm and he had met a number of interesting people. What more could he ask of his holiday?

The way back took him close to the ruined windmill. He would have liked to take the opportunity of examining it nearer at hand, but a glance at his watch showed him that he had barely enough time to reach Janet's at the hour he was expected for tea.

He studied the mill as he passed, however, and it was as a result of his interest that he caught sight of the figure of a man coming from behind the derelict building.

He was a burly individual, dressed in a fisherman's jersey and thigh boots. Although Tremaine was not close enough to see his expression clearly he had the impression of a heavy, lowering face that carried the marks of ruthlessness. He quickened his pace so that he would be well ahead before the other reached the road.

It was then that he noticed that another man was striking across the rough ground towards the mill. He recognized the dumpy figure of Hedley Latinam.

In almost the same instant Latinam heard his footsteps on the road and turned quickly. Tremaine thought that the other made a sudden urgent movement with his right hand.

'Good afternoon!' he called. 'Going to have a look at the old mill?'

Latinam did not reply immediately. He glanced over his shoulder in the mill's direction. He seemed disconcerted, but when Tremaine drew nearer he saw that the normal jovial expression had settled upon the plump man's features.

'No,' he returned. 'Taking a short cut, that's all. What about you?' he added, reluctantly. 'Are *you* making for the mill?'

Tremaine shook his head.

'I can't spare the time just now. But it's a place I mean to have a look at as soon as I can. There's rather an intriguing story attached to it, isn't there?'

'Is there?' Latinam said sharply, and then he relaxed. 'Oh, you mean the miller? Can't say I've much belief in ghosts myself but the islanders give the place a wide berth.'

His smile had a fixed, unreal quality, as though it was a mask behind which he was trying to adjust himself to an unexpected situation.

'I think I'd keep clear of it if I were you,' he added, after a pause. 'It's in a dangerous state. Should have been pulled down long ago. It's easy to fall through the boards, and if you were on your own it could be pretty serious. Might lie there for hours with a broken leg or something before anybody found you.'

'I see what you mean,' Tremaine said.

Clearly Latinam was waiting for him to go. He looked at his watch.

'I must be getting on or my friends will be wondering what's happened to me.'

'Me, too,' Latinam said.

He made no move, however, and it was Tremaine who was the first to turn away.

Fifty yards along the road he glanced back. Latinam was still standing in the same position.

The plump man's behaviour seemed decidedly odd. Despite his denial he *had* been making for the ruined mill. Why had he been so secretive about it?

And there was another queer point. The rough-looking man in fisherman's clothes had vanished; he had never reached the road.

Had that quick gesture Latinam had made anything to do with it? If he had not imagined it and the incident had really happened, what had been the reason for it?

He was still preoccupied when he reached the bungalow.

'I happened to meet someone on the way back,' he replied, to Mark's bantering enquiry.

'Anyone we know?'

'Mr. Latinam.'

Mark's eyebrows rose.

'Why should meeting him give you such a furrowed brow? He's usually overpoweringly full of the joy of living!'

Tremaine did not answer the question directly.

'Do you know anyone in the district who's rather a rough-looking character, Mark?' he said slowly. 'Might be wearing a fisherman's clothes. Big, burly fellow, with a scowling appearance?'

'The description's a bit wide,' Belmore observed with a frown. 'Plenty of fishermen live on the island, you know. There are scores of small boats around the coast. Big, scowling sort of chap, you say? There *is* one of the locals who might fit. His name's Le Mazon—Gaston Le Mazon.'

'What's his reputation like?'

'Not very good. He's been in trouble with the police once or twice. Why?'

'I saw him coming from the ruined windmill this afternoon.'

'What happened? If he tried to cause trouble I'll take it up with the police.'

'It wasn't anything like that,' Tremaine said quickly. 'We didn't get very close to each other. You say his reputation isn't very good? Then you don't think he's likely to be acquainted with Mr. Latinam?'

'What put the thought that he might be acquainted with Latinam into your mind?' Mark said evasively. 'Did you see them together?'

'Not exactly. I've no real reason for connecting them at all. But Le Mazon was coming from the mill at the same time that Latinam was going towards it. The impression I had at the time was that they were going to meet each other.'

'That was easily proved, surely? Didn't you wait to see what happened?'

'That's the odd thing about it. Latinam and I saw each other at the same time. We spoke for a moment or two and when

I looked round to see what had become of the man you've called Le Mazon he'd vanished.'

'I dare say he went off somewhere when your attention was being taken up with Latinam.'

'But where could he have gone without my seeing him?' Tremaine persisted. 'You know what it's like around the mill. It's open ground. He couldn't possibly have crossed it without my seeing him.'

'It's *your* mystery. What do *you* think happened?'

'I had a feeling at the time that Latinam had signed to the other man to keep out of sight and that Le Mazon had ducked down somewhere until I'd gone. But that means that Latinam and Le Mazon must be on fairly close terms and you don't seem to think that's possible.'

'I didn't say that,' Belmore objected. 'I just wanted to find out exactly what had happened before I committed myself. There's something about Latinam I can't place although he always seems open and cheerful enough when you meet him. It isn't surprising that he wasn't anxious that you should see him with Le Mazon. He wouldn't want the news to get around that he's keeping that kind of company.'

Tremaine adjusted his pince-nez.

'What do you imagine they can have in common? They certainly appear to be an oddly-assorted pair.'

At that moment Janet came into the lounge where they were holding their conversation.

'Tea's ready when you are.' She glanced from her visitor to her husband. 'You're both looking very serious about something.'

'I met Hedley Latinam on the way back,' Tremaine said, 'and I was just telling Mark that I had the idea he was going to meet a local fisherman called Gaston Le Mazon but that my coming along rather upset him.'

'Le Mazon?' Janet frowned. 'Isn't that the man who was supposed to have been smuggling tobacco, and wines and spirits across to the mainland, Mark?'

'He's supposed to have been mixed up in a good many shady things,' her husband returned. 'He's usually well supplied with money, but nobody seems to know just where he gets it. There's no doubt that it doesn't come from the fish he catches.'

'So he was seeing Latinam—' Momentarily there was a shadow in Janet's eyes, and then she shrugged. 'Mordecai's on holiday. He doesn't want to be bothered with our local affairs.'

It was clear that she did not wish to pursue the subject any further. It remained on Tremaine's mind, however, and he was still puzzling over it when he went to his room that night.

What was it that was troubling Janet? There *was* something, and an unresolved mystery represented a challenge. He would have to try and persuade her to tell him what was in her mind.

He was sitting on the edge of his bed, facing the open window with its view over the bay, and suddenly he thought that a speck of light winked and vanished again out in the darkness.

At first he was not sure that he hadn't imagined it, but a few minutes later he saw it again. An answering speck somewhere along the coast showed briefly. He counted three quick flashes.

He peered out of the window but although he watched the area from which the flashes had come they were not repeated. Nor did he observe a repetition of the light he had noticed out at sea.

He waited for a long while but there was nothing more. The excitement that had flared within him subsided into a faint disappointment. He undressed and climbed into bed.

6

THE WOMAN IN THE BACKGROUND

THE continued fine weather was attracting the majority of the holiday-makers in Moulin d'Or to the local bay rather than to the numerous other beaches scattered around the island's coast. It was difficult for Tremaine to find a quiet spot on the stretch of rocks he had come to regard as his own. Various small boys were clambering over his favourite resting place.

He liked small boys and appreciated their need for self-expression, but he sighed as he searched for some other refuge. He was engaged upon this activity when he came upon Alan Creed and his wife.

The gaunt man gave him a friendly smile.

'Enjoying your stay on the island?'

'Very much so,' Tremaine returned. He glanced at Valerie Creed. 'Have you had your regular dip yet?'

'Not yet. But we'll be going in soon,' she added, indicating the bathing towels they had brought with them.

Despite her heavy features and the thickness of her body there was something shy about her; something that was almost shrinking, as though she was not at her ease and didn't know quite what to say to him.

'I think your friends are trying to attract your attention,' Creed remarked suddenly, and Tremaine had a feeling that he had been glad of the opportunity to take the interest away from his wife.

Several people were coming from the dunes. He saw Nicola Paston's fair hair glinting in the morning sunshine, with Ruth Latinam beside her. Geoffrey Bendall's tall figure was just behind, and a yard or two in front, as if leading the cavalcade, was Hedley Latinam's plump form.

It was Latinam who had seen him and waved; his arm was still in the air in slightly over-hearty greeting.

Tremaine waved back but he did not go over to meet them. He did not wish to appear discourteous towards the Creeds and he expected that in any case they would come in his direction.

They did not do so, however, but chose a place further down the beach, spreading out wraps and towels. Tremaine glanced at his companions. Valerie Creed was staring towards the water. She seemed to have become rigid, as though she was on guard against something; the fingers of her right hand were probing nervously among the pebbles around the base of the rock against which she was leaning. Alan Creed was outwardly unconcerned, but there was a slight twitching of a muscle along the side of his jaw.

'Mr. Latinam appears to be taking advantage of the fine weather, too,' Tremaine observed carefully.

'Latinam? The Rohane hotel man?'

There was an enquiring note in Creed's voice and Tremaine gave him a look of surprise.

'Yes. There he is, with the people who've just come on to the beach. They're from the hotel.'

Creed shaded his eyes against the sun.

'Yes, I see. Latinam's the short, rather stout fellow, isn't he?'

Somehow his choice of adjective seemed to strip away Latinam's good-natured joviality, leaving him a figure who was vaguely coarse.

'I thought you knew him,' Tremaine said.

'I know him by sight, of course,' Creed rejoined. 'I've seen him about the district. But we haven't been introduced.' He studied the group sitting with Latinam on the sand. 'I had an idea the others must be from the hotel. I've noticed them here quite a lot. I suppose one of the two girls is Latinam's sister. I know she's running the hotel with him.'

'The dark-haired one is his sister. The other is Mrs. Paston. They're rather a jolly crowd.'

'I'm afraid Valerie and I don't mix very much. Unsociable of us, I suppose, but we get along.'

Valerie Creed had been sitting in silence, still with that guarded, taut look upon her face, but now she stirred and looked at her husband.

'Shall we go in for our swim now, Alan? I'd like to get back fairly early. There are one or two things I must do before lunch.'

'Of course, my dear,' Creed said quickly. He rose to his feet. 'You'll excuse our leaving you?' he added to Tremaine.

'By all means,' Tremaine returned.

He watched them as they went down to the water. They plunged straight in and began swimming strongly. He went slowly across the beach. Latinam saw him approaching.

'Come and join us. I see your friends have gone in. Local people?'

'I understand they've been living here for some months now,' Tremaine returned. 'Their name's Creed.'

'Ah, yes.' Latinam nodded. 'I've heard of them. Husband's an artist or something.'

Tremaine made no comment. Latinam and Creed had been talking very confidentially indeed when he had stumbled upon them several days previously, and yet each of them had now pretended that he knew the other only casually. It was more than a little curious.

Geoffrey Bendall slipped off his bathing robe.

'I think I'll go in myself. Anybody else coming. Nicola? Ruth?'

'Not for me,' Ruth Latinam said. 'I'm not in the mood.'

When Bendall and the fair-haired Nicola had gone down towards the water, Tremaine glanced at the dark-haired girl who was sitting up with her arms around her knees. There was a note of enquiry in his voice but he did not put a direct question.

'I notice Mr Holt isn't here today.'

'No,' she returned, without looking at him. 'He had to go over to the mainland.'

'I hope he hasn't had to cut short his holiday.'

'He expects to be back in a day or two.'

She sounded disinclined to pursue the subject and it was her brother who persisted with it.

'I had no idea he was going until he mentioned it after breakfast this morning. What made him decide in such a hurry?'

'He had a letter,' she said. 'He told me he had to go over on business.'

'Pretty important business to make him go off—under present conditions, eh?' Latinam said, with an expressive wink in Tremaine's direction.

Tremaine adjusted his pince-nez. He was rather embarrassed. He didn't want to offend Latinam, but on the other hand it wasn't likely that his sister would be anxious to talk about Ivan Holt.

'You don't go in for the local growing hobby?' he asked, after a pause.

'Growing?'

Latinam's plump face looked blank.

'Tomatoes,' Tremaine explained.

'Oh, tomatoes. No, can't stand 'em,' Latinam said. 'Suppose it's the sight of so many baskets of 'em around here.'

'It's quite a science—much more so than I imagined. I've been talking to one of the growers, Mr Exenley. I expect you know him.'

'Exenley?' Latinam frowned. 'No, can't say I do.'

He stared down over the beach to where Bendall and Nicola Paston were splashing about in the water. Tremaine stroked his chin unhappily. He didn't appear to have been very successful in trying to change the subject.

But to his relief Latinam didn't return to the question of Ivan Holt. When he abandoned his pensive study of the figures in the water he was his usual jovial self.

'Never mind the tomatoes,' he said breezily. 'Suppose we talk about you. I've been hearing quite a lot about you since we first met. Something of an amateur detective I'm told. Are you only over here for a holiday or is there more to it?'

Ruth Latinam stirred. Her dark eyes went from her brother to Tremaine, speculative, shadowed.

'It's just a holiday,' Tremaine said hurriedly. 'Nothing more, I assure you. Anyway, there's nothing in the nature of crime on the island, is there? Real crime, I mean.'

'As distinct from motoring offences?' Latinam grinned. 'I know that's about all the crime the local newspaper carries. But you never can tell. All sorts of things go on under the surface. If you keep your ear to the ground you may be surprised at what you'll pick up.'

'You sound as though you've found something yourself,' Tremaine said, probing.

'I'm as interested in crime as the next man,' Latinam confessed. 'Most criminals are small fry, of course, but now and again you do come across somebody who's really worth studying. Somebody to whom you can take off your hat as a master of his profession. Like Smooth Jonathan was, for instance.'

'Smooth Jonathan?'

'Why, yes.' Latinam raised his brows. 'Don't tell me you've never heard of him?'

'I'm afraid I haven't,' Tremaine admitted.

Latinam chuckled, a rich, rumbling sound.

'Hear that, Ruth? It's a tribute to a rogue if ever there was one! Smooth Jonathan always did cover his tracks.'

'Who was he?' Tremaine asked.

'One of the cleverest crooks who ever kept out of the way of the law. As far as I know he was never put behind bars—which is why not many people have heard of him.'

'Is he still alive?'

'Very much so,' Latinam said, as if he was savouring the words. 'Enjoying his ill-gotten gains and snapping his fingers at the police.'

'What was his line?'

'He didn't have a line. That was the beauty of it. There was no *modus operandi* record to trip up Smooth Jonathan. Safe cracking, the confidence trick, or just plain fraud—you never knew what he was going to do next. He must have got away with thousands in his time.'

Tremaine regarded him doubtfully.

'You sound quite enthusiastic about him.'

'I admire efficiency,' Latinam rejoined, 'wherever it's to be found. You have to give the fellow his due even if he *was* a crook. He kept himself in the clear and then retired to live on the proceeds of his criminal activities just like any respectable bank clerk living on his pension. He even found time to get himself married. His wife died a long while back, but I think there was a daughter. Yes, I'm sure there was a daughter.'

'Although the police may not have been able to prove anything against him,' Tremaine said thoughtfully, 'I dare say they knew all about him and how he made his living. Even when he committed his last crime and retired, as you termed it, that wasn't the end of the matter. There's always a chance of additional evidence turning up and all criminals must spend their days wondering whether they covered their tracks as well as they imagined. This Smooth Jonathan is probably still living in uncertainty, even now, not knowing whether his next visitor is going to be someone to tell him that his past has caught up with him.'

'Death the only release, eh?'

Latinam sounded amused.

'The police aren't his only worry,' Tremaine persisted. 'There isn't any honour among thieves. Your Smooth Jonathan must be just as worried about some of his old colleagues catching up with him as he is about the police. They wouldn't be above blackmail if they thought they could get away with it.'

'I don't think that's very likely,' Latinam said. He was less eager, as though he had grown bored with the topic. 'I don't doubt that he's taken good care to protect himself—wherever he is.'

He broke off. Bendall and Nicola Paston were coming back up the beach.

'Good swim?' he asked.

'Fine,' Bendall returned, rubbing himself down vigorously.

'Meet any interesting characters?'

Bendall nodded cheerfully.

'We always do, don't we, Nicola? You ought to come in some time. Maybe you'd find out some of the things that come our way.'

The plump man laughed and stretched lazily.

'No need to go plunging about in the water like a porpoise. That's the hard way. I'm willing to back my intelligence service against all competitors.'

'You don't leave many stones unturned,' Bendall agreed, his voice muffled in his towel.

'Isn't that the mail boat out there?' Ruth Latinam said suddenly.

She pointed to the drifting smoke rising beyond the headland where a ship was just coming into view. Her voice sounded so eager that there was a faint shrillness in it.

Bendall shielded his eyes.

'It's about the right time for the mail boat,' he confirmed. He glanced around the beach as he finished towelling the wet from his body. 'Hullo, isn't that Mrs. Burres?'

'I thought she was going into St. Julian Harbour this morning,' Nicola said. 'That was why she came downstairs early. She must have changed her mind. The major's with her.'

'Let's get them over,' Bendall said. 'No objections are there?'

His eyes went to Latinam. The plump man met his gaze with a wide smile.

'Carried unanimously. No point in having an odd man out. Or would it be two odd men out?'

Bendall came across the beach with the two people he had indicated. The woman, heavily built and in late middle-age, walked with difficulty, leaning on the arm of Major Ayres. As they drew nearer Tremaine saw that the major was carrying her knitting bag.

'Always the gallant soldier, Major!' It was Latinam, boomingly cheerful, his voice carrying down the beach. 'I like to see the man of action who also knows how to be the squire of dames!'

'Hrrm,' the major said. 'Like to see the ladies are all right, eh, what?'

'Nothing like it, Major,' Bendall agreed. 'Personally, I think that any man who calls himself a woman-hater must be more than slightly deranged. I've heard of people carrying it to the most amazing lengths. Wouldn't hear of anybody getting married, for instance.'

'Surely not?' Latinam said, unwillingly, but obviously the person from whom Bendall expected a reply.

'Chap I heard of in Yorkshire was quite fixed on the idea. Wouldn't budge from it. Made all kinds of difficulties for his relatives.'

'What sort of difficulties, Mr. Bendall?'

It was the middle-aged woman who had just joined them who put the question. She had a round, broad-featured face which would have been pleasant, although not attractive, but for the shadowed, almost sullen expression it now bore. It was both defensive and aggressive; a strange mixture that Tremaine found hard to analyse. She looked vaguely unhappy; when she smiled her eyes did not share in it.

Bendall's reply was evasive.

'Family troubles,' he told her. 'Over money and so on.'

'Couldn't the law do anything about it?'

Bendall turned back to Latinam, from whom this last question had come.

'Apparently not. There was a will. This other fellow had worked it all out very cunningly.'

'Which other fellow?'

Bendall looked surprised.

'Didn't I mention him? He's the key figure in the whole thing. He managed to get hold of the old fellow I was telling you about—the one who was a woman-hater—and got him to make a new will. There wasn't anything to be done about it.'

'Too bad,' Latinam said. 'But wasn't it possible to prove something against this villain of the piece? Couldn't he have been shown to have murdered the old man in order to benefit under the will or something?'

Bendall shook his head regretfully.

'No, I'm afraid it was quite a natural death. But I think the family still have hopes. They're after the villain of the piece—thanks for the apt description, by the way—and I imagine they'll catch up with him sooner or later.'

'I hope it's sooner,' Latinam said. 'For the family's sake. I don't doubt that they're feeling sore about it.'

'Oh, they are.' Bendall was very definite. 'You can't imagine the things they've said.'

Tremaine had the feeling that he had come in half-way through the second act of a play and was still trying to sort out who was responsible for saying what and why they were saying it. He was on the point of asking to be enlightened when he caught sight of Ruth Latinam's face, and the misery in her eyes stilled his resolve.

He turned instead to Mrs. Burres, who had now taken her bag from the major and extracted her knitting. Her needles were working busily.

'A new jumper, Mrs. Burres?'

'A pullover for my nephew,' she told him.

This time her eyes were included in her smile; it transformed her face and gave him an entirely different impression of her.

'I hear you've been staying on the island for some time,' he went on. 'You find it suits you?'

'It suits me very well,' she returned. 'I've been here just over a year. Before that I was on the south coast—Eastbourne.'

Geoffrey Bendall, who had sprawled on his towel on the sand, raised himself on one elbow to glance back at them.

'They tell me you're leaving us, Mrs. Burres. I hope it isn't true. We shall miss you about the place.'

There was a momentary hesitation in the busily clicking needles and then they went on as steadily as before.

'Nonsense,' she said practically. 'In any case, I don't suppose you'll be staying here very much longer yourself, Mr. Bendall. Holidays don't last for ever, you know.'

'Sometimes mine have a good try. I'm a lazy individual and I like it here. The place interests me.'

'That's dangerous,' Latinam said. 'It's unwise to take things too deeply on a holiday. Keep a blank mind, that's the best policy.'

'The policy of stagnation!' Bendall countered, with mock horror. 'But you won't let Mrs. Burres desert us, will you? Tell her she can't leave us in the lurch!'

'My dear chap, it isn't up to me to tell any of my guests what to do—least of all a lady. If Mrs. Burres has decided that she wants to leave us then I must accept her decision philosophically.'

'I see your point,' Bendall said. 'But I still think you ought to get to work on her. It'll be a pity to break up the party.'

'Isn't it broken up already?' Mrs. Burres interposed, without taking her eyes from her needles. 'I thought Mr. Holt left this morning.'

'It's only a temporary departure,' Latinam explained. 'He's coming back as soon as he's dealt with some business matter or other. You could hardly expect him to stay away for long in view of local conditions.'

Major Ayres looked up suddenly.

'Local conditions?'

Latinam made a significant gesture in his sister's direction and the major cleared his throat noisily.

'Hrrm. Quite so, quite so.'

Tremaine fancied that there was a faint shadow in his face, a hint of disappointment. He looked as though he had rather hoped that Ivan Holt would not be coming back.

Surely the major wasn't jealous of Holt? *That* couldn't be the reason?

He dismissed the thought as absurd, but it still troubled him. Although the rest of the conversation dealt with trivialities and Latinam was his usual hearty self towards each of them in turn, when the party broke up at lunch-time Tremaine left the beach with a queer feeling of doubt in his mind.

There was something that wasn't quite right; something that didn't seem to be as it should be.

It wasn't just that Ruth Latinam had been very quiet, hardly saying a word. That was understandable. It was, in fact, really very satisfactory. She was missing Ivan Holt.

He was still trying to find some explanation for his sense of uneasiness when Mrs. Burres came into his mind. He saw her as she had been for most of the morning, a heavy, brooding figure sitting on the fringe of the group on the beach, her needles moving indefatigably.

There had been something forbidding about her. She made him think of the knitting women who had sat at the foot of the guillotine when the streets of Paris had been red with blood.

7

INTERLUDE IN AN OLD MILL

CLOUDS hung low over Moulin d'Or, moving sullenly before a wind which had suddenly swung to the north-east.

'I think it'll be all right later on,' Mark Belmore commented. 'The glass is going up again. But it won't be too good on the beach for a while. The wind's blowing straight into the bay.'

'In that case I think I'll take a look at the old mill,' Tremaine said. 'Is there any prospect of your coming, Mark?'

'Sorry. One or two chores to do yet. Sure you'll be all right?'

'Quite sure. Dare say I'll call at Exenley's place on the way back.'

'You seem to have made a hit there. Old Ralph isn't too eager to talk to people as a rule. In fact, in the ordinary way he's something of an oyster. Watch your step at the mill, by the way. It must be half-rotten by now.'

When he went out to the roadway and was no longer sheltered by the boundary walls of the bungalow Tremaine encountered the full force of the wind, and was glad that he had made up his mind to keep away from the beach. He began to walk briskly.

To get to the mill he had to go through a gateway leading to a small field in which cattle were grazing, and then across a stretch of rough and slightly rising ground beyond. It was situated about a mile beyond the limits of the scattered dwellings forming the main part of Moulin d'Or.

When he reached the wooden framework, which was creaking eerily in the wind, he experienced a sense of isolation. Although the houses were not a great distance away he felt that he was in a remote and lonely place, far from any human presence.

It was, no doubt, the mill's evil reputation which was responsible. It had given the place an atmosphere, and of all people, Mordecai Tremaine regarded himself as susceptible to atmosphere.

The split and broken sails, splinters of wood hanging drunkenly downwards, stirred uneasily in the breeze. Their movement was stiff and slow, as if resentment at being thus roughly disturbed was finding expression; it added to the sullen menace of the place.

Tremaine glanced around. There was no one else in sight. He almost repented of his visit and then he took himself to task and climbed the narrow flight of worn stone steps that led up to the battered door.

It gave to his touch and he was aware of a shameful sense of disappointment. Now there would be no excuse for not exploring further.

The interior of the mill was gloomy but not as dark as he had expected, for the daylight invaded it through a dozen gaps in the main structure. He stepped cautiously through the doorway, feeling his way before entrusting his weight to the boards. They felt loose but they seemed sound enough.

When his eyes had become more accustomed to the gloom he looked about him. In one corner lay a pile of rotting sacks, but otherwise the place was empty apart from a flight of wooden steps leading to the upper portion of the mill.

He moved towards the steps and put his hand on the guard rail. He tested the neighbouring boards, glancing down as he did so. There were a number of light-coloured particles scattered near the foot of the steps and he stooped for a closer examination.

Surprise at what they appeared to be made him collect several of them in the palm of his hand and carry them across to the door. As he had thought, they were food particles—crumbs of bread and cake.

Puzzled, he went back towards the steps. What would crumbs of food be doing in this deserted, dilapidated ruin?

Stray picnickers? Children playing? Neither alternative convinced him. The gloomy mill, thick with dust and grime, seemed hardly likely to be chosen by picnickers, and he did not think that the local children would number it among their playgrounds in view of its sinister reputation.

A tramp? On this small island tramps were non-existent.

Who then? He stood with his hand on the rail, hesitating. And at that moment there was a loud creak from somewhere above him that echoed through the gloomy building.

His heart thumped violently. He waited, taut, for what would happen next.

The answer was anti-climax. He heard the slight jar of the sails as they reacted to the wind; heard the sigh of it through the broken walls above his head. But there was nothing else; nothing that spoke of terror or alarm.

He loosened his grasp of the rail and pushed back his pince-nez. His forehead felt moist and he was trembling. He was glad that he had come to the mill alone; he would not have liked Mark to see him giving such a display of nerves.

In an old structure such as this it was inevitable that there should be all kinds of queer sounds. They didn't mean anything abnormal. He had been allowing the story of the miller and his fate to disturb him unnecessarily.

He set his foot on the second step. The rickety structure that led into the darkness above trembled dangerously. He ascended to the third step and felt it sway even more.

It would be foolish to go any further. If the steps gave way and he was thrown to the ground he might suffer an injury which would detain him in the mill until either chance help arrived or until Mark came to look for him.

Janet would be worrying about him if he did not get back to the bungalow when he was expected. It would be unfair to place such a burden upon her.

He was grateful for the opportunity of retreating without admitting that he had shrunk from pressing his exploration to its end. Trying to avoid any appearance of haste he went carefully back to the entrance to the mill.

The daylight seemed bright and inviting after the gloom within. He descended the steps and set off across the field. A hundred yards away he stopped and glanced behind him. There was no sign of life about the mill; gaunt against the sky it bore its accustomed air of desertion.

As he walked towards Ralph Exenley's bungalow he saw that the clouds were breaking; the wind had driven wedges between the dark threatening banks and the blue sky was showing through.

Exenley was picking in his greenhouses, but he saw his visitor come down the gravel path and waved a greeting.

'You won't mind if I don't stop?' he called. 'I just want to get these baskets finished before I knock off.'

He indicated a pile of empty baskets stacked by the door of the greenhouse in which he was working. Tremaine seated himself on a nearby wooden crate from which he could face the entrance.

'Go ahead,' he returned. 'I know that you're one of the labourers of society. I'm just a parasite.'

Exenley had been giving him an intent scrutiny.

'You don't look on form this morning. Anything wrong?'

Instinctively Tremaine's hand went up to his pince-nez. It was a revealing gesture.

'No,' he said. 'No, nothing wrong. Why?'

'When I saw you coming down the path I thought you looked as though you'd had a shock of some kind.'

'I've just been to the old mill,' Tremaine said carefully.

'Prowling among the ruins, eh? Nothing much to see bar dirt and cobwebs, is there?'

'I'm not sure.' Tremaine tried to sound casual. 'Do people use it at all?'

'As a rule they give it a pretty wide berth. Don't want to meet up with the ghost of the miller!' Exenley said with a chuckle. 'What's on your mind? You don't think anybody is using the mill now?'

'Well, not exactly using it in that sense. But I did notice crumbs on the floor inside—as though somebody might have had a picnic meal there recently.'

'Oh.' Exenley's tone reflected the deflating of his excitement. 'I suppose that's possible enough.'

'I'm wondering whether it is,' Tremaine said, trying not to give the appearance of struggling to preserve a subject which was already dead. 'I don't suppose any of the local people would choose it for a picnic and it's hardly likely to attract visitors who are over here on holiday.'

'Why not? It might have been some young and romantic couple looking for a little colour.' Exenley shrugged the matter aside carelessly. 'Excuse me a moment. I want to see how my water tank's getting along.'

He walked over to the wooden framework on the top of which the water tank was perched and began to climb the ladder. Tremaine, recalling his experience in the mill, regarded him anxiously.

'It looks rather unsafe. Shall I steady the bottom of the ladder for you?'

Three steps up the ladder Exenley turned to grin at him.

'Unsafe? Don't you believe it! Years of life in it yet!'

He shook the sides of the ladder vigorously to prove his point and then climbed up to the tank. He peered over the edge of it before coming back to the ground.

'Enough water there to be going on with. I'll switch off the pump.'

Tremaine stayed for half an hour, watching Exenley as he went on with his tasks, putting questions to which the other replied with a cheerful tolerance. When eventually he got back to the bungalow he found Mark Belmore busy in his garden.

'We've had a visitor,' Mark said, as he approached. 'We've been invited to a dance.'

'A dance?'

'Up at the Rohane. Latinam's throwing something of a party. Nothing elaborate, so he said. Just the people at the hotel and a few others from round about. He's hired a small dance band from St. Julian Harbour. Wants to know if the three of us will go tomorrow night.'

They went into the bungalow where Janet was busy with preparations for lunch.

'Mark's told you?' she said. 'About the dance?'

'You'd like to go, my dear?' Mark said.

'We don't get much in the way of excitement, Mark. And I'd like to look inside the Rohane hotel.'

'But I thought you weren't at all keen on Latinam,' her husband said doubtfully.

'Perhaps I was prejudiced. Besides—'

Janet broke off. Fleetingly her eyes went to Tremaine. He resisted the impulse to question her but her glance puzzled him. It belonged to the strangeness he had noted before in her attitude. He wondered what mystery lay behind it. If, indeed, there *was* a mystery and he was not imagining things.

The wind was still spraying sand against the dunes, and the three of them spent the afternoon in St. Julian Harbour. It was a thought that seemed to have occurred to most of the holiday population of the island, for the narrow streets were crowded. They were making their way back to the quayside where Mark had parked the car when they caught sight of Geoffrey Bendall and Nicola Paston some distance ahead.

'I wonder what the relationship is between those two?' Tremaine said, musingly. 'They aren't engaged, are they?'

'I haven't heard so,' Belmore said. 'But they seem to spend a good deal of time in each other's company.'

'Maybe it's because of Mr. Holt and Miss Latinam,' Tremaine went on. 'As the remaining members of the foursome they naturally tend to pair off, even if there isn't really anything in it.'

Geoffrey Bendall puzzled him. He did not seem to be in love with Nicola Paston, although she was an attractive young woman. At times, indeed, his manner was casual towards her. And yet there was a certain intimacy between them, hard to define and yet indisputably there.

The next morning the wind had dropped and Tremaine took his newspaper down to his accustomed seat on the rocks.

The Armitage affair was still on the front page. Marfield, who had made such a daring escape from Parkhurst prison, was still at liberty despite an intensive man-hunt.

As usual, the scent was being confused by conflicting reports from people who claimed to have seen or to have spoken with the fugitive. He was said to have been recognized in a dozen different places between Yorkshire and the south coast. The official police view was that he was lying low somewhere in London, and a thorough search was being carried out in the neighbourhoods he was likely to have chosen.

In the afternoon Tremaine spent a pleasant hour with Exenley at his bungalow. He raised the matter of the dance, wondering whether Latinam's invitations had been scattered with a lavish hand over Moulin d'Or, but Exenley smiled.

'I don't know Latinam well enough to receive invitations from him. I doubt whether he's even aware of my existence.'

'He seems to be making quite an occasion of this dance.'

'You mean he's going into the highways and by-ways?' Exenley chuckled. 'Well, I suppose it's one way of getting publicity for his hotel. From all accounts it isn't doing too well. If what I hear is correct it would pay him to turn over to growing tomatoes!'

'I don't think he's concerned about making money. And I'm sure he isn't likely to become a grower. I tried to draw him out the other day about the growing industry but he didn't seem very interested in tomatoes. He started talking about someone called Smooth Jonathan.'

'Smooth Jonathan? That's an odd sort of name.' Exenley frowned, pulling thoughtfully at his dark chin. 'Something familiar about it, though.'

'According to Latinam he was a highly successful criminal,' Tremaine explained. 'He made a good living out of crime—which is unusual enough—and managed to retire without being caught.'

'One of the exceptions, eh? I'm sure I've heard the name before, although I can't quite place it. I wonder what made Latinam refer to him?'

'We were talking about crime and Latinam mentioned Smooth Jonathan as being a master of his profession. He seems to have a high opinion of his talents.'

Exenley raised his eyebrows.

'Hardly the type of hero you'd expect a respectable citizen to have!'

'Oh, I don't know. Crime has a fascination even for people who wouldn't dream of doing anything against the law themselves.'

Exenley put down the chip of tomatoes he had been carrying, his brow wrinkled.

'I've got it now,' he said slowly. 'I've read a bit of criminology, as I told you the other day. This chap was an artist all right. When he decided that he'd made enough out of his crooked activities he disappeared without leaving a trace. So Latinam thinks a lot of Smooth Jonathan, does he? He was almost boasting about him in fact. H'm. Interesting.'

'What's in your mind?' Tremaine asked curiously.

'Latinam came here and bought the Rohane hotel—a place, by the way, nobody over here wanted—and yet he doesn't seem to be in any hurry to make it a paying proposition. I wonder why? And I wonder where all his money came from?'

'You don't think—you're not suggesting——?'

'That Latinam is—or *was*—Smooth Jonathan?' Exenley pursed his lips. 'That sounds to me too much like slander. But I must say it's an intriguing thought. A *very* intriguing thought.'

Tremaine was in a pensive mood when he left his companion. It had been difficult to be sure whether or not Exenley had been joking; he had a habit of saying things with a perfectly straight face but with his tongue metaphorically in his cheek.

Had he meant what he had said about Latinam? Or was it merely that he had seen the opportunity for a little gentle leg-pulling, and, knowing his visitor's preoccupation with crime, had been unable to resist making use of it?

8

PROBLEM FOR TWO LOVERS

OVER tea at the bungalow the conversation turned naturally upon the Rohane hotel and the night's dance. Tremaine waited for the right moment to put his question.

'Where did Latinam live before he came to the island, Mark?'

'Somewhere in Yorkshire, I fancy.'

'Has he any business connections?'

Belmore looked blank and Janet prompted him.

'What Mordecai wants to know is where he got his money. Isn't that it?'

'Well, yes,' Tremaine admitted.

'I'm afraid I can't help you there,' Belmore said. 'He certainly hasn't carried out any business deals over here. Apart from buying the hotel.'

'There wasn't any difficulty about that? I mean because he isn't an islander?'

'The place was up for sale for a long while although the previous owner kept it going. Nobody on the island wanted it—too expensive a white elephant, I suppose—so there wouldn't have been any objection to Latinam's taking it on.'

Janet looked thoughtfully across the table.

'You seem very interested in Hedley Latinam, Mordecai.'

'I suppose it's my natural curiosity,' he smiled. 'Anyway, I feel I ought to know something about him since he's invited me to the dance tonight.'

'Is that all?' she said, and he fancied that her voice held a faint note of disappointment.

When they drove towards the Rohane hotel several hours later a number of cars were already parked in the drive and lights were blazing all over the building although it was not yet dark.

Latinam received them, resplendent in evening dress and with the air of a plump penguin.

'Glad you were able to come. Straight ahead. We're using the bar lounge as a ballroom.'

At one end of the long room overlooking the sea a drummer, a saxophone player, and a pianist had established themselves. A few couples were already circling the floor. Most of them were strangers to Tremaine, but he recognized Geoffrey Bendall. When the music stopped Bendall escorted his companion to a chair and then sauntered towards him.

'Mrs. Paston not coming?' Tremaine enquired.

'Oh, Nicola will be here in a few moments,' Bendall returned. 'She's just putting the finishing touches to her war-paint.'

Tremaine found the expression slightly jarring—Bendall seemed to have an unhappy facility for saying things that impacted harshly upon his sentimental soul—and tried to save himself from making an over-sharp rejoinder by looking about the ballroom. He saw Ruth Latinam standing by the doorway, her dark hair acting as a foil to her pale face and her creamy shoulders with the barest golden tan emerging from her low-cut evening gown.

'Is Mr. Holt back?' he asked.

'He's back from his trip,' Bendall said. 'But he doesn't seem to be here yet.'

There was a whisper of curiosity in his voice. He turned to gaze in Ruth Latinam's direction, and then strolled towards her, Tremaine following. She saw them approaching and made a visible effort to appear at her ease. She smiled, but it was a sad smile in which there was a hint of fear.

'What's happened to Ivan?' Bendall said.

She met his question with a careful unconcern.

'I thought he must be with you.'

'Haven't seen him since just after he got back. Haven't seen anybody,' Bendall said, with a mock air of tragedy. 'Nicola's been missing for hours.'

'Never mind,' she told him, with an attempt to match his manner. 'I'm quite sure your loneliness is only temporary.'

'I hope so. We've made a pleasant little party. I wouldn't like anything to happen to any of us.'

She met his gaze steadily.

'Is anything likely to happen?'

'I gave my crystal-gazing outfit away,' he said lightly. The band struck up again and he touched her arm. 'May I?'

Her hesitation was only slight.

'Of course.'

Bendall waltzed expertly. Tremaine watched them, wishing that his own limbs were as supple as they had once been.

He did not, however, spend the evening as a mere spectator. He took the floor several times with Janet, and twice with Nicola Paston after her appearance, beautiful and elegant, her fair hair gleaming against the clinging black gown she wore.

Once, as they passed Bendall, he saw the other's grey eyes upon her, openly admiring as though he was seeing her for the first time. So it *was* possible to arouse some real emotion in that young man!

Tremaine surprised himself by the intensity of his feelings. So much so that he hesitated in his step and Nicola Paston gave him a rueful glance.

'You aren't very flattering!'

'What do you mean?' he said guiltily.

'You know quite well what I mean! Here I am doing my best to charm you and you're allowing your attention to wander all over the place! What's Geoffrey been doing to you?'

Her shrewdness momentarily disconcerted him, but despite her smile there was a note in her voice that was urgent and feverish.

'I've been a little worried about Mr. Bendall,' he said deliberately, and he felt her become suddenly rigid.

'Worried about him?'

'He hasn't seemed to me to be enjoying his holiday. He's given me the impression that he has something on his mind.'

'Why on earth should you think that?'

'He's inclined to be a little cynical at times. People who talk like that often do so because they're unhappy about something. It's a method of hiding their feelings.'

'I think you're mistaken,' she said. 'About Geoffrey, anyway.'

'There's one explanation that might account for it.'

'What explanation?' she said quickly.

'He may be in love.'

The rigidity went out of her body and he felt her relax against him. Her laughter was vibrant with relief.

'Poor Geoff! You think he may be suffering from a secret passion! Who's the lady in the case? Surely not Ruth?'

'Oh no,' said Tremaine, shocked. 'Not Miss Latinam. Yourself.'

She did not reply for a moment or two. Her face had become suddenly serious again.

'You must think me a very rude and interfering old man,' Tremaine said, with a shameful pretence at contrition. 'But you did ask me about Mr. Bendall just now.'

'Yes, I know,' she said quietly. 'It's on my own head, isn't it? But I'm sure you're wrong. Geoffrey doesn't feel like that—at least, not about me. I know you've seen us about together a good deal. But that's because—'

She broke off, and a flush came into her cheeks.

'Put me down as a sentimental old bachelor who doesn't know when to keep a still tongue,' Tremaine said hastily. 'I hope I haven't offended you?'

'Of course you haven't,' she reassured him, smiling. 'I've been a married woman. I'm not starry-eyed from the convent.'

Nevertheless, there was a certain constraint between them now which lasted until the music had stopped and he was escorting her back to her seat. It might have been coincidence, but somehow he thought not, that Bendall should have imme-diately taken the vacant chair next to hers.

It was growing warm. Tremaine went out to the terrace beyond the open window facing the sea and strolled slowly around the hotel. It was well past dusk now and the cliff ended in a dark line from beyond which came the gentle sigh of a calm sea washing against the shore.

As he turned the corner of the building he heard footsteps coming up the path towards him. A moment later a figure came into view and in the faint light that glowed from a curtained window near at hand he recognized Ivan Holt.

He saw that Holt was holding a handkerchief to the side of his head. The handkerchief was stained and there were smears of dirt and what appeared to be dried blood on his face.

'You look as though you've had a nasty blow,' Tremaine said levelly. 'Are you all right?'

'Yes, quite all right, thanks,' came Holt's voice in reply. 'It's nothing to worry about. I slipped coming up the cliff—hit my head on a rock. It was my own fault for being so careless.'

They could hear the sound of the dance-band, and Holt made a gesture towards the hotel.

'Is everything in full swing?'

'Just getting nicely warmed up.'

'I dare say there've been a few enquiries after me. I'll get cleaned up and then go along and show myself.' Holt's manner bore a trace of hesitancy. 'Look here, do me a favour, will you?'

'Of course.'

'Don't tell anyone you've seen me. Not like this, anyway.' He indicated his head with a slight movement of the hand still keeping the handkerchief pressed against it. 'I don't want to cause any fuss.'

'I quite understand. I won't tell Miss Latinam.'

'I didn't mention Miss Latinam particularly.'

'I know you didn't. But it was Miss Latinam you really meant, wasn't it?'

For an instant or two Holt stood facing him with a grim expression, and then his features relaxed into a smile.

'Maybe it was. I wish I knew a little more about you,' he added ruminatively. 'You and I might—'

Tremaine waited.

'You and I?' he prompted, but Holt shrugged.

'Nothing. You won't say anything?' he added, and then he turned and went quickly round the building.

Tremaine followed him slowly. He liked Ivan Holt. He was a dependable type of young man. He wished he had been a little more communicative.

Had he really been injured in the way he had said? If so, what had he been doing on the cliff path when he was supposed to be attending the dance at the hotel? And what had he been on the point of saying when he had turned and gone off so hurriedly? Frowning, Tremaine continued along the narrow path that circled the hotel.

He came to an open doorway, and mechanically, immersed in his thoughts, he passed through. It was not until he found himself in a dark passage inside the building that he realized what he had done. He could hear the dance-band plainly, however; it should be an easy matter to find the ballroom.

A door in front of him appeared promising. He pushed it open. The light was on and he saw at once that he had made a mistake; the room he had entered possessed only the one door.

He looked about him curiously, guessing that it must be Latinam's office. There was a big desk in the centre of the floor and a filing-cabinet stood against the left-hand wall.

Standing on the desk was a picnic basket. It seemed incongruous in its present setting and instinctively he moved closer to examine it.

He lifted the basket's wicker lid and saw a thermos flask, a package wrapped in greaseproof paper that looked as if it might contain sandwiches, two small tins of pressed meat and a tin opener, with several other small parcels packed around them. Tucked down at one side was a packet of cigarettes.

He realized then what he was doing. Since the light was on someone—probably Latinam himself—was likely to return shortly. Explanations would sound painfully thin if he was caught in such a compromising situation.

He went out of the room, closing the door cautiously behind him. He could see now the way he should have taken, and after traversing another short passage, found himself approaching the ballroom.

Hedley Latinam was blocking the entrance. The plump man's smile was as pleasant as ever but there was a perceptible narrowing of his eyes.

'Been taking the air?'

Tremaine nodded, hoping that he did not look as guilty as he was feeling.

'I suppose I'm not used to this kind of thing!'

'You could have gone out on to the terrace,' Latinam said, pointing. 'Get the sea breezes there, you know.'

He sounded casual, but to Tremaine's uneasy conscience there was suspicion underlying his words.

'I know,' he returned, as carelessly as he could. 'As a matter of fact I did go out that way. I went for a stroll round the building intending to come back through the main entrance. I must have been day-dreaming and came in through the wrong door.'

'Day-dreaming! That's a bad sign!' Latinam said jovially. 'You found your way all right?'

'Oh yes, quite easily. It was just a matter of following the sound of the music.'

Latinam made no comment but stood aside to allow him to pass into the ballroom. Facing him Tremaine saw Ruth Latinam, sitting where she could watch the doorway. Her expression was troubled and her hands were nervously twisting a handkerchief in her lap.

He wanted to do something to help her; it was wrong that there should be unhappiness in her face. But he realized that if Ivan Holt came in and saw them together he could not fail to suspect that his confidence had been betrayed; young men in love couldn't help being suspicious even at the best of times.

Cautiously he glanced back towards the doorway. Latinam was no longer there.

During his absence the ballroom seemed to have filled; the floor was almost uncomfortably crowded. Idly Tremaine watched the dancing couples, and suddenly his eyes widened; moving in his direction to the rhythm of the slow fox-trot which was being played were Alan and Valerie Creed.

It needed only one glance at Valerie Creed's face to see that she was a woman very much in love; it had added grace to her clumsy figure. She looked, Tremaine reflected approvingly, almost beautiful.

They were level with him when the music stopped. They came over to the vacant chairs nearby, Creed's arm still possessively about his wife's waist.

'Good evening,' Tremaine said. 'I was watching you dance just now and feeling very envious.'

Alan Creed's gaunt features softened into a friendly smile.

'It isn't often Valerie and I attend an affair of this sort. We thought we'd make the most of it.'

'I was surprised to see so many people here. It's quite an occasion for Moulin d'Or, isn't it?'

'I suppose it is,' Creed said. 'I fancy that quite a few invitations were unexpected.' It was clear that he had recalled the incident on the beach when he had said that he knew little of

Hedley Latinam and felt that some explanation was needed. 'I didn't know, for instance, that Latinam knew of our existence,' he added.

As usual Valerie Creed said little. Some of the light that had invested her with such charm had gone out of her face, and Tremaine was regretfully aware that he was the cause of it. He was relieved when the band struck up again and they got up to dance. He did not enjoy the role of the skeleton at the feast.

Ivan Holt had put in an appearance now and was dancing with Ruth Latinam. Holt seemed pale and there was a discolouration at the side of his head. It was not, however, particularly noticeable; Tremaine thought if he had not been looking for it he might not have been aware that it was there.

He wondered whether other people had seen it. Hedley Latinam had come back; he was watching his sister and her partner as they danced. His expression was thoughtful. Possibly it was the lighting, but to Tremaine it seemed also a little sinister.

He sat out a number of dances and then found himself beginning to nod; it was difficult to combat the soporific warmth of the crowded room. He compelled himself to get to his feet and walk out on to the terrace.

The cool night air playing on his face quickly revived him. He descended the few steps leading from the terrace and strolled over the turf towards the cliff edge.

The blaze of light and the sound of the dance-band coming from the hotel behind him offered a sharp contrast to the darkness in which he stood; he felt translated, suspended between two worlds. He closed his eyes, the light sea breeze drifting over him.

The voices seemed at first to come whispering out of space, and then, as the speakers moved closer to him, he was able to distinguish the words.

He did not listen consciously; in his state of disembodied exaltation it did not occur to him that he was eavesdropping.

'But why not? Surely there's a reason, Ruth?'

It was Ivan Holt's voice, urgent, passionate, and pleading. He sounded like a man who had decided to settle an issue one way or another.

'Yes, Ivan,' came Ruth Latinam's low tones, 'there is a reason.'

'Then tell me what it is. Tell me what's troubling you. At least let me try to help. That's all I ask. You know—you know that I love you.'

'Don't, Ivan—please.'

'You *do* know it, don't you? It must have been plain enough. I'm not very good at hiding my feelings and I don't think your brother at least has any doubts.'

'Yes, I know it, Ivan. It makes me very—proud.'

Although Tremaine could not see them, for they were standing on the far side of a cluster of bushes, he knew that Ivan Holt had taken the girl into his arms.

'Tell me what it is, darling. Let me do something to get rid of this thing that's hanging over you.'

'You mustn't ask me, Ivan. You mustn't. It's better that you shouldn't know. Believe me, my dear, you don't know what it is you're asking.'

'I know that I love you. And you love me, Ruth. That's true, isn't it? You *do* love me?'

Her reply was so low as to be almost inaudible.

'God forgive me,' she said. 'Yes, I do love you.'

9

UP IN THE MORNING EARLY

TREMAINE performed his routine exercises in front of the open bedroom window at his usual time, and then dressed and went quietly out of the bungalow. Mark and Janet would doubtless want to lie on this morning; there was no point in disturbing them.

He walked through the garden to the road, deliberating whether he should make his way down to the beach or stroll in the other less familiar direction. He chose to go inland but it was not until he found himself staring at the old mill that he realized what thought had been in his mind.

He fancied that he detected a movement at the side of the building; in the next moment a figure left the shelter of the mill and began to walk across the rough ground on which it was situated.

The figure made no effort at concealment but kept on towards the roadway. He recognized Ivan Holt.

He hesitated, uncomfortable at the thought of the conversation he had overheard on the previous night, although he did not think that either Holt or Ruth Latinam had been aware of his presence. Holt came straight on.

'Oh, it's you,' the younger man said, as he drew nearer. 'I was wondering who it might be taking a stroll so early.'

'Good morning,' Tremaine returned. 'I was wondering the same thing.'

'I couldn't sleep. Went to bed too late, I dare say. After tossing and turning for a few hours I thought I might as well get dressed and try and walk it off.'

'Anything of interest at the mill?'

Holt gave him a steady look.

'What should there be?'

'I'm sure I don't know. But I thought you seemed to be having a look around.'

'I happened to come this way,' Holt said. 'That's all.'

Now that he could study the other more closely Tremaine could see that his face was white and drawn and that there were dark patches under his eyes. He looked haggard and ill; the mark on the side of his head showed now as an ugly bruise.

The fact that he had had little sleep would, of course, have explained his appearance in some degree; but there was,

Tremaine thought, more to it than that. In some subtle way Holt's attitude had changed; he seemed older, and on his guard.

'I was at the mill myself the other day,' he volunteered.

He waited, leaving the opening. But beyond a brief tightening of his lips Holt gave no sign that he understood.

Tremaine tried again.

'You gave me the impression last night that there was something you wished to discuss with me.'

'Did I?'

'I think you were doubtful about the best way to begin. I'd like you to know that if there is any way in which I can help you I shall be only too pleased to do it.'

'I've no idea what you mean,' Holt said. 'There's nothing I want to discuss.' He glanced pointedly at his wrist-watch. 'I must be getting back otherwise I shall be missing breakfast. Dare say I'll be seeing you later on.'

He nodded and turned away, his stride making it obvious that he did not wish to be troubled with anyone else's company.

Tremaine stared after his tall, retreating figure. Then he took off his pince-nez and polished them thoughtfully, gazing into space.

If Holt didn't wish to talk there wasn't very much to be done about it. Which was a pity, for if there was a way in which the course of love could be made to run smooth he would have been delighted to lend a hand.

But where did the mill come into it? He stared at the gaunt building with its tattered arms raised supplicatingly to the morning sky. It no longer seemed evil; there was merely a tragic helplessness about its splintered framework.

When he eventually reached the bungalow Janet was up and the smell of frying bacon filled the kitchen.

'You certainly believe in getting up early, Mordecai!' she called, as she saw him approaching.

'It's a bad habit,' he returned deprecatingly. 'I've reached the stage where I just can't help myself!'

Mark, shaving in the bathroom, pushed open the window as he heard the voice of his guest.

'See anybody about?'

'Ivan Holt,' Tremaine returned. 'I met him over by the mill.'

'I noticed last night that he'd had a knock on the head,' Janet remarked. 'Did he say how it happened?'

'He told me he'd slipped coming up the cliff path.'

'He seems to have been another early bird.' Janet gave him a quizzical look. 'Ruth wasn't with him?'

'No.' Tremaine shook his head. 'No, she wasn't with him.'

'I've been waiting for an interesting announcement concerning those two,' Mark said, emerging from the bathroom. 'There isn't much doubt over which way the wind's blowing.'

In this, Tremaine reflected, as he took his seat at the breakfast table, Mark was mistaken; but to embark upon explanations would be a little too complicated.

He spent a quiet morning on the beach with his newspapers, seeing nothing of anyone from the Rohane hotel.

There was a small wooden kiosk on the edge of the sand dunes where it was sometimes possible to buy cigarettes, ice-cream, and soft drinks. Mark had mentioned casually at breakfast that he was running short of cigarettes and Tremaine made a detour towards the kiosk in order to obtain a packet to take back with him.

Two people were sitting on the rocks on the other side of the kiosk, which had hitherto been out of his sight, and he recognized Major Ayres and Mrs. Burres.

The major saw him and nodded in a friendly fashion, and when he had bought his cigarettes he strolled over to them.

'I didn't see you at the dance last night, Major.'

'Hrrm. No.' The major prodded his stick into the pebbles at his feet. 'Not a dancing man, y'know. Never was. Getting too old for it, anyway.'

Seated on the other side of the major's spare figure Mrs. Burres was still knitting indefatigably. Her lips came together at her companion's comment and her knitting needles seemed to move a little more quickly.

'It doesn't look as though your nephew will have long to wait,' Tremaine commented.

'I want to get it finished,' she said. 'Before—'

She broke off with a sudden exclamation. It might have been because her needle had slipped, but Tremaine suspected that the needle had been an excuse to cover the fact that she had changed her mind about what she had been going to say.

'Mr. Latinam seems to have invited quite a number of people in the district to last night's dance,' he observed. 'Perhaps he intends to bring the hotel more into the limelight.'

'I don't doubt that he has a good reason for whatever he's doing,' Mrs. Burres said tartly.

There was an awkward silence.

'How is Mr. Holt?' Tremaine asked, after a moment or two.

'Holt?' Major Ayres looked puzzled. 'Didn't know there was anything wrong with him? Has he been taken ill or something?'

'Not exactly that. He had an accident last night—slipped and hit his head against a rock. He said it wasn't anything to worry about but I fancy it was worse than he admitted.'

'Accident, eh? Hrrm. Haven't seen anything of him this morning,' the major said.

'I happened to run across him quite early,' Tremaine said. 'I didn't think he looked at all well then. That's why I enquired.'

Mrs. Burres had still not brought her needles back into play. Her eyes were thoughtful.

'You saw him early this morning. I would have thought—'

'That he would have been lying on for a while?' Tremaine smiled. 'I met him over by the ruined mill—just before seven.'

He caught the sudden glance the major gave his companion; it was a speculative, shrewd glance.

'Hrrm. Up with the lark, eh?' The major cleared his throat. 'Did he—did he say what he was doing?'

'Only that he couldn't sleep and was taking a stroll.'

Tremaine left them with the feeling that he had put a question into their minds. He had an idea that it was a question which was going to receive a good deal of discussion when he was no longer within earshot.

In the afternoon Mark suggested a run to the rocky promontory in the south-east of the island upon which Mortelet lighthouse was built. They left the car parked on the spongy turf bordering the narrow road and climbed the cliffs to an open stretch of ground from which they could overlook the treacherous coast, fringed by jagged outcrops of rock, against which the lighthouse served as a warning.

Three men lay sprawled upon the grass.

'Hullo,' Mark exclaimed. 'Isn't that Latinam over there?'

'Yes, it is,' Tremaine said. 'Bendall and Holt are with him. I don't see the ladies, though.'

The sound of their voices had carried, although their words could not have been distinguished at such a distance. They saw Latinam turn, stare, and then wave an arm.

'Come and join us!'

The plump man was all smiles, and Bendall, too, seemed friendly enough. Ivan Holt, however, did not look pleased at their appearance; he merely nodded briefly.

'It looks like a stag party,' Tremaine said.

'Oh, Nicola and Ruth are somewhere about.' Latinum made a vague gesture. 'They're feeling energetic. We mere males couldn't keep up with them. Worn out with our efforts last night, eh, Holt?'

'Speak for yourself,' Holt returned shortly. 'I thought the girls wanted a stroll on their own. Besides, I thought we might have had a few moments to ourselves.'

He glanced at Bendall, a little sourly, as if he resented the other's presence. Mark and Janet sat down near him.

'How are you feeling?' Janet asked. 'I noticed last night that you'd given yourself rather a nasty knock.'

Holt made a visible effort to be civil.

'It's no more than a bruise. It looks a bit fierce but it's nothing really.'

'Enjoy yourselves last night?' Latinam enquired.

'Very much,' Janet smiled. 'The Rohane hotel's likely to become the centre of Moulin d'Or's night life!'

'I'm thinking of going in for that sort of thing more often. I don't think I've been progressive enough in the past.'

'I wouldn't say that,' Bendall commented. 'I think you've been highly progressive. It's just that your talents have lain in different directions.'

Latinam's jovial expression became fixed. He turned away, looking along the cliffs.

'Here come Ruth and Nicola.'

The two girls were about two hundred yards away, coming slowly towards them. They were about the same height, and Tremaine thought they made a charming picture with their striking contrast of colouring and with their light summer dresses blowing gracefully about them in the breeze. Nicola Paston was slightly in advance of her companion. Her fair hair tumbling about her head, its tresses stirred into gleaming life, possessed a golden radiance.

'Behold a fair woman,' Geoffrey Bendall said softly.

He was not looking along the cliffs; he was looking at Latinam.

Tremaine saw a tautness come into the plump man's face. He did not cease to smile, but there was murder in his eyes.

10

THE NIGHT IS FATAL

STUMBLING back down over the uneven surface of the cliff to the roadway Tremaine was close to Ruth Latinam and her brother. He heard Latinam's voice, rough with anger despite his guarded undertone.

'What have you been up to?'

'Nothing,' the girl said. 'Nothing. I swear it.'

'If you've been talking—'

Latinam broke off. Although he could not see it Tremaine sensed the suspicious glance the plump man cast in his direction.

It was an uncomfortable journey; the tension in the atmosphere was palpable. Once Tremaine caught Holt's eyes on Latinam. They were close to the edge of the cliff, with the jagged, ugly reef lying more than a hundred feet below them, and the expression on the younger man's face made it plain what he would have liked to do.

They parted company with Latinam and the others when they reached the roadway. The plump man had parked his car further round the headland.

'What was wrong with Ruth?' Janet asked, as they drove off.

'I didn't notice anything,' Tremaine returned uneasily.

'Either you're losing your powers of observation or you're being diplomatic,' Janet said quietly. 'She looked upset. I'm pretty sure she'd been crying. And Ivan wasn't in a very friendly mood. What's gone wrong between them? They haven't quarrelled?'

'I dare say it was the effect of the late night,' Tremaine said evasively. 'People aren't at their best on the morning after.'

'I suppose not,' Janet said, unconvinced.

Mark had obtained tickets for the repertory theatre in St. Julian Harbour that evening, and Tremaine enjoyed the fast-moving farce which was being performed. By the time the final curtain fell he had forgotten Ruth Latinam's unhappy, haunted face and the look in Ivan Holt's eyes.

The town itself was a blaze of light but once they had left it behind and were travelling through the narrow, twisting roads that led to Moulin d'Or, they were in almost complete darkness.

Mark used his headlights most of the way, otherwise there would have been a danger of scraping the big car against the overhanging walls.

As they turned into the lane leading to the bungalow the car sent a flare of light along the hedge, picking up the figure of a man. They saw his face briefly outlined.

Tremaine gave an exclamation.

'That's the fellow!'

'What fellow?' Mark said.

'The one I told you I'd seen coming from the old mill.'

'It was Gaston Le Mazon,' said Janet's voice, from the rear of the car. 'I recognized him in the headlights.'

'So it *was* Le Mazon you saw with Latinam.'

'I didn't say I *saw* him with Latinam,' Tremaine objected. 'It looked as though they *might* have been going to meet, that's all.'

Janet was peering through the rear window, although by now they had left the burly, sullen-looking man far behind.

'What do you suppose he's doing out at this time, Mark?'

'Probably up to no good,' her husband returned dryly. 'But he lives in Moulin d'Or, so I suppose we can't complain if he wants to take a stroll before going to bed.'

The conversation stopped there, for they had reached the bungalow and Mark needed all his attention for the task of swinging the big car through the narrow entrance between the stone boundary walls.

In the morning Tremaine announced his intention of going over to see Ralph Exenley.

'Ask him if he'd like to look in tonight,' Janet said. 'He hasn't spent an evening with us for some time.'

When Tremaine arrived Exenley was standing on the wooden ladder leading to his water tank. He glanced down and waved a hand.

'Shan't be a moment or two. Just checking up on the level. Pump's been a bit temperamental.'

In a few moments his thickset figure came agilely down the ladder, and Tremaine seated himself upon his usual upturned crate whilst Exenley busied himself with the motor that worked the pump.

'Your friend Latinam's making himself a reputation,' he observed after a while, removing his head from the interior of the engine. 'The news of the gay doings at the Rohane has been sweeping through the district.'

'He says he's going to do more entertaining in future.'

'It'll all be good for business. I'm not sure, though, that I want to see Moulin d'Or becoming too popular. I like it well enough as it is.'

'I've a message for you from Janet,' Tremaine said. 'She wants to know if you'd like to come over this evening.'

'I'll be delighted,' Exenley returned. 'It's some time since Janet and I had one of our arguments. When we get on to politics we have to be held apart. It's a good job Mark's there as a peacemaker!' And then his face fell. 'No, confound it, I can't make it. I'd forgotten I'd fixed up an appointment for tonight.'

'You couldn't put it off?'

'I'm afraid not,' Exenley said disappointedly. 'It's a matter of business. I've not been altogether satisfied with the prices I've been getting lately and I've arranged to thrash the whole thing out with the distributors. I had to cancel the meeting once before because I couldn't get into St. Julian Harbour, and if I cry it off again they may get the idea that I'm not all that worried.'

'Business must come first, of course.'

'Make my apologies to Janet and tell her I hope she won't hold it against me.'

'She won't do that. Look here, if you've an appointment in town tonight you won't want me hanging around getting in your way.'

Tremaine rose to his feet. There was a hint of reluctance in his face. His glance went to the tall framework supporting the water tank.

'What is it?' Exenley asked.

Tremaine cleared his throat in an embarrassed fashion. He adjusted his pince-nez unnecessarily.

'Well, the fact is,' he said awkwardly, 'I promised myself that the next time I came to see you I'd ask you whether I could climb up your ladder there and have a closer look at your water tank.'

Exenley, who had been wearing a rather doubtful expression, not sure what was coming, put his head back and laughed delightedly.

'Is that all! My dear chap, go right ahead now!'

'No, not at this moment,' Tremaine said, his confidence returning. 'You're busy and I'd rather do it when I can examine it at my leisure and ask all kinds of questions.'

'Why on earth didn't you mention it before?'

'I suppose it was because I felt it was a bit—well, childish. I thought you might tell me to be my age!'

'It's a change to meet someone who still believes in simple pleasures,' Exenley replied. 'Well, you'd better come along tomorrow morning. I'll be fairly straight then and you can try your hand at whatever takes your fancy—exploring the water tank, picking in the greenhouses, stripping the leaves; the place will be yours!'

'I'll be over in the morning just after breakfast,' Tremaine said, relieved.

He left Exenley stacking a pile of empty baskets. It was a pleasant world—that part of it, at least, which was centred upon Moulin d'Or. He had been allowing his unruly imagination to slip its reins again when he had begun to think otherwise.

He spent the afternoon in the garden of the bungalow with a book of love stories he had managed to extract from Janet's bookshelf unobserved; he was in the mood for their pleasantly sentimental style.

After supper he decided to take a stroll before going to bed and set off in the direction of the beach. As he neared the end of the lane leading to the road skirting the dunes he heard the sound of voices, and in a moment or two he distinguished the sharp, repeated tapping of a stick. He peered through the gloom at the tall, spare figure, with the thickset, much shorter one at its side.

'Good evening, Mrs. Burres. 'Evening, Major.'

Major Ayres turned abruptly, clearing his throat.

''Evening. Hrrm. Fine night for a stroll, eh, what?'

'Delightful. There's nothing better than a quiet walk in the cool of the evening. Helps one to think.'

'It does if one wants to think,' Mrs. Burres returned. He thought how odd she looked without her knitting, almost as though she was lacking some essential part of her apparel. 'We don't all come out for that particular purpose, do we, Major?'

'Hrrm. No,' Major Ayres said gruffly.

He leaned heavily on his stick, as though he was feeling tired; his tall figure did not have its usual upright air.

'It's strange to think in this peaceful place,' Tremaine commented as they came out upon the beach road, 'that there are big cities where it isn't safe to wander alone after dark.'

'Crime wave, eh?' the major observed. 'Things are in a bad way.'

'We're far away from all that here, of course. The sound of the sea instead of the sound of traffic; seagulls instead of barrow boys.'

Mrs. Burres gave a sudden, unexpected chuckle that held something of irony.

'You're almost lyrical about it. But don't be too sure that you're right.'

'You don't agree with me?'

'Crime is where you find it,' she said dryly, and he raised his eyebrows.

'You sound very cryptic!'

'I'm a cryptic person,' she returned, again with that deep and rather odd chuckle. She took the major's arm. 'What about it, Major? Shall we go back?'

The major's voice held a note of surprise but he did not oppose her suggestion.

'Hrrm. Yes. Suppose we ought to be getting along.'

'We'll say good night, Mr Tremaine. I dare say you'll be going in the other direction.'

Tremaine thought she was being rather obvious and he smiled ruefully in the darkness.

'Yes, I'll be strolling along by way of the dunes.'

He watched them until they were lost in the gloom stretching towards the Rohane hotel, and then he turned and went slowly down the road. They were a strangely assorted pair; he wondered what was the link that bound them, and surprised himself by the realization that he had taken it for granted that there *was* a link. Surely there was nothing odd about two people similar in age and staying at the same hotel accompanying each other on an after-supper stroll?

Occupied with his thoughts he almost collided with someone coming in the opposite direction. Ivan Holt had to step quickly aside.

'Sorry,' Tremaine said apologetically.

'You're out late,' Holt said.

It was obviously a question. Deliberately Tremaine evaded it.

'You and I seem to make a habit of meeting each other at the extremities of the day!' he countered lightly. 'We must be kindred souls. Or perhaps we have kindred interests.'

It was difficult to see Holt's face clearly and his voice gave nothing of his thoughts away.

'Perhaps,' he returned non-committally. 'I suppose you're on your way back now?'

Everybody seemed to be anxious to get him back indoors. Tremaine felt an urge to resist the general pressure.

'No, not just yet. I've had a lazy day. I think I'll wander about for a little while longer.'

'I wouldn't overdo it,' Holt said. 'The air's beginning to grow chilly. It doesn't do to stay about too long, you know, once the sun's gone down.'

'I'll be careful. I'm enjoying my stay too much to want to spend any of it in bed.'

'Very wise,' Holt observed.

It was an innocent enough conversation. When Holt had gone on his way Tremaine asked himself why he had felt that the younger man hadn't been altogether pleased at meeting him. It wasn't as though they were on bad terms.

Without doubt the answer went back to the intimate scene at which he had been an eavesdropper on the night of the dance. It was Ruth Latinam who held the clue to Ivan Holt's present behaviour.

His sentimental soul was in full flight, due no doubt to the literary diet in which he had been indulging during the day. He had not settled down with his favourite periodical, *Romantic*

Stories, for so long that his reading during the afternoon had been like suddenly calling upon an empty stomach to cope with a rich meal.

He left the road, and, crossing the dunes, sat down in a little hollow facing the sea. The exercise of walking had naturally warmed him, but Holt had not exaggerated when he had said that the air was growing chilly; it was agreeably sheltered in the hollow. It was peaceful to sit facing the beach, listening to the gentle fall of the water upon the sand.

The grass deadened the footsteps of the people who were coming over the dunes, and it was not until they were almost level with him so that their voices were clear that he was aware of their presence.

'There's something going on. I'm certain of it. He's bound to give himself away sooner or later.'

It was Geoffrey Bendall. He recognized the crisp, clipped tones, edged now with an unexpected grimness. It was that grim note which caused him to remain where he was instead of standing up to greet them.

'Don't take any risks, Geoff. I'm sure he's beginning to suspect and sometimes he frightens me.'

Nicola Paston's voice was softer, much lower than her companion's and lacking his confident firmness.

Bendall laughed.

'He won't do anything. He won't dare. He's got too much to lose.'

Tremaine did not hear Nicola Paston's reply, for by now they had gone well past him and he caught only a vague murmur of sound.

It was clear that they had not seen him. He scrambled up, brushing the sand from his clothes. As far as the Rohane hotel was concerned it seemed to be a regular night out.

But, after all, it was the biggest place in the neighbourhood and it was natural that other people should have experienced the desire to go for a stroll before retiring. And that Mrs. Burres and Major Ayres should have been together and that Nicola Paston and Geoffrey Bendall should have chosen each other's company was no more than he might have expected.

The only odd man out had been Ivan Holt. If only he and Ruth Latinam had been walking hand in hand the sentimental picture would have been complete.

Already Tremaine had made up his mind that, rebuff or no, he would see what could be done in that direction. He took the road back to the bungalow, wondering whether he would encounter any more of the Rohane hotel's inhabitants before the night was done.

He did not have long to wait. Just ahead of him, dark and shuttered now, was the wooden kiosk on the dunes. A figure detached itself from the shadows.

'You're early. She must mean a lot—'

The faintly sneering voice broke off. Tremaine stopped. For an instant he had a queer feeling that he was reliving a scene in which he had already played once before. The voice, the darkness, the short, squat figure in front of him—all these he had known on some previous occasion.

The figure moved nearer and he recognized Hedley Latinam.

'Oh, it's you, Mr. Latinam.'

The plump man's face bore a strange expression that was almost a grimace.

'Mistook you for someone else,' he growled. Only slowly did the habitual smile come back to his features and the jovial note to his voice. 'Hope I didn't startle you. Might have given you heart failure!'

'I wasn't really surprised to see you,' Tremaine told him. 'As a matter of fact, I rather expected to.'

Latinam stared at him. His podgy fingers went to his collar.

'You expected to! What do you mean?'

'Nothing sinister! But ever since I've been out I've been coming across people from your hotel. You all seem to have decided to take the air at the same time!'

'People from the hotel?' Latinam echoed him, as though he didn't quite know what to say and was making conversation whilst he collected his thoughts. 'What people?'

'The major and Mrs. Burres. One or two of the others.'

'Ruth? My sister? Have you seen Ruth?'

There was a sudden sharpness in Latinam's voice. Tremaine looked at him in surprise.

'No, I haven't seen Miss Latinam.'

The plump man seemed to realize then that he had made himself too obvious.

'She hasn't been too well today. I don't want her to stay out in the night air. It isn't good for her.'

'I expect she's safely indoors,' Tremaine said. 'She strikes me as being a sensible young woman who doesn't take foolish risks.'

He said good night and left Latinam still standing by the kiosk. When he glanced back he could no longer see the plump man's form, but whether it was because he had left the spot or because he had moved back into the shadows he could not be sure.

Despite the exercise he had taken it was not easy to get to sleep. Finally he climbed out of bed again and, going across to the open window, he leaned on the sill, staring out into the darkness.

His mind was still active. Why had Hedley Latinam been waiting by the kiosk? Had he been expecting to meet someone?

From somewhere in the distance he heard a faint, rhythmic sound. It was vaguely familiar, and he frowned, trying to place it.

Determinedly he drew back from the window. At this rate his brain would be going round in circles until the morning.

Over breakfast on the following day he told Janet and Mark of his arrangement to see Ralph Exenley.

'It won't be putting you out?' he said anxiously.

'Of course not,' Janet told him. 'I'm glad you and Ralph are getting on so well.'

When he reached the bungalow Exenley was just clearing away the remains of his meal. The task completed, they walked out into the garden towards the greenhouses. As they passed the timber framework supporting the water tank Tremaine gave it a long, reflective glance. Exenley saw it and smiled.

'Of course, you want to go climbing the rigging! All right, aloft you go then. But don't blame me if you don't get much for your pains!'

Tremaine set his foot on the ladder and began to climb. It took his weight without a quiver, unlike the rickety ladder at the mill. He went up hand over hand, and, reaching the top, stared over into the tank.

The colour went out of his face. He pushed his pince-nez back into position falteringly, gripping the top of the ladder hard with his free hand.

He compelled himself at last to lean further over the tank in order that he might be quite certain, and what he saw convinced him that there was nothing he or anyone else could do.

He turned and looked down for Ralph Exenley but there was no sign of him and, shakily, he began to descend the ladder.

When he reached the ground he saw that Exenley had walked over to the boundary wall of the bungalow where it flanked the road and was talking to someone who stood on the other side of the wall.

He turned as he heard Tremaine approach and gestured to him to come nearer.

'You know Miss Latinam, of course.'

The girl's dark hair was tumbled about her pale, strained face, and her eyes were full of fear.

'It's my—brother,' she said haltingly. 'He hasn't been back all night.'

'I've just been saying,' Exenley remarked reassuringly, 'that I don't think there's any real need for alarm. He'll show up again soon. You're quite sure you haven't made a mistake and that he isn't at the hotel now?' he added, turning back to her. 'He wouldn't have used a different room last night for any reason?'

She shook her head.

'No, he wouldn't have done that. His bed hasn't been slept in,' she went on, her voice trembling with her effort to restrain the hysteria. 'He went out late and didn't come back.' She looked pleadingly, despairingly, at Tremaine. '*You* haven't seen him, Mr. Tremaine? I know you sometimes go out early in the morning. Mr. and Mrs. Belmore told me I'd find you here.'

'Yes,' Tremaine told her gravely. 'Yes, I *have* seen him.'

'You have? Oh, thank God! Where? Where?' she said quickly, the relief flooding her face.

Tremaine glanced briefly back towards the water tank on its tall, wooden framework, the horror of the thing he had seen mirrored in his eyes.

'I'm afraid it's bad news,' he said slowly. 'Very bad news. You must prepare yourself for a shock, Miss Latinam. Your brother is—dead.'

'Dead?' They saw the grey look creep into her face, the more dreadful to watch because of the relief it was superseding. 'Dead? Oh no. *No!*'

The last word broke horribly. Her body wilted, and if Exenley had not been quick to reach out to her she would have fallen in a faint against the wall.

II

INTERVIEW WITH THE CHIEF OFFICER

DISCONSOLATELY Mordecai Tremaine scooped up a pebble and lobbed it into a nearby rock pool. He had wanted to enjoy his holiday. And now there were policemen swarming all over Moulin d'Or and there was a corpse about to make the headlines.

Things had moved swiftly since that dreadful moment a few hours earlier when he had stood looking down into Ralph Exenley's water tank at the distorted, dead face of Hedley Latinam. The local constable, informed of the tragedy, had communicated at once with his superiors at St. Julian Harbour;

police cars had brought the island's senior officers hurrying to the bungalow.

It was a long time since the authorities had had to deal with murder; the constable's message, Tremaine reflected, must have stirred up a hornets' nest judging by the fury of activity which had been going on ever since.

No doubt the sightseers would be arriving soon; the peace of Moulin d'Or would be shattered by an avalanche of curious humanity with time to spare coming in the wake of the policemen and the reporters. Murder was a magnet that could be depended upon to draw everything towards it.

He sighed, and, slipping down from the rock upon which he had been sitting, walked over the soft, clogging sand towards the dunes.

The constable who had been sent in search of him watched him speculatively from twenty yards off, comparing what he could see with his own eyes with what had been imparted to him by others, and, judging by his slightly puzzled expression, finding it difficult to reconcile the two.

He saw the slight, stooping figure of an elderly man with whom it seemed incongruous to associate violence. His air of harmless benevolence was accentuated by the pince-nez which had slipped to the end of his nose and were apparently on the point of sliding off completely.

So this was the Mordecai Tremaine he'd heard so much about. This was the chap who solved murder mysteries and got himself in the headlines.

Well, you never could tell.

As Tremaine clambered up to the grass bordering the dunes the constable moved towards him.

'Excuse me, sir. You're Mr. Tremaine?'

'That's right, Constable. What can I do for you?'

'The Chief Officer wants to know if you can spare him a few minutes, Mr. Tremaine.'

'Of course.' Tremaine nodded. 'Is he still at the hotel?'

'Yes, he's still there, sir.'

The police had made the Rohane hotel their headquarters. It had been the dead man's home, so that extensive enquiries had been necessary there; and it was in any case much more convenient as a centre of local operations than the bungalow where the body had been found.

Geoffrey Bendall and Nicola Paston came down the short roadway over the headland as Tremaine and the constable approached the hotel. They nodded briefly. Bendall's grey eyes rested curiously upon the policeman and his thin eyebrows rose slightly.

Tremaine was annoyed with himself for feeling suddenly uncomfortable. It wasn't as though there was anything especially significant about his being sent for by the police. Everybody had been interviewed, Bendall included; it was just routine.

He noted, however, that Nicola did not share her companion's air of flippant aggressiveness. She was tense, as though she was struggling to keep up an appearance of unconcern which she did not feel. He thought that she was a little afraid.

He glanced after them when they had passed. Their heads were in close proximity. He had a brief impression of something conspiratorial.

It disturbed him. It made him recall the remark Bendall had made a day or two earlier on the cliffs near Mortelet. It was a remark which had troubled him with its elusive familiarity.

But because Nicola Paston was still young, although she was a widow, and because her fair hair framed a face of appealing beauty, he hadn't wanted to think about it.

He knew how unwise it was. Because a woman was fair to look upon it didn't mean that all was well within.

The constable on duty at the door of the hotel stood aside to allow his colleague to enter, giving Mordecai Tremaine a salute as he did so. Tremaine began to suspect why he had been sent for, and he wondered whether the same thought had occurred to Geoffrey Bendall a few minutes earlier.

Chief Officer Colinet, responsible for the efficient running of the island's police force, was a big man whose bulk dwarfed the desk at which he was seated. He heaved himself upright and held out his hand.

'They didn't take long to find you, Mr. Tremaine.'

'I was on the beach. Not very far away.'

The Chief Officer pushed forward a chair. Tremaine sat down. He waited expectantly.

'As the person who found the body you're our most important witness so far,' the Chief Officer remarked conversationally, returning to the desk. 'I'd like to talk things over with you as fully as possible.'

'I'm ready to give you all the information I can, of course.'

'Superintendent Boyce assured me of that,' the Chief Officer said, and Tremaine gave him a thoughtful glance.

'Superintendent Boyce?'

'I've been speaking to him on the telephone. I believe you and the superintendent are on very good terms?'

'You might put it like that,' Tremaine agreed. 'Jonathan Boyce and I have been friends for a long time.'

The Chief Officer's manner was affable. It was clear that the impression he wanted to give, although without using words, was that a witness who enjoyed the close friendship of Superintendent Boyce, of Scotland Yard, was in a very different category to a witness who was of purely civilian status.

Tremaine wondered what Jonathan had said. He could imagine what his friend's reaction had been when the Chief Officer had told him who had found the body.

But it wasn't *his* fault that he seemed to have a remarkable propensity for discovering corpses. He didn't go around looking for the bodies of people who'd been murdered; they just happened and there wasn't anything he could do about it.

He couldn't have known, for instance, what he was going to find when he'd climbed that ladder.

He hoped that Jonathan hadn't been too humorous about it—or too complimentary. It was always a strain trying to live up to a reputation. Especially when secretly you weren't alto-gether sure you could do it.

Someone in the neighbourhood of Moulin d'Or had told the Chief Officer about him and the call to the Yard had been the result. All the signs pointed to his being both a witness and a party to the investigation.

Well, it might be interesting. The island formed a little world of its own, separated from the mainland by no more than a few miles of water and yet, with its own government and its own courts of law, as remote from it as if it lay on the other side of the ocean.

Chief Officer Colinet was in much the same position as a Chief Constable at home. All the threads of the investigation would pass through his hands; it would be exhilarating to enjoy his confidence.

The trouble, of course, was knowing the people who were concerned too well. People like the Creeds, and Ruth Latinam, and the others. There was no telling what would come out once the thing got started, and it wasn't easy when suspicion began to grow up around people you knew and liked.

'In the early stages, of course,' the Chief Officer was saying, 'we're so busy covering the facts—just to make sure we don't overlook anything vital—that we don't go beyond the routine questions. But now that we've had time to see just where we are we can start to look for the details.'

Tremaine pushed his pince-nez back into position.

'Yes, I see,' he observed dutifully.

'Let me just refresh my memory.' The Chief Officer consulted his notes. 'You've been staying with Mr. and Mrs. Belmore since your arrival?'

'In their bungalow here at Moulin d'Or,' Tremaine agreed.

'And it was through them that you came to meet Mr. Exenley?'

'Yes. I was introduced to him shortly after I got here—about three weeks ago. I understand that Mr. Exenley and Mr. and Mrs. Belmore have known each other for some years.'

'They are close friends?'

'Hardly that.' Tremaine pursed his lips. 'I suppose you might say they're on neighbourly terms. At any rate, that was the basis on which I was introduced to him. They visit each other occasionally, but I can't say that I've noticed that their acquaintance is any more than a casual one—just neighbourly, as I said.'

'Sufficient, though,' the Chief Officer pursued, 'to induce Mr. Exenley to invite you to call and see him.'

'That was largely my doing,' Tremaine explained. 'When I heard that Mr. Exenley was a tomato grower I couldn't resist asking him all sorts of questions. He told me that if I cared to go over and see him at any time he'd take me through his greenhouses and explain everything to me.'

'And you did go over?'

'Oh yes. I developed the habit of dropping in for a chat with him. It was as a result of that first visit that I went over this morning.'

'Had Mr. Exenley started work in his greenhouses when you arrived?'

'No. He'd only just finished breakfast and was still clearing up indoors.'

'Before you climbed the ladder to the water tank you had no suspicion that there was anything wrong?'

'None whatever.'

'Did you meet Mr. Latinam at any time during your visits to the bungalow?'

Tremaine shook his head.

'No. Ralph—Mr. Exenley—knew Latinam by sight, but that was all.'

'So that there was no reason as far as you know why the dead man should have been anywhere near that particular spot,' the Chief Officer said thoughtfully. He leaned back, overflowing his chair. 'You met Mr. Latinam on several occasions yourself,' he added. 'What was your opinion of him?'

Tremaine hesitated. This room had been Latinam's office; the plump man must many times have occupied the chair now barely coping with the Chief Officer's bulky form. It seemed a little indecent to be dissecting Latinam's character in such a setting.

But murder had been done and the truth must needs be told.

'I had the impression,' he said slowly, 'that there was something not quite *right* about him. It's difficult to describe. It's just that sometimes I felt that he didn't mean what he was saying and that his smile wasn't really as open as it looked.'

The Chief Officer made no comment, but a sudden glimmer came and went in his alert, grey eyes. He tapped reflectively with a pencil on the surface of the desk. He surveyed his visitor steadily for a moment or two and then he leaned forward.

'I've been glancing through the statements we've taken so far and I think that you can help me a great deal.'

'Help you?'

Tremaine sounded deliberately vague. He thought he knew what was coming and he didn't want to look as though he was anticipating.

Chief Officer Colinet nodded. His thick fingers idly ruffled the loose papers in front of him.

'At the moment these accounts are all more or less disconnected. They're about the same thing but they're so many separate versions of it. *You* can link them up. You know all these people. I dare say you've already formed a pretty good idea of how their minds work. I'd appreciate it if you'd tell me about your contacts with them—in such a way that all these different statements coalesce into one coherent story. Do I make myself understood?'

'Yes,' Tremaine said. 'Yes, I think you do.'

'And I can rely upon your co-operation?'

'There is only one possible answer to that.'

The Chief Officer smiled broadly.

'I must admit that after talking to Superintendent Boyce I was hoping that you would see it like that. Go ahead and tell it in your own way. I promise you I won't interrupt. And don't worry about how long you take. I've given instructions that we're to be left undisturbed.'

Thus reassured, Mordecai Tremaine pushed back his pince-nez and began his story.

12

LADY IN DISTRESS

TREMAINE stopped. Now that he could no longer hear the sound of his own voice the room seemed very quiet.

Chief Officer Colinet was sitting hunched forward in his chair, his bulk resting against the late Hedley Latinam's desk.

'Thank you, Mr. Tremaine. You've been extremely helpful.'

'I think,' Tremaine said slowly, 'that I should make one point clear. In talking to you I've emphasized certain things which seem to me to need emphasis now in view of what has happened. But at the time, before Latinam's death, they didn't appear to be as important.'

The Chief Officer nodded.

'When you write the story backwards you see all the things that escaped you before because then you didn't know what the end was going to be. It's always easy to be wise after the event but it isn't so easy to put your finger on trouble before it happens. You've nothing to reproach yourself with. That's what you mean, isn't it?' he added shrewdly.

'Yes, I suppose it is. Ever since I looked into that tank and saw Latinam's body I've been asking myself whether I could have done anything to stop it happening.'

'Coming events and their shadows? In an affair like this the shadows aren't as obvious as that. The murderer can't afford to let them be.'

The Chief Officer turned over the pages of the note-book he had been using. He ran his thick fingers down a list of names, pursing his lips thoughtfully.

'Have you any—ideas?' Tremaine asked, probing.

The big man looked at him with a wry smile.

'Ideas in plenty,' he returned. 'You've given me a good deal to work on. Whether we shall get very far, though, is a matter for time to decide.'

With difficulty he extricated himself from his chair. Walking across to the door, he opened it and glanced outside. Tremaine heard him speaking to the constable on duty there and in a few moments a police inspector came in, glancing curiously at the Chief Officer's visitor as he did so.

'I heard you were with Mr. Tremaine, sir. Anything promising so far?'

'Quite a bit,' the Chief Officer said. He tore off a leaf from his note-book and handed it to his subordinate. 'Rope in your friend Gaston Le Mazon and find out what he was doing last night. And then I want this enquiry put through to the Record Office at Scotland Yard.' He turned to Tremaine. 'This is Inspector Marchant. You'll probably be seeing a lot of him in the next few days.'

'I've heard of you, of course, Mr. Tremaine,' the inspector said. 'Glad to have the opportunity of seeing you in action.'

Marchant was a tall, well-built man who looked as though he knew his job. Clearly he wasn't the type who went around handing out flattery to every stray witness.

Tremaine, embarrassed, glanced at the Chief Officer to see how he was taking it but Colinet had turned away again to study his note-book.

At least it was a relief to know that they didn't think that *he* might have killed Latinam even though he *had* found the body.

He rose to his feet as the door closed behind Inspector Marchant.

'Have you any—instructions?' he asked.

'For the time being,' Colinet returned, 'be like Brer Fox. Lie low but see and hear everything. Sometimes it's the chance unguarded word that starts the hunt in the right direction. But I don't need to tell *you* that!'

The desk creaked protestingly as he leaned against it, the open note-book in his hands.

'At the moment it's an open field. The doctor puts the time of Latinam's death at something after eleven o'clock last night. We know that he was alive when you saw him at ten-forty-five and his watch stopped at eleven-thirty so that it's reasonable to suppose that he was killed at some time during that three-quarters of an hour. At least five people staying in the hotel were out during the most likely period of the murder. Mrs. Burres, Major Ayres, Mr. Bendall, Mrs. Paston, and Mr. Holt.'

'Are there any discrepancies in their stories?'

'They've all admitted frankly that they *were* out of the hotel last night. No attempt to keep it back.' The Chief Officer frowned. He shut the note-book and slipped it into his pocket. 'But they know that *you* saw them. They might have argued that since it wouldn't be any use denying they were out they might as well gain a reputation for frankness by admitting it straight away.'

'A rather cynical explanation,' Tremaine said. 'But I see what you mean. It doesn't apply to Mr. Bendall and Mrs. Paston, though. *They* didn't see me.'

'You mean they gave no sign of it. Maybe they *did* see you but had their own reasons for not allowing you to suspect it.'

Tremaine studied the big man thoughtfully as he released the desk from bearing his weight and moved across to the window. Colinet was acting on the assumption that it would be wise to be suspicious of *all* the characters in the drama; that way he would make sure of alighting sooner or later upon the murderer.

'What about Ruth Latinam?' he asked.

'Had a headache,' Colinet said, without turning and without consulting his notes. 'Went to bed just after ten.'

'Has the doctor been able to confirm the cause of death? Was it drowning?'

'No. His skull was fractured before he was put into the tank.'

Tremaine wrinkled his brows, calling back the grim scene upon which he had gazed earlier. Two iron supporting bars ran from side to side of the water tank and about six inches from the top. They had prevented Latinam's twisted body from rising to the water level, which had been an inch or two above the bars.

It had been a macabre sight. No movement on the surface of the water, and the body, face turned partially sideways, pinned beneath the iron supports.

He glanced at Colinet.

'The weapon?'

'The old-fashioned blunt instrument. We're looking for it now. Not that we expect it to be very helpful as far as finger-prints are concerned. Only the most careless of crooks leave that kind of trade mark nowadays.'

'And you don't think that this was the work of one of the careless variety?'

The Chief Officer moved away from the window.

'It's rather too early to be thinking anything—officially. But between ourselves, no, I don't think it was the work of anybody either careless or lacking in intelligence. None of the people staying here seem to me to be the type likely to give themselves away through stupidity.'

Tremaine's eyebrows went up. He eyed the big man guardedly.

'It doesn't follow that whoever killed Latinam must have been staying at his hotel.'

'No,' the Chief Officer agreed. 'No, it doesn't follow. That's why I'm going after Gaston Le Mazon. I'm not leaving any stone unturned. But in this kind of affair the best place to look for suspects is among the people who made up the victim's immediate circle. I'm no believer in the mysterious individual who turns up out of the blue, does the fatal deed, and then vanishes again.'

'You're satisfied about the staff?'

'I'm not dissatisfied—yet. They're all locals with back-grounds we can check. The cook, a chambermaid, a waitress, and an odd-job man Latinam employed to look after the bar, act as porter, and make himself generally useful. There's no suggestion that any of them had a grudge against him.'

'It's true,' Tremaine said, 'that there's usually some evidence of what was coming to be found in the victim's relationships with the people around him.'

'That's why I asked you to give me your account of things. And admirably you did it. What about Ivan Holt, for instance?'

Tremaine sighed.

'I was afraid it was coming. There's certainly been something odd about Holt's attitude lately. But I wouldn't say that it adds up to a reason for murder.'

'Ruth Latinam's a very attractive woman.' Colinet's voice was deceptively soft. 'She's also a very frightened one. Women do get frightened for themselves, but more often they get frightened for someone else. Do you think she *is* in love with Holt?'

'Yes, I do. I also think it shows that Holt couldn't have had anything to do with the murder. He wouldn't have been tactless enough to kill the brother of the woman he wanted to marry.'

'It doesn't sound the best approach to matrimony,' the Chief Officer agreed dryly. 'But I don't think we can altogether ignore enquiries in that direction. Then there's Mr. Bendall. According to what you've just told me he's been carrying on some kind of under-cover feud with Latinam. His talk sounded normal enough but gave you the impression that there was more to it. I remember in particular something being said about rich men not knowing where to leave their money.'

Tremaine kept his eyes on the shrewd, grey ones regarding him from the Chief Officer's impassive face. Colinet didn't miss anything.

'That was the note?' he said. 'The note you gave to Inspector Marchant just now?'

'I think,' Colinet said, evading a direct admission, 'that the sooner we find out where Latinam acquired the money he was living on the quicker we'll find out who killed him.'

There was a tap on the door. The Chief Officer looked up enquiringly as it opened and a constable came in.

'It's Mrs. Burres, sir. She's asking to see you. I thought it was all right to let you know, sir, since the inspector's been in.'

'Yes, that's all right, Constable. Bring her along, will you.'

'Perhaps I'd better go,' Tremaine said.

'I'd like you to stay,' Colinet told him. 'She knows you and if she really wants to see me all that badly the fact that you're here won't make any difference to what she intends to say. Besides, I dare say she knows all about your connection with crime and she's probably expecting to find you here anyway.'

After placing a chair for his expected visitor the big man seated himself at the desk again. Tremaine removed his own chair to a corner where he thought he would be less conspicuous.

Mrs. Burres, broad and determined, her drab brown costume shapeless upon her bulky form, swept into the room past the constable who had escorted her. She gave Tremaine no more than a glance; evidently Colinet had been right in his judgment.

'Sit down, Mrs. Burres,' the Chief Officer said. 'You have fresh information you wish to give me?'

'I want to see justice done.'

'Very creditable.' Colinet nodded gravely. 'You may rest assured, madam, that we share your desire.'

Mrs. Burres settled herself in her chair.

'It's easy for the wrong people to be accused. That's why I've come to see you—before any mistakes are made.'

There was a glint of amusement in Colinet's grey eyes.

'I'm sure we shall appreciate anything you can do to prevent us making fools of ourselves,' he said gravely.

'I'm not blind,' she said, apparently unaware of his faint irony, 'although a lot of people take me for a stupid old woman. If you're thinking that Mr. Holt had anything to do with what's happened just because he's in love with Ruth Latinam you're mistaken. Her brother was asking for all that came to him. He was playing with fire and he got himself burnt.'

The amusement had gone from Colinet's eyes now. He leaned forward, his tone quiet but incisive.

'What do you mean by playing with fire?'

'Who was it he went out to see at night?' she countered. 'What was he doing creeping out of the hotel when he thought nobody was watching him?'

'Do you mean last night? The night he was killed?'

'Not only then. There were other times as well.'

'What are you trying to tell me, Mrs. Burres?'

'That it wasn't anyone here who killed him,' she said tensely. 'Whoever did it had something to do with what he's been doing outside. He was a bad man—wicked right through the soul of him!'

Her voice wavered. Surprisingly her face crumpled, as though she was going to cry. It was so unexpected in a woman of her build that it clearly took Colinet aback. He waited a moment or two for her to recover.

'That's a drastic accusation, Mrs. Burres,' he observed evenly. 'I imagine you must have very strong reasons for making it.'

'He liked to torture people,' she went on, her voice steady again although her face still showed traces of her emotion. 'He enjoyed putting them in a position he knew was painful to them and then deliberately saying things to make them suffer. He even did it with his own sister!'

Colinet's heavy lids drooped over his eyes, veiling the quick, probing intelligence.

'Can you be more explicit, Mrs. Burres?'

For reply she twisted suddenly in her chair to face into the corner of the room.

'Ask Mr. Tremaine there,' she said, revealing that she had all along been aware what his presence meant. '*He'll* tell you.'

Colinet's lids were raised, unmasking the enquiry that lay behind them.

'I'm afraid you're making a mistake, Mrs. Burres,' Tremaine said quietly. 'I can hardly tell the Chief Officer anything because I really don't know what you mean. I haven't had a great deal to do with Miss Latinam.'

Her lip curled.

'I would have thought you'd have seen enough. You can't be as good at observing things as I imagined.'

The Chief Officer coughed deprecatingly behind a large hand. His gaze held that of his visitor across the table.

'Is there anything more, Mrs. Burres?'

'No, that's all,' she said, and her lips came together. 'I wanted to be sure you knew about Latinam.'

She was on her way to the door when Tremaine's casual question brought her to a sudden halt.

'Shall we be seeing anything of the major?'

She turned round slowly; she gave the impression that she wanted to gain time to think.

'The major? Major Ayres? I imagine so. I suppose we shall all be here until the police give us permission to leave.'

'I wasn't meaning that. I was wondering whether he might have anything to say to the Chief Officer.'

'How should I know that?' she retorted sharply. 'I can't tell you what the major is likely to do.' Her glance flickered to Colinet and then came back to Tremaine. 'The major's a fine man,' she said. 'A good man. He didn't have anything to do with this.'

'I assure you I wasn't suggesting anything to the contrary,' Tremaine said levelly.

She stood looking at him for a moment or two, uncertain what was in his mind and yet reluctant to risk a question. And then she turned and went out. As the door closed upon her broad, powerful figure Colinet heaved himself upright again; all his movements seemed to call for a large expenditure of effort.

'What was all that about?'

'My part in the proceedings?' Tremaine said. 'Or hers?'

'Both. I felt that I was on the outside looking in. It's a bad place for a policeman to be when he's investigating a murder.'

'There's something between Mrs. Burres and the major. Once or twice lately they've looked like conspirators.'

'And Mrs. Burres certainly didn't like Latinam,' Colinet observed. 'I wonder where we go from there? She's powerfully built for a woman. Do you think she could carry a man up a ladder?'

'And push him into a tank?' Tremaine said. 'After she'd first knocked him on the head? It would have been an awkward business, especially in the dark.'

'But with the major to help it might have been managed.' The Chief Officer gave him a quizzical glance. 'I've been thinking aloud rather a lot. I don't want you to imagine that I make a habit of it. Only in this case I thought it might help.'

Tremaine appreciated what was in the big man's mind. He was showing the extent of his confidence and was trying to induce a reciprocal frankness. It showed that Jonathan Boyce must have been very friendly indeed over the telephone from Scotland Yard.

'I won't let you down,' he said. 'Sometimes it's useful to make a shot in the dark. It clears things up, helps you to see the right way out of the wood.'

Colinet clasped his hands behind his back and stared up at the ceiling, standing with feet planted solidly apart, a great, leaning mountain of a man.

'As you said,' he remarked, 'getting up to that tank must have been awkward. Even with two people concerned. Only room on the ladder for one at a time. Those two supporting struts running across the inside of the tank meant that the body had to be forced underneath them whilst whoever did it was also busy balancing on the top of the ladder.'

'Yes,' Tremaine agreed. 'Yes, they did.'

'Damned inconvenient, I'd imagine. When the job was done, of course, the struts came in useful; kept the body down under the water. If Latinam had still been alive when he was pushed in they'd have stopped him coming to the top and would have made sure that he drowned without too much time being wasted. *And* without the murderer needing to hang about on top of the ladder to make sure his victim was dead. Dangerous to have spent too long up there. People don't usually go around the district looking at water tanks after dark, but it was always possible that somebody might have passed by and noticed what was going on, even at that late hour.'

A memory came into Tremaine's mind of Hedley Latinam's dead face, all the joviality distorted out of it. He shivered.

'You make it sound—gruesome. Up there on top of the ladder in the darkness, with a dead man on your hands. Or at least a man you intended to make sure was dead very soon. Your heart pounding with fear and every movement in the shadows making you wonder whether you were being watched!'

'Murder's a gruesome business. But once you've made up your mind to it,' Colinet said practically, 'you've got to go through with it or you're done for. If it hadn't been for you that tank might have been a good idea.'

'Why me?' Tremaine said defensively.

'It was your excursion up the ladder that produced the body! Any notion of how often your friend Exenley goes up aloft?'

'No, I don't think he's actually mentioned it although I've seen him go up to the tank once or twice.'

'He says that if the pump's working normally it's usually days and may even be a week or more between inspections. And he checked it only a couple of days ago because it hadn't been satisfactory. He made sure it was in order and unless it had started to give trouble again he wouldn't have examined the tank for a while. The body might have stayed there with no one any the wiser until the murderer was ready to get rid of it permanently at his leisure.'

'Then the murder wasn't premeditated?'

'That's the way it looks,' Colinet said. 'Let's see where we are.' He enumerated the points on his thick fingers. 'Latinam left his hotel fairly late at night. According to Mrs. Burres he did it furtively, as though he didn't want to be seen, although he doesn't seem to have been very successful in preventing *her* from noticing him. He went to the kiosk on the sand dunes where he'd arranged to meet someone. *Your* story confirms that.'

'He thought I was the person he was waiting for. He wasn't very pleased when he found he'd made a mistake.'

'So whatever the meeting was about it was something he didn't want to make public. It looks as though when the meeting did take place there was an argument and Latinam had the worst of it. The murderer found himself out in the open with a body on his hands. Not a happy state of affairs, even though it was dark. So what did he do? He looked for somewhere to hide the corpse until he could do something about getting rid of it without bringing suspicion on himself.'

'Hence the tank?'

'Hence the tank,' the Chief Officer agreed. 'Your friend Exenley's bungalow is some distance from the kiosk by the road, but it's possible to take a short cut to his greenhouses across a couple of hundred yards of rough ground between the bungalows separating his place from the beach. The murderer dragged the body across this ground, possibly with some idea of hiding it among the brambles and weeds, and then he saw the tank and thought of a better plan.'

'You sound definite about it,' Tremaine said, and the big man nodded.

'There was still a distinct track this morning showing where something heavy had been dragged from the road towards the back of the greenhouses. And we found traces of grass and weeds in the tank and still clinging to Latinam's clothes. The soil wedged between his rubber heels and his shoes was the same as that where the track was made.'

'I see. Latinam might have been reported as missing, but there would have been no proof that he was dead. And nobody would have thought of looking for him in a water tank.'

'Which makes it all the more satisfactory from our point of view that you've been taking such an interest in growing tomatoes. Instead of the murderer going quietly about his preparations, he—or she—must now be in a state of panic, wondering just how much we've found out. And when people get in a panic they're liable to make mistakes.'

Colinet glanced at his wrist-watch. He had an air of satisfaction.

'I'm due back at St. Julian Harbour in half an hour for a routine conference with the Governor. Inspector Marchant or one of his men will be here. I'll leave instructions that you're to be given any assistance you may ask for. Unless the Governor has anything important in mind I'll probably be out again myself later on.'

'It's very good of you,' Tremaine murmured. 'I know I haven't any official standing.'

'I'm casting my bread on the waters,' the big man said. 'I see no virtue in ignoring the fact that you're here and that you've had what might be called a ring-side seat.' His tone became graver and the humorous light in his grey eyes was replaced by a more sober expression. 'I realize that it isn't going to be any joyride. You've been seeing a good deal of the people here. I dare say you've got to like at least some of them. Investigations of this kind are a thankless business. But they have to be carried out.'

'Yes, I understand,' Tremaine said quietly.

He waited for Colinet to say what was in his mind.

'I'd like to know,' the Chief Officer went on, 'what's been worrying Mr. and Mrs. Belmore. There's no need for me to become all official and send Marchant out to talk to them. But I've got to find out.'

'Of course. Yes, I'll ask them.'

'Good man.'

Colinet smiled. It was a friendly, understanding smile, and instinctively Tremaine returned it.

He liked the Chief Officer. It was clear that he was a shrewd man who would not be easily fooled; the attitude of his subordinates towards him had shown that he demanded a ruthless efficiency. But he possessed a sense of humour and he was ready to unbend.

It was a pity that the background to their relationship should be a murder investigation in which people he had come to know and like were involved.

If Colinet was right and the murderer was to be found among Hedley Latinam's immediate circle, the days to come were going to be very difficult. Very difficult indeed.

13

THE SUSPECTS FORM PAIRS

THERE were knots of sightseers in the neighbourhood of the hotel. Curious eyes watched Tremaine as he came down the path from the headland. He supposed he would have to get used to it; the affair would be a nine days' wonder and anybody who was believed to have the remotest connection with the murder would be an object of interest.

He reached the bungalow to find Janet and Mark eager for news.

'Any arrest yet?' Mark asked.

'Not yet. So far it's just been routine procedure—photographs, interviewing of witnesses and so on.'

'Are you in?' Janet said.

He did not pretend that he did not know what she meant.

'Yes, I'm in,' he said, and went straight to the point. 'The Chief Officer asked me if I'd begin with you.'

'With us?' Janet looked startled. 'Surely he doesn't think *we* had anything to do with it?'

'No, of course not. But he does think you may know something that might help the investigation.'

'I wonder,' Mark said thoughtfully, 'where he got hold of that idea?'

'He got it from me,' Tremaine admitted. 'I haven't asked questions, Mark, when it's been obvious that you didn't want to talk. But now it's murder and things are different. The questions *must* be asked—and answered. I'm sure you'd rather they came from me than from the police. That's what the Chief Officer thought.'

'I'm not sure,' Mark said slowly, 'that I know what you're getting at, but if you've been given the job of putting certain questions to us, then go ahead. I'll answer them as well as I can.'

'I know that, Mark. I don't want it to sound like an inquisition. Maybe there's nothing much in it, anyway. It's just that several times you've given me the impression that there was something on your mind, but whenever I've tried to find out what it was you've put me off by changing the subject or saying that I wouldn't be interested in your local affairs. Now that your local affairs have turned into something more, perhaps you'll feel that you can take me into your confidence.'

'Have we been so obvious?' Janet looked at her husband. 'I don't know quite what to say about this, Mark. When you try and put it into words it sounds so—so vague.'

'Is it anything to do with Latinam?'

'It *might* be. That's the trouble,' Mark said.

'What he means,' Janet explained, 'is that we think it's something to do with Latinam but we can't be sure about it.'

'And the Creeds aren't the kind of people you can cross-examine,' Mark said.

'The Creeds? *They* come into it, do they?'

'What it amounts to,' Mark said, 'is this. Alan Creed and his wife came here at the beginning of the year and took the cottage where they're living now. At first they seemed willing enough to be friendly, although they were on the reserved side; they even came here with us on one or two evenings. And then, quite suddenly, they changed. They wouldn't accept any invitations and didn't seem to want to speak to people.'

'But didn't you tell me they were newly-weds? Surely that would account for their wanting to keep to themselves?'

'Up to a point. But you'd have thought that even if they hadn't been married very long and were wrapped up in each other they'd gradually have become more ready to mix. The odd thing is that it seems to have worked out in the opposite way. They began by appearing ready to be sociable and then without any warning they started to cool off.'

'And that led to fewer invitations being given to them?'

'When people realized what was happening the natural result was that they said that if the Creeds didn't want to have much to do with the rest of us then nobody was going to bother with *them*.'

'But I thought they seemed friendly enough when we met them on the beach?'

'If you happen to meet them when there isn't anyone else about they seem quite willing to talk, but when there are people around they tend to go all distant and don't say a word more than is necessary.'

'Mark and I talked it over,' Janet put in, 'and it seemed to us that the whole thing started when Hedley Latinam came to the Rohane hotel.'

'Did you ever see them with Latinam?'

'No.' Janet shook her head. 'I know it sounds odd and I shan't blame you for thinking there's nothing in it. Maybe they just decided that they didn't like us, after all.'

'What made you think of Latinam as the cause? Is he the only person who's come to live here recently?'

'Apart from one or two island people who've moved into the village. I suppose we really thought of him because he seemed to be such a mystery man.'

'A mystery man?' Tremaine pushed back his pince-nez. 'Now you're really making the plot thicken. What made you look on him in that way?'

'Just a lot of small things that appeared to add up to something that didn't seem quite right.' Janet wrinkled her brows. 'Like his taking over the Rohane hotel, paying a lot of money for something that was a bit of a white elephant and then not seeming to bother whether it paid its way or not.'

'You know something about the other reasons already,' Mark added. 'He was seen about with several not very reputable characters—Gaston Le Mazon, for instance. He kept some queer company. Now and again he had visitors to the hotel—not exactly guests, they didn't stay more than a day or two as a rule—who didn't look the right type for a self-respecting hotel proprietor to have.'

'And, of course, Ruth Latinam was scared of him,' Janet said casually, as one who stated an obvious truth.

Tremaine stared at her.

'Ruth was afraid of her brother? You're not serious?'

'She didn't dare to lift a finger unless he gave her permission. When they first came here she never went out unless he was with her.'

'But surely I've seen her several times since I've been here when her brother wasn't about?'

'Just lately things have seemed different. Ever since Ivan Holt arrived, as a matter of fact. She's been much more approachable.'

Tremaine smiled; this, he felt, was ground he understood.

'I think there's a simple explanation for that. Ivan Holt is in love with her and she's in love with him.'

'She's only been in love,' Janet said, 'as far as her brother would allow her to be.'

Tremaine gave her a doubtful look. He did not like the implication behind the words, but he respected Janet's shrewdness in such essentially feminine matters and there was in any case the disturbing memory of the conversation he had overheard that night on the cliff outside the hotel.

'When the Latinams first came here,' Mark said, 'there were one or two rumours about them. I know that gossip is easy to start and that it doesn't always have any foundation, but these rumours were fairly persistent for a while.'

'What sort of rumours?'

'They were—unsavoury,' Mark said. He glanced at his wife. 'Let's leave it at that, shall we? What's your programme now?'

'I thought of going over to Ralph Exenley's. I haven't had the chance of a real chat to him since all this began this morning.'

'Poor Ralph!' Janet gave a rueful smile. 'He can't be very pleased at all the attention he's getting. He likes to be left alone. You'll probably find him complaining bitterly about having policemen all over the place and asking what he's done to deserve it!'

There were several groups of people in the neighbourhood of Exenley's bungalow, obviously intent upon viewing the scene of the crime, but the police constable stationed at the entrance gate was dealing firmly with any attempts to linger. As Tremaine approached he saw one of the sightseers point out the water tank to his companion; clearly the details were becoming known.

'Why me?' Exenley said, as he greeted his visitor. 'Why pick on me? Out of all the tanks in Moulin d'Or, why choose mine for such an inconsiderate piece of dumping?'

'That's what Chief Officer Colinet would like to know,' Tremaine returned. 'Although he has an idea about it already.'

'What might that be?'

'That the murderer chose it because it was near at hand and he wanted to hide the body until he could get rid of it for good.'

'So that's the theory, is it?' Exenley stroked a chin already beginning to darken with a persistent stubble. 'I hear you spent quite a time with the Chief Officer,' he remarked. 'Does that mean that you've been called in?'

He sounded so carefully unconcerned that Tremaine eyed him thoughtfully. The solution to a minor mystery presented itself.

'Was it *you* who told him about me?'

'I might have mentioned in passing that you were the Mordecai Tremaine who made a hobby of clearing up murder cases,' Exenley said. His blue eyes twinkled suddenly behind his glasses. 'I thought it might clear the way for you, so to speak. I hope you aren't going to hold it against me! After all, I thought you *ought* to take a hand since it was your unhealthy curiosity about my water tank that turned the place into a policeman's paradise in the beginning!'

'I was wondering just how it happened. The Chief Officer seems to have got in touch with Jonathan Boyce at the Yard. I won't hold it against you, Ralph. I was involved enough, anyway, since I found the body and I was also the last-known person to speak to Latinam before he was killed.'

'Of course, you met him by the kiosk last night. Didn't you say that you got the idea then that he was waiting to meet someone?'

'Yes. At first he mistook me for someone else.'

'He didn't say who it was?'

'No. It was pretty clear that he didn't want to talk.'

'Judging by what happened he was up to no good,' Exenley said dryly. 'Latinam was a queer fellow and he kept some mighty queer company.'

There was an echo of Mark Belmore in his voice.

'Like Gaston Le Mazon, for instance?' Tremaine observed.

'Yes, like Le Mazon. What was a chap like Latinam doing with that kind of shady character?'

'It's certainly a point.'

'It may turn out to be *the* point. If I was in charge of this investigation I know where I'd start looking for the man I was after.'

'If *that's* the answer,' Tremaine said quietly, 'it clears the people at the Rohane hotel. At present they're naturally all under suspicion. It isn't a very pleasant situation for them.'

'It isn't a very pleasant situation for anybody in Moulin d'Or,' Exenley said ruefully. 'Nor will it be until the thing's been settled once and for all. The sooner the murderer's laid by the heels the better.' He turned slowly, glancing along the path to where the gaunt framework bearing the water tank reared itself against the sky. 'As far as *I'm* concerned it's a personal matter. It was on *my* property that the body was found. I'm in the limelight. And I don't like it much.

I can't look at a policeman now without wondering what's in his mind and how soon he's going to come out with the handcuffs!'

Despite his apparent banter there was a serious note in his voice; he was more concerned than he had revealed.

'From what I've seen of the Chief Officer, Ralph,' Tremaine said reassuringly, 'he isn't the type to go leaping to conclusions. You don't have to worry.'

'You're probably right,' Exenley returned, smiling. 'But I can't help feeling like the man who's standing up to be shot! As a matter of fact, that's why I told the Chief Officer who you were. I'll feel a lot safer knowing I've a friend at court! After the grilling I had this morning from Colinet and Inspector Marchant I was afraid anything might happen!'

'Naturally, they wanted as much information as possible. But I know that at the moment the police are keeping an open mind.'

'Which means that the list of suspects is pretty open, too. I'd like to see the field narrowed a bit. You're the expert in this kind of thing. Where do *your* suspicions lie?'

'I haven't even begun to sort them out,' Tremaine admitted frankly. 'I'm hoping you'll be able to help, Ralph. Did you hear anything out of the ordinary last night? Or see anything that might possibly have had some connection with the murder?'

Exenley shook his head.

'Not a thing. Whoever did the job didn't make any noise about it. There's a chance, of course, that it was all over before I got back. I was on the last bus from town, and I suppose Latinam's body could have been in the tank already. I certainly didn't notice anything unusual as I walked in. I've been scratching my head ever since Inspector Marchant left to see if I could remember anything that might help, but I'm afraid I'm a complete blank. I was pretty tired when I got in and I must have slept like a log.'

'Even if it didn't happen until after you were back,' Tremaine said, 'it's unlikely that you would have heard anything. The murderer—or murderers—would have taken care to be quiet.'

'You think there might have been more than one person in it?'

'I think there might have been,' Tremaine returned carefully. He studied his friend reflectively. 'The other day, Ralph,' he went on, 'you said something about a man called Smooth Jonathan—a crook who was supposed to have retired and to be living on the profits of his past crimes.'

Exenley nodded, clearly wondering what was coming.

'Yes, that's right. I remember our talking about him. Why?'

'You suggested that Latinam might be Smooth Jonathan, living here under a false name. Did you mean it? Mean it seriously enough to tell the police about it?'

Exenley's eyes twinkled behind his thick spectacles in that irrepressible sense of humour. He chuckled.

'My dear Mordecai, you'll get me put behind bars for leading the police up the garden path!'

'Then you *were* joking?'

'Sorry. I couldn't resist it. When you mentioned that Latinam had been talking so knowledgeably about this Smooth Jonathan character it seemed too good an opportunity to miss. I thought that with your interest in crime, putting the idea into your head might start you off on something!'

'So that was all?'

Tremaine sounded regretful. Exenley stood facing him for a moment or two, still with his half-amused expression; and then a more serious look came into his face.

'Look here,' he said slowly, 'I'm afraid that *was* a leg-pull. But there was no question then, remember, of Latinam's being killed. This rather alters matters.'

'You mean,' Tremaine said, 'that if Latinam had already been murdered you wouldn't have suggested that he might have been Smooth Jonathan?'

'After all, the thing would have been too near the bone. I don't want to get a reputation with the police for trying to be funny at their expense. But that doesn't mean that I think that Latinam was a virtuous character. In fact, I think he was anything but. He was mixed up with all sorts of people who might turn out to know something about his being murdered.

You've already mentioned Le Mazon, and I don't doubt that when the police get down to it they'll find plenty of others.'

Walking back from the bungalow Tremaine occupied himself in forming a mental list of the people whom he must now, even if it was against his inclinations, regard as suspects. It was curious—and disturbing, too—how they paired off.

First, Mrs. Burres and Major Ayres. They had been out of the hotel at the critical period, and although he had watched them walk in the opposite direction to the kiosk where he had encountered Latinam, there was no proof that they had in fact gone straight back indoors. The time of their arrival, according to the statements they had made to Colinet, was uncertain. They had been unable to produce any witnesses because they had gone immediately to their rooms without speaking to or seeing anyone else.

Opportunity, then, was there. But motive?

What was there to link either of them with the murder? No more than the vague hostility which had seemed to lie between Latinam and the major, and the way in which Mrs. Burres had gone to Chief Officer Colinet and then said nothing of importance; her statement that Latinam had been an evil man, violently though it had been made, could hardly be accepted as evidence.

Had it been a clumsy attempt to put the police off the scent? It presupposed a powerful motive, and so far no sign of anything of the sort had emerged.

Next, Geoffrey Bendall and Nicola Paston. They, too, had been out of the hotel; and although they had also appeared to be walking away from the place where Latinam had been waiting it did not follow that they had not made contact with him later.

Tremaine frowned. Had they seen him sitting in the hollow in the dunes and purposely ignored his presence so that he should imagine that they were unaware that he was there?

It was true that they had seemed genuinely preoccupied when they had passed. But if his instincts were wrong and they *had* seen him, what then? A mere desire not to have their conversation interrupted at such a moment? Or had they wished to give him the impression that they were returning to the hotel when the reality had been something quite different?

That interpretation, of course, made the incident decidedly sinister. He wondered what they had been talking about. Nicola Paston had sounded agitated.

'*Don't take any risks, Geoff. I'm sure he's beginning to suspect and sometimes he frightens me.*'

Was it Latinam she had meant? There was no proof, no suggestion, even, that she had had the dead man in mind. But it was something that couldn't be ignored.

Bendall at least had something on his mind that concerned Latinam. Antagonism had existed between them. It had been masked by polite words but it had been there.

Tremaine recalled the sand racing at Firon and the talk about making money and finding rich old men with no near relatives. It had sounded innocuous enough, the kind of banter people might exchange in an idle moment. But there had been that odd feeling that Latinam hadn't been enjoying it as much as his jovial expression had implied; and in both Nicola Paston and Ruth Latinam he had noticed a guarded nervousness, as though they had been anxious for the conversation to stop before it took the wrong turning.

Thinking of Ruth Latinam brought Ivan Holt into his mind. They formed the third pair of suspects—ugly but inevitable word.

He realized that he had subconsciously been regarding them as the most likely of the people at the Rohane hotel to have been involved in the murder. That was dangerous. That was the way to make appearances fit the crime instead of tracing the crime back to its source.

It was true that the relationship between Holt and the girl appeared to be on a tangled level, but that did not mean that the tangle had anything to do with Latinam. In fact, Latinam had always seemed to favour his sister's interest in Holt; it had been Ruth who had been distant and unwilling to commit herself.

There was no sound reason for suspecting Holt. There was no shred of evidence to suggest that he had struck down Hedley Latinam with murderous force and then tried to hide his crime by carrying the body to a nearby water tank where he had hoped it might remain undetected until he was better able to dispose of it.

Except, perhaps, the peculiar incident of the injury to his head on the night of the dance at the hotel. But on that occasion Latinam had been inside the building; it hardly seemed possible that he could have been concerned in the affair.

Ivan Holt had undoubtedly been at large on the night of the murder. Could he have been going to meet Ruth, and could they both have been implicated in what had taken place?

No, that was straining too much to build up a case. Ruth Latinam had not left the hotel. There was nothing at all to justify such a theory.

Tremaine did not know whether to be relieved or disappointed at the results of his mental exercise. He had all but convinced himself that none of his suspects could have been responsible for the murder.

It was just as well to know that one probably didn't need to fear that one had been on familiar terms with a murderer; but it wouldn't be very satisfactory from Chief Officer Colinet's point of view. He would have to look elsewhere for a solution, and the wider you made the field the more difficult your problem became.

And then he remembered that one more pair remained to be added to his list of suspects.

Alan and Valerie Creed. It was true that he hadn't actually seen them on the night of the murder, but their cottage had been close at hand; there was nothing yet to prove they *hadn't* been in Latinam's company.

Memories came crowding into his mind. A memory of Creed and Latinam talking earnestly in the shelter of the rocks in one of the island's bays; a memory of Creed later denying that he knew Latinam well enough to have any dealings with him; a memory of Creed and his wife appearing unexpectedly at the dance at the Rohane hotel given by the man they did not know; a succession of memories of Valerie Creed, her clumsy figure taut and her face betraying an incessant attempt to keep on her guard.

Against what?

He recalled then the strange feeling that he had seen her before that she had given him on their first meeting. He had never been able to place her; the thought had remained a vague irritation in the back of his mind.

He would have to make a determined effort to call back recognition. Had he really met her before? Or was the vagueness a sign that at some time he had merely seen a likeness of her, perhaps a photograph in a newspaper?

Suddenly he felt that the answer would tell him a great deal about the death of Hedley Latinam.

14

EXAMINATION OF A DOUBTFUL
CHARACTER

GASTON LE MAZON was as truculent and uncommunicative as his burly figure and his rough appearance had suggested that he would be. He brought an atmosphere of menace and violence into the severely furnished room at the Rohane hotel which had served Hedley Latinam as his office and which Chief Officer Colinet was now using as his local headquarters.

'There is nothing you have against me,' he growled. 'You cannot keep me here. I know my rights.'

His voice was harsh and guttural but he spoke with a slight island accent which softened his natural belligerence.

'It always surprises me,' the Chief Officer remarked, 'how often people who have something on their minds start talking about their rights.'

Le Mazon's eyes narrowed suspiciously.

'There is nothing on my mind. It is a trick. I do not know anything about this man's death.'

'What makes you imagine, my friend, that I think you do?'

'Why are you here? Why did you send your men for me? It is obvious what you think! Well, you are wrong. I know nothing about murder.'

'I agree that it hasn't been in your line so far, Le Mazon,' the Chief Officer admitted. 'But when a man makes a habit of going outside the law murder sometimes finds its way where it was never intended to go. Your reputation is hardly spotless. Didn't the magistrate have some remarks to make a few weeks ago?'

'Can I help it if the police are always suspicious? If anybody else on the island forgets his licence, or drives at more than the limit, or touches another car on a corner because a road has not been widened, that is to be expected, that is natural. But if it is Gaston Le Mazon who is responsible, that is different. That is a great crime which needs to be punished!'

'Everybody is punished when they break the law,' Colinet said. Tremaine saw the hint of amusement in the big man's eyes and guessed that he was recalling to his own satisfaction a scene in the island's police-court when Le Mazon had been fined for some minor offence. 'You can hardly blame the magistrate when he has a chance of saying a few well-deserved words to someone who's been a thorn in his flesh for a long time, even if the actual occasion doesn't call for more than a fine.'

The Chief Officer leaned back in the inadequate swivel chair behind the dead man's desk. He turned over the pages of the note-book which was almost lost in his massive palms. He glanced at Le Mazon and his tone became harder.

'I am sure you have business to attend to,' he said, with a deliberate sarcasm. 'So let us get down to the matter. You knew this Mr Latinam who has been murdered, did you not?'

'Why should you say that I knew him?'

'You were seen in his company. Not once but several times.'

Le Mazon relaxed. He did not appear to be alarmed.

'It is the truth,' he agreed. 'I knew him.'

'What did you have in common? You, an islander, and this man from the mainland who was running his hotel for visitors who would not wish to associate with such–doubtful–characters.'

'I have a boat,' Le Mazon returned. 'I am a fisherman. Sometimes I do not catch many fish and life is hard. But there are visitors who do not have to fish for a living who are willing to pay well to amuse themselves. It is more profitable to me that they should fish than that I should do so. Unfortunately, there are not many visitors here in Moulin d'Or. It is not easy to find such customers. But a man like Mr Latinam is able to help me.'

He stopped, looking very pleased with himself. Colinet glanced at Tremaine.

'A very natural story,' he commented. 'So Latinam was finding people for you to take out fishing in your boat. Who were the last of his visitors to go with you?'

This time Le Mazon hesitated. He moistened his lips with his tongue.

'It was a new thing this, you understand,' he said at last. 'We had not yet begun.'

'Yes, I understand.' Colinet's tone was very dry. 'You have not taken any of Mr Latinam's visitors yet, nor have you made a firm arrangement to take them. But you were going to. It was a profitable business.'

Le Mazon spread his hands wide in an injured fashion.

'You are too quick. You want to go too fast. But of course there was an arrangement.'

'With whom?'

'I am not sure of the name. It was, I think, a Mr. Bendall. Yes, now I am certain. It was Mr. Bendall.'

Colinet gave him a long, shrewd look. He extricated himself from the swivel chair and went to the door.

'Constable,' he called, 'ask Mr. Bendall if he can spare me a moment.'

He came back to the desk. Le Mazon betrayed no anxiety at this evident sign that his words were to be put to an immediate test. He rubbed his chin with a grimy forefinger.

'I am a simple man. I do not understand all that is taking place. But I know that you suspect me and I think you should be frank. I have heard that Mr. Latinam is dead but I do not know when or how.'

'Indeed? Dear me, I thought you would have had all the details by now.' Colinet sounded surprised; it was impossible to tell whether his surprise was genuine. 'His dead body was found yesterday morning in a water tank belonging to one of the bungalows here at Moulin d'Or.'

'So? Then it was not here at his hotel.'

'No, it was not here. Do you find that strange?'

'Why should I find it strange? You said that it was yesterday morning that he was found? But when did he die? You know that, too?'

'Yes, we know that.'

Colinet was watching the burly fisherman closely. Le Mazon was frowning. It seemed that he would have liked to ask further questions and yet was scared of doing so.

A knock came at the door and it was opened by one of the constables Tremaine had already noticed on duty at the hotel.

'Mr. Bendall's here now, sir.'

'Thank you, Constable.' Colinet nodded. 'Ask him to come in.'

Bendall's step was jaunty. He eyed Le Mazon curiously, gave a careless glance in Tremaine's direction, and then turned to the Chief Officer.

'More questions?' he asked, with a lift of his eyebrows.

His tone was flippant, but the flippancy was not reflected in his face; it was a mask, not an indication of his real feelings.

'Not many more, Mr. Bendall,' the Chief Officer said easily. 'I'm sorry to be such a nuisance. I'm afraid all this is making rather a mess of your holiday.' He indicated Le Mazon. 'Do you know this man?'

Bendall nodded.

'I've seen him before if that's what you mean. His name's Le Mazon, isn't it?'

'Yes. When did you meet him?'

'A couple of days ago. I didn't exactly meet him. Latinam pointed him out to me.'

Le Mazon turned in his chair and regarded Tremaine significantly. Virtue was in every line of his burly form.

'Would you mind telling me,' Colinet went on, 'whether Mr. Latinam had any particular reason for pointing him out to you?'

'Yes, as a matter of fact, he did. I thought about taking a boat out with Nicola—Mrs. Paston. There isn't much of that kind of thing organized around here, as you know, and when I mentioned it to Latinam he suggested Le Mazon and said he'd fix up a trip for us.'

'I see. Thank you, Mr. Bendall.'

Bendall stood facing him uncertainly, a look of surprise on his face.

'That all?'

'Yes, that's all. Just a matter of confirming things. We like to do it step by step. It saves a great deal of time that way.'

The door closed behind him. Colinet fixed his gaze once more upon the fisherman.

'Well, it hangs together. So that *was* why you were having dealings with Latinam. *One* of the reasons, anyway.'

'I told you it was just that you were suspicious,' Le Mazon returned, in an aggrieved tone. 'I am an honest man. I like nothing more than to be allowed to go about my business.'

'All right,' Colinet said. 'All right. It doesn't mean that I'm expecting to see wings sprouting from your shoulders. Since you're being so frank maybe you'd like to tell me where you were on the night before last from ten o'clock onwards.'

Again there was a noticeable hesitation in Le Mazon's manner.

'I was at home. Where should I be?'

'And you did not see Mr Latinam?'

'No, I did not see him.'

The sound of his own voice seemed to be giving him confidence. It was almost as though he thought that his explanation was better than he had imagined. Tremaine leaned forward. He glanced enquiringly at the Chief Officer.

'Go ahead,' Colinet said.

'I was wondering,' Tremaine said, his eyes on Le Mazon, 'whether arranging fishing trips was the *only* business contact you had with Mr. Latinam.'

Le Mazon had turned to face his questioner but now he swung back towards Colinet. A lowering, sullen expression blanketed his features.

'You don't *have* to answer,' the Chief Officer said. 'But you can regard any questions from Mr. Tremaine as having the same effect as if they'd come from me. So that any refusal to answer will be open to the same construction. Which means,' he added, seeing the play of emotion in the other's face, 'that we shall start wondering what you're trying to hide.'

'I have told you already why I met Mr. Latinam,' the fisherman growled.

'What I meant,' Tremaine persevered, 'was what did you find to interest you at the old mill?'

The truculence in Le Mazon's face had been joined by an unmistakable trace of fear. He moved uneasily.

'The mill? What should we be doing at the mill?'

'I don't know.' Tremaine sounded benevolent and disarming. 'I thought you might be able to tell me something about it. And then there were those lights I saw out at sea the other night. You being a fisherman who knows the coast hereabouts I thought you might be able to explain them.'

Le Mazon's face had gone a grey colour. He looked like a man taken by surprise, and anxious to be gone before worse came upon him.

Colinet, watching the display with interest, tapped suggestively upon the surface of the desk with his pencil.

'I haven't heard your answer.'

'What answer should there be?' Le Mazon muttered. 'Lights? The old mill? What should Gaston Le Mazon know about them?' He stood up. He was deliberately ignoring Tremaine. 'I ask that I should be allowed to go.'

Colinet nodded amicably.

'All right, my friend. There's the door and you're free to use it if you want to.'

Slowly, as if he could not quite bring himself to believe there was no trick intended, Le Mazon moved towards the door.

'Remember,' the Chief Officer's soft voice came after him, 'we'll be checking on that alibi. Don't do anything rash like trying to get away from the island. We might have to get annoyed with you and none of us would care for that.'

Le Mazon's hand was on the door when he turned back. He had the air of a man who had at last been stung into speech.

'Why do you always look for Le Mazon when there is something wrong? Is Le Mazon the only one who can be guilty? Why do you not look at the others in Moulin d'Or? Ask them what they fear! *He* knew where to go and what to look for!'

He stood facing them for an instant or two, his face contorted, and then he wrenched the door open and his burly figure thrust its way from the room. The Chief Officer looked expressively at Tremaine.

'Exit with thunder and lightning. You certainly did something to him.'

'I wish I knew what,' Tremaine said. 'It was a shot in the dark. What about his alibi? Do you think it's genuine?'

'I don't know,' Colinet said. 'But we'll soon find out. He lives in a cottage here in Moulin d'Or. We'll see whether his wife confirms his story.'

'His wife?'

Colinet nodded.

'Yes. Our friend Gaston doesn't seem to fit in with a domestic background, does he? But he's married all right. By all accounts his wife doesn't get much of an existence but she sticks by him. Regards him as her man for better or worse, I suppose.'

'In that case won't she be likely to support his alibi whether it's false or not?'

'Probably she will. But we can't lose,' Colinet said philosophically. 'If she does back him up we're no worse off, and if she *doesn't* we'll have the best lead we've had so far.'

Tremaine left the big man in the office—a great deal of routine work needed to be done and he was anxious that his subordinates should deal with it without delay—and left the hotel. On his way down from the headland he met Bendall. It was not a chance meeting; he knew intuitively that the other had been waiting for him.

'What's happening?' Bendall's tone was friendly but urgent. His features, always finely drawn, seemed sharper now; the skin was stretched tight over his cheek-bones in a nervous tension. 'Do they know who did it?'

'If they do,' Tremaine countered, 'they haven't told me. But why should they, in any case?'

Bendall smiled thinly.

'I thought we understood each other. There's been a murder. You're an amateur criminologist.'

'Solving a murder case is a job for professionals. The police don't encourage amateurs.'

'Is that why you've been spending so long with Chief Officer Colinet?' Bendall rejoined disbelievingly. 'All right, I know it was you who found the body. But I don't think it needed as many conferences to hand over the essential information about that.'

Tremaine met his gaze steadily.

'No,' he admitted, 'perhaps it didn't. The Chief Officer thought that since I was staying in the district and had seen quite a lot of Mr. Latinam and his friends I might be able to assist him a little in his investigations.'

'And was the Chief Officer right?'

'That's a question which I don't think I'm at liberty to answer.'

Bendall shrugged.

'Be difficult if that's the way you feel. I don't suppose I can blame you.'

There was a weary, resigned droop to his shoulders. His face lacked the cynicism which had been there so often.

'You might win more confidences,' Tremaine observed quietly, 'if you were more disposed to give them.'

Bendall's head went up.

'Meaning?'

'I think you could tell the police more than you have so far. It might clear the air if you were to be frank with them.'

'I didn't come here merely for a holiday. I'll tell you that much because I dare say you've guessed it anyway. But I didn't come to kill Latinam. You can believe that or not, just as you like. It all looked straightforward and I knew what I was going to do. Now it isn't working out the way I thought.'

It seemed to Tremaine that Bendall was weakening; that he was on the verge of revelation.

'Why not tell me what the trouble is?' he said persuasively. 'You'll get reasonable treatment from the Chief Officer. I can guarantee that. If there's anything you don't want made public that hasn't any real bearing on the case I know he'll do what he can to meet you. His chief consideration is to clear up the murder and to do it as quickly as possible.'

'You're trying hard,' Bendall said wryly. 'And you mean well. But it won't do.'

'What's the difficulty?'

'When you've been giving your mind to something,' Bendall returned grimly, 'and then you find that you can't have what you've been after without doing damage in another direction that you hadn't bargained for, you've got to stop and think.'

Tremaine nodded gravely, trying to catch his mood.

'Sometimes that's the way of it. But in the long run it pays to speak out openly.'

'It doesn't happen to be my right to speak,' Bendall said. 'I'm afraid that settles it.'

He turned and began to walk on up towards the hotel. Tremaine let him go. It wouldn't be any good to go on trying to talk him out of it. At least, not yet.

15

A CHANGE IN THE EVIDENCE

ALTHOUGH it was a warm and sunny afternoon the lounge of the Rohane hotel was full. Nobody had been anxious to brave the stares and whispers of the clusters of sightseers still being drawn to the district by the magnet of murder, and the Chief Officer had in any case made it plain that he would prefer them to stay within reach so that they would be easily available for further questioning if necessary.

Glancing around Tremaine was dismayed by the change that had come over their relationships in so short a time. Instead of the general conversation which would have existed two days earlier there was a taut gloom broken only by an occasional brief and hushed remark.

Ivan Holt saw him come in and tossed the periodical he had been reading into an empty chair.

'Seems to me there's a lot of unnecessary fuss being made. Anybody would think we were all under suspicion.'

It was meant to be a challenge. Tremaine accepted it.

'I'm afraid,' he said, 'that that's just what we are.'

He studied the reaction that went around the room, from Nicola Paston's quickly stifled gasp to the tightening of Geoffrey Bendall's already compressed lips.

Major Ayres laid aside the newspaper he had been pretending to read. He cleared his throat with a great deal of noise.

'Hrrm. You're not serious? Joking, eh, what?'

'Dear me, no, Major,' Tremaine returned. 'A man's been murdered. We're the people who made up his immediate circle and are therefore most likely to know something about his death.'

Major Ayres flashed a quick glance at Mrs. Burres, who was knitting determinedly in one corner; she remained steadfastly watching her needles.

'See what you mean, of course. Hrrm. Difficult situation.'

'It seems to me,' Ivan Holt said deliberately, 'to be a typical obtuse piece of official reasoning. Latinam's murderer might have come from anywhere.'

Ruth Latinam looked across at him, her dark eyes fixed on him in appeal.

'Must we go into all that again, Ivan?'

Her expression discomfited him; that much was evident from his heightened colour. But he persisted doggedly.

'You're not going to agree that it was one of us, Ruth?'

'Of course not,' she told him sharply. 'That's absurd, Ivan. But you can't blame the police for seeing it that way.'

Her voice trembled. She looked as though she was going to cry. Tremaine thought that it was up to him.

'You're looking a bit under the weather, Miss Latinam,' he remarked. 'Why not come out into the sunshine for a few moments?'

She came to her feet automatically; it was clear that she was responding because it was expected of her, not from any personal desire.

Walking with her towards the terrace Tremaine was uncomfortably aware that every other eye in the room was turned upon them. He had the confidence of the police. He knew what they had discovered; he knew what else they wished to know.

It was easy enough to imagine the questions that would be in the minds of people around whom hung the suspicion of murder. What was he going to ask her? What pregnant questions did he propose to put?

Ruth Latinam accompanied him mechanically, without a backward glance. They went down the steps of the terrace and out across the cliffs.

'What is it you wish to know?' she said.

She was facing him now, her dark eyes probing. The breeze drifted a strand of hair across her forehead. She pushed it back into place with a gesture that seemed to give her an air of challenge.

Tremaine smiled.

'I think you misunderstand,' he said, but she gave him a quick denial.

'No,' she told him, 'I don't think I do. But please don't feel that I'm annoyed about it. I realize that questions have to be asked and I can quite see why the police should think that you might be better able to find out the things that need to be known than someone official who's never met us before.'

'You make me sound rather an unpleasant individual.'

'Do I? I'm sorry. I don't mean to. It's just that I seem to be past caring any more.'

'I'm quite sure that everyone understands how you feel. It's been a dreadful shock for you. It happened so suddenly, without warning. There's been so little time for you to adjust yourself to a new life.'

'A new life!' she echoed quietly. She turned away from him, staring out over the water. The breeze, blowing her dress about her, emphasized her slender form as it had done that day on the cliffs near Mortelet lighthouse. Despite the sunshine she was dark with tragedy. 'A new life!' she repeated. 'I wonder? I seem to be moving in a dream. I can't bring myself to believe that Hedley's dead.'

'It's a mercy we're granted in a time of suffering. Being numbed we don't feel the full extent of the shock, and when at last we do we've had time to prepare ourselves.'

'I'm not going to pretend,' she said steadily. 'I don't feel any grief because Hedley's dead. Not real grief. I think it's more because of the *way* he died than because it actually happened.'

'In that case,' Tremaine said, 'perhaps it will be easier for you to discuss it without pain. Can you think of anyone who might have wished harm to your brother?'

She had evidently been expecting the question, for her answer came without hesitation.

'No,' she said. 'I can think of no one.'

'No—business associate?'

'He had more than enough money to live on. This hotel was his business, and I think you know that it was more a hobby with him than a business in the true sense. I hardly imagine that anyone could have been afraid he was setting up too much in competition.'

'I noticed that he liked to have people around him, although in so short a time I didn't get to know him really well.' He ignored the bitterness that had been in her voice. He was distressed at the hard lines that had settled around her mouth. 'What about the guests at the hotel? Did you notice any signs of discord between your brother and anyone staying here?'

'I imagine you already know the answer to that,' she returned. 'After all, you've seen a good deal of us.'

'Yes, that's true,' he admitted. 'But the onlooker doesn't always see most of the game. Sometimes the players hide their real feelings just because there *is* an onlooker present.'

He studied her thoughtfully and decided that there was little to be gained by any more fencing.

'I was thinking chiefly of Mr. Holt,' he observed, and was rewarded by her sudden hiss of indrawn breath.

'Why should you think of Ivan?'

'Because he's in love with you,' he told her calmly. 'And because I'm not altogether certain about your brother's attitude.'

'Aren't you being rather personal?'

She was breathing quickly and her body had become taut with what might have been either anger or dread.

'Yes, I'm afraid I am. It isn't very pleasant for either of us, but I'm sure you can see that if the questions were to be left to the police it might prove to be even more unpleasant—for you.'

'You're talking in riddles,' she said, in a low voice.

'But riddles I think you understand. Believe me I want to help you. Why not tell me all you can?'

For an instant she looked very young and very helpless, and his sentimental soul went out to her.

'I can't,' she whispered. 'I—daren't.'

She realized that she had been on the point of betrayal, and her lips came together. She made an effort to speak formally.

'I think I'd like to go in again. It was very good of you to come out with me but I feel better now.'

It was palpably untrue but Tremaine was not aware of any way in which he could have challenged her without being discourteous.

They went back into the lounge. As they stepped through the open windows he came face to face with Mrs. Burres. She had dropped her knitting and was openly staring at them. He knew that she would have given a great deal to have known the subject of their conversation.

The atmosphere was too strained for comfort; after a moment or two Tremaine made his way to the office where he knew he would find Colinet. Inspector Marchant was there; he had obviously been in conference with his chief.

'How are they taking it?' Colinet asked, with a lift of his eyebrows. 'Any noticeable reactions?'

'They aren't talking much,' Tremaine said. 'Everybody seems to be waiting for someone else to make a move. I've just been having a word with Ruth Latinam,' he added. 'She wouldn't open out but she's hiding something.'

'I wouldn't be surprised,' the Chief Officer returned, and the dry note in his voice made Tremaine give him an intent scrutiny.

'There've been—developments?'

'Marchant's been digging,' Colinet said. 'It's surprising how much you can turn up when you really get started. Better let him tell you himself.'

Tremaine glanced at the inspector. Marchant nodded.

'I've been going through the staff. Just to make sure.'

'Apparently,' Colinet said, 'there's been some high life below stairs.'

'The barman-porter,' Marchant explained, 'and the chamber-maid. Crevicher—that's his name—seems to have been turning the young lady's head.'

'The barman? But he's quite elderly, isn't he? I'm not sure of the chambermaid but if she's the girl I've noticed about once or twice when I've been here she isn't much more than a child.'

'Quite so. This is her first job. Her parents live in the village. They've always kept an eye on her and I suppose she's been growing up a little faster just lately. Anyway, Crevicher's been making the most of his chances.'

'A distressing business, certainly,' Tremaine said. 'Did Latinam know what was going on?'

'If he did he wasn't doing anything about it. But on the night he was killed Crevicher and the girl went out for a little—er—dalliance.'

'You mean, they saw something?'

'They saw *someone*,' Colinet intervened. 'Ruth Latinam.'

'Oh.' Tremaine's hand went up to his pince-nez. 'So she *wasn't* indoors, after all.'

'Not if the girl's speaking the truth. And Marchant believes that she is.'

'She's telling the truth all right,' the inspector said. 'It was plain when I started to question her that she wanted to hide something and it didn't take long to find out what it was. She's scared of the news of what she's been up to getting back to her parents. They're respectable folk who believe in old-fashioned remedies. That's why she told me about Miss Latinam. She didn't like doing it—I understand that Miss Latinam's always treated her well—but she wanted to shift the limelight away from herself. Once she had told me, of course, it was too late to go back on it.'

'What about Crevicher? Does he confirm her story?'

'As far as seeing Miss Latinam is concerned.' The Chief Officer was laboriously disentangling himself from his chair. 'They're waiting in one of the other rooms. I'll have them in.'

He went over to the door and despatched a constable with the necessary instructions.

'You say the girl comes from this part of the island?' Tremaine said. 'What's her name?'

'Geffard,' Colinet told him. 'Ena Geffard. It's a well-known name hereabouts.'

'Yes, I believe I've noticed it on one or two shops in the district. You don't suppose there could be any local antagonism against Latinam and his sister? I mean on account of his being a newcomer to the island?'

Colinet shook his head.

'Too many of our people make a living out of catering for summer visitors for that kind of insular idea to last very long! You're trying very hard on Miss Latinam's behalf,' he added shrewdly. 'But I'm afraid it won't do. The girl saw her right enough.'

Tremaine was saved from embarrassment by the arrival of the constable with his two charges. Ena Geffard was a plump, dark girl, clearly in that difficult transition stage when new maturity of body has not yet been matched with a similar maturity of mind. She was wearing a tight-fitting black dress, obviously chosen with the purpose of emphasizing what she believed to be her seduction of figure. Under normal conditions he might have considered her pretty, but at the moment she was not at her best for her face was red and tear-stained.

Crevicher, slight, grey-haired, and more than old enough to be her father, came in diffidently just behind her. He looked uncomfortable; Tremaine guessed with satisfaction that Marchant had been exceeding his authority and passing caustic judgment on the barman's behaviour.

'Sit down,' Colinet said to the girl, not unkindly. 'Before I ask Miss Latinam to come in I want to make quite sure that you haven't made a mistake. You're certain that you *did* see her?'

The girl nodded miserably.

'Yes, sir. I couldn't be wrong about her.'

Colinet switched his glance to the barman. His voice became harder.

'And you?'

'It's true what she says, sir. It was Miss Latinam. Both of us saw her. She didn't see us, though, because—well—'

'Because you took good care not to let her. Under the circumstances,' Colinet said grimly. 'All right. We won't go into *that*. And the time?'

'Just after eleven o'clock, sir. I was surprised to see her out so late by herself and when she'd gone by I looked at my watch.'

'It won't make any trouble?' the girl broke in tremulously. 'I don't want to say anything against Miss Latinam, not to do her harm.'

'Your job is just to speak the truth, my girl,' Colinet said sternly. 'The rest doesn't concern you.'

He looked significantly at Marchant and the inspector nodded and went out. There was complete silence in the room during the few moments it took to bring Ruth Latinam from the lounge; Tremaine sensed that the Chief Officer was doing his best to bring the gravity of the situation home to his two witnesses.

Ruth Latinam was plainly surprised to see Crevicher and the girl but she made no comment. She took the chair Marchant set for her facing the desk.

'You know these two people, of course, Miss Latinam?' Colinet said, and she made a brief inclination of her head.

'Of course.'

'Naturally,' the Chief Officer went on, 'a great deal of time is taken up in an investigation of this type in checking up on what seems to be the obvious. We set one person's statement against another's, and then if we come across a discrepancy anywhere we have to try and sort things out.'

'A—discrepancy?' she said, with a slight catch of her breath.

'That's right. Like this one that's just turned up,' Colinet remarked casually. 'In *your* statement you said that on the night your brother was killed you went to bed early because you had a headache, and now we've just been hearing that over half an hour after you were supposed to have gone to your room you were seen walking over the sand dunes.'

Ena Geffard half-rose to her feet.

'I didn't mean to tell them, miss,' she broke out. 'I didn't want to do anything to hurt you. But I—I was frightened. I didn't know what I was saying.'

'Am I to understand, Ena,' Ruth Latinam said, 'that you saw me on the sand dunes just after eleven o'clock that night?'

'I couldn't help it, miss. They kept on asking me questions. I—I was afraid of what would happen.'

For a second or two Ruth Latinam sat facing her. And then she smiled.

'It's all right, Ena,' she said gently. 'There's nothing for you to be worried about. After all, if you saw me there's no reason why you shouldn't tell the Chief Officer.'

'Then you admit,' Colinet said, 'that you were there?'

'Certainly I was there,' she told him calmly.

The big man glanced at the constable who was still standing at the door.

'In that case we don't need to detain these two,' he observed with a nod towards Ena Geffard and Crevicher.

The constable escorted them from the room, Crevicher moving quickly with relief—not once had he been able to meet Ruth Latinam's eyes—and the girl with a last tearful backward glance.

Ruth Latinam was frowning.

'They were out together? Crevicher and Ena? I saw nothing of them. Why didn't they speak to me?'

'I gathered,' Colinet said, 'that they were embarrassed at the thought of your seeing them and kept under cover.'

Understanding came into her face then.

'I see. But Ena's hardly more than a child! Surely Crevicher didn't—'

'Apparently the girl's come to no harm. The affair was still in its early stages. And after this little episode I don't think either of them is likely to try and take it any further. But that's by the way, Miss Latinam. The question I want answered now is why you should have lied to me.'

'You sound very serious. You don't imagine, surely, that I murdered my brother?'

'Why didn't you tell me that you left the hotel?'

'I didn't think it was important.'

Colinet raised his eyebrows. He allowed the disbelief to sound plainly in his voice.

'Not important! I find it difficult to accept that you're being serious, Miss Latinam. Why *did* you go out?'

'I've already explained that I had a headache. When I got to my room I–I felt stifled. I just had to have some air before I got into bed, otherwise I knew I'd never sleep. I went for a short walk over the dunes.'

Her voice was level and emotionless. It was as though she was reciting a well-rehearsed lesson.

'Did you see your brother?'

'No. I didn't see anyone. I didn't realize,' she added, 'that anyone had seen *me*.'

'How long were you out?'

'I'm not sure. Perhaps a quarter of an hour, perhaps twenty minutes. I didn't notice.' Her dark eyes met Colinet's grey ones. 'Nothing important happened. I didn't think it would have any bearing on the case. That's why I didn't trouble to mention it before. I'm sorry if I've made things difficult.'

'It certainly doesn't help when people forget essential pieces of information,' Colinet said. Deliberately he emphasized the word forget and Tremaine thought he saw her flinch. 'Is there anything further you would like to add now, Miss Latinam?'

'No, I don't think so. I've told you all I can.'

'Very well.'

There was a pause. She looked at him innocuously.

'Does that mean you've finished with me? I can go?'

'Yes,' Colinet said. 'You can go.'

Her face was a little white but she moved quietly and without haste to the door. It closed behind her.

'Very cool,' Marchant observed. 'Very cool indeed.'

The Chief Officer leaned back in his chair. He was frowning.

'I don't like it,' he said. 'I don't like it at all.'

Tremaine pushed back his pince-nez. He glanced at his companions. *He* didn't like it very much either.

16

THE FRIGHTENED MAN

INSPECTOR MARCHANT had evidently been busy. It was the morning after the unsatisfactory interview with Ruth Latinam. Watching the road leading to the headland Mordecai Tremaine had seen the Chief Officer's car making for the Rohane hotel and had set off in the same direction himself. The inspector had arrived shortly afterwards and the three of them were now seated in the familiar office.

Colinet had settled himself in the swivel chair behind the desk but he had the air of a man who had not come to stay.

'I'll be leaving you to it, Marchant,' he observed. 'I'm in for a pretty full day back in town. The arrears have been piling up. But you'll know where to find me if anything turns up.' He glanced at Tremaine. 'Any news since yesterday?'

Tremaine shook his head.

'Nothing fresh.'

'Miss Latinam not decided to take us into her confidence?'

'No, I'm afraid not.'

'I've been sorting out Le Mazon's alibi, sir,' Marchant said. 'It isn't looking too healthy.'

'You mean for Le Mazon? His wife isn't backing him up?'

'I didn't start with his wife,' the inspector returned. 'I thought she mightn't be inclined to be helpful, so I made a few enquiries in the village. When I'd found a couple of witnesses who were prepared to swear that they'd seen Le Mazon round about eleven o'clock on the night of the murder I went along and tackled both of them.'

'Any results?'

'Le Mazon tried to bluff it out at first. Swore he hadn't been out of his cottage after ten and that the witnesses must have been mistaken. But it didn't take long to make him change his tune. Funny thing, sir,' the inspector went on, 'I wouldn't have expected him to break up as he did. He seemed to go right to pieces.'

'He admitted his alibi was a fake?'

'Not directly. He didn't say straight out that he *had* been out. But he started in on a lot of wild talk about how he was always being persecuted and how we wouldn't leave him alone. I've never seen him in such a state before. He was practically on his knees and that's a sight I didn't imagine I'd see.'

'It sounds as though you've got something,' Colinet said thoughtfully. 'So Le Mazon's alibi isn't worth a bean and he's really scared. Maybe you'd better keep working in that quarter. Find out if anybody in the village can throw any light on what he was up to with Latinam. Let him see what you're after. Fear's a great loosener of tongues; you may force him into the open.'

He was lifting himself to his feet when there was an urgent knock on the door.

'It's Gaston Le Mazon, sir,' said the constable who came in. 'He's here asking if he can see you. Seems in a bit of a panic, sir.'

Colinet glanced significantly at his companions. Slowly he levered himself back into his seat.

'Maybe we'd better have him in and find out what's troubling him. All right, Constable, bring him along.'

It was clear from his appearance and the shambling, hurried manner of his entrance—as though he could not get in quickly enough and yet feared to come—that Gaston Le Mazon's nerves were under a severe strain. He seemed unable to control his hands, and he looked like a man who had not slept for some time.

He made straight for Colinet.

'I want to know what it is you have against me.'

'Sit down,' the Chief Officer said coldly. He glanced at his watch significantly. 'I can spare you exactly five minutes.'

His disinterested, deliberately hostile tone sobered Le Mazon. The burly fisherman lost something of his air of impetuous aggression; he sat down obediently; he was still agitated but he was obviously trying now to control himself.

'You think that it was Le Mazon who killed Latinam,' he muttered.

'You mean,' Colinet said, 'that *you* think that is what I believe.'

'Then why do the police come to me? Why do they keep asking me questions?'

'Maybe it's because we're not satisfied with your answers. For instance, we're not satisfied with the reason you've given for your connection with Latinam. And we're not satisfied that you *were* safely indoors at the time of the murder.'

Le Mazon did not reply for a second or two. His eyes flickered towards Inspector Marchant. A cunning look settled upon his sullen features.

'Always it is Le Mazon you suspect. You do not trouble to look anywhere else. It is too easy to say that it is Le Mazon who is guilty. But there are things you do not know—things that would make you change your mind.'

Colinet studied him thoughtfully.

'In that case,' he observed, 'perhaps you could tell us about them.'

Le Mazon drew a deep breath, as though he was about to embark upon some laborious task.

'I was to have taken my boat,' he said, 'with Mr. Bendall and Mrs. Paston. It was Latinam who told them that I would arrange it for them.'

'So much we know already,' Colinet remarked. 'It was for a fishing trip,' he added, making his irony plain. 'For you it was good business. The money was to have been good.'

'The money was to have been good,' Le Mazon agreed. 'But it was not for a fishing trip.'

There was a different note in his voice now; it held a strange mixture of triumph and reluctance. His burly figure leaned towards the Chief Officer.

'There would have been an—accident. Mr. Bendall and Mrs. Paston would have been drowned.'

Colinet brought his hands down upon the desk. His grey eyes were hard and stern.

'And who was it who desired this—accident?'

'It was Latinam. He said that I knew the currents; that I could see to it that no one suspected that anything was wrong. People have been drowned here before; it is a very dangerous coast for those who do not know. He said that he would pay me well if I would do what he asked.'

'In other words you're telling me that Latinam wanted you to murder Mr. Bendall and Mrs. Paston in such a way that it would look like an accident?'

'That is what he wanted.'

'And just why was he suggesting that you should murder two of his guests?'

'I do not know. He did not tell me and he was not a man you would ask questions.'

Colinet frowned. He gave Le Mazon a long, reflective stare.

'And did you agree to do this thing?'

The fisherman shifted in his seat. He raised his big hands in a deprecating gesture. There was almost a note of hurt in his voice.

'But no,' he said virtuously. 'Gaston Le Mazon has done many wrong things. I admit it. But murder is not one of them. Gaston Le Mazon does not kill. I told him that I would have none of it.'

'How did Latinam take that?'

'He did not like it. He wanted it done, you understand. But what was there he could do? He could not tell people that Gaston Le Mazon would not kill for him.'

Colinet coughed behind a massive hand, concealing his quick smile at the man's assumption of rectitude.

'Why did you not tell the police that this offer had been made to you?'

'Would the police have believed Gaston Le Mazon? Would they have taken his word against that of the respectable Mr. Latinam? It was best that nothing should be said.'

'What made you decide to talk about it now?'

The cunning expression deepened in Le Mazon's face. Watching him closely Tremaine was aware that this was the crux of the matter; this was the reason for the man's visit.

'Now it is different. You are accusing Gaston Le Mazon, but all the time it is to this Mr. Bendall you should look. Maybe he knew that Latinam wanted him killed. Maybe he thought that he would do something about it first.'

The fisherman stopped, breathing heavily, his face flushed. He faced Colinet challengingly.

The Chief Officer gave no sign of having been impressed by what he had heard.

'Is that all you came for?'

Le Mazon looked discomfited. Slowly the elation drained away from his eyes; fear and uncertainty took its place. His glance went to Inspector Marchant and then came back to Colinet.

'You do not believe me! You think that I have lied! It is the truth I have told you!'

'Your five minutes are up,' Colinet said. He nodded to the constable. 'All right, see that he leaves.'

Reluctantly Le Mazon came to his feet. He looked like a man who had played what he had imagined to be a winning card and had seen it make no difference to the game. There was a hint of desperation in his voice.

'There were other things, too. You will see. I will find them out and I will tell you!'

The constable closed the door firmly upon his protests. Colinet raised an eyebrow in Marchant's direction.

'Did you say you'd scared him?'

'Sounds like an understatement now, sir,' Marchant said. 'Do you think Latinam really wanted him to get rid of Mr. Bendall and Mrs. Paston?'

The Chief Officer looked at Tremaine.

'What about it?' he said significantly.

'There was certainly something odd going on between Bendall and Latinam,' Tremaine admitted. 'I don't know that it was big enough for murder.'

'It isn't going to be easy to make sure,' Colinet said. 'Maybe that's what Le Mazon's depending on.'

'You mean he made up the story because he wanted to throw suspicion on Bendall in order to save his own skin?'

'If ever I've seen a man in a state of panic it was Le Mazon just now. That means he must have good reason to be scared. Is it because he's afraid we're trying to pin Latinam's murder on him? If it is then he thinks there's a case against him.'

'Either he's guilty,' Tremaine said slowly, 'or he knows we're liable to discover something that will make it look as though he might be. So he's trying to confuse the trail. If Bendall and Nicola Paston knew that Latinam was likely to make an attempt to kill them they aren't likely to say so now because that would mean admitting he must have had a reason. And the reason might work in reverse. It might give us a motive to explain why *they* might have killed Latinam.'

'Exactly. Le Mazon's succeeding in creating a reasonable doubt. Even if we confront Bendall with the story and Bendall tells us it's nonsense we can't be *sure.*'

Walking down from the hotel after the Chief Officer had gone back to St. Julian Harbour and Inspector Marchant had proceeded about his business, Tremaine thought the matter over. Was Gaston Le Mazon merely a badly frightened man casting about for some way of diverting suspicion from himself? Or was he a very clever rogue deliberately trying to obscure the issue?

He was in no hurry and he allowed his stroll to follow a devious route which brought him eventually into the straggling village which was the heart of Moulin d'Or. Occupied with his thoughts, he almost collided with Ralph Exenley at the entrance to the small general stores.

Exenley was carrying a shopping basket. He noticed Tremaine's glance.

'Just been replenishing supplies,' he explained. 'I've been chary about moving very far with so many people all coming to gaze on the scene of the crime. Been a bit embarrassing. Interest seems to be slackening a bit now, though. I don't feel quite so much like a prize exhibit when I walk down the road.'

He nodded to an elderly man who was sitting smoking on the lawn of the house they were just passing. Tremaine regarded his companion speculatively.

'You're one of the locals, Ralph. What's the gossip?'

'It's all on one topic,' Exenley returned. 'But that's what you mean, isn't it?'

'It isn't often,' Tremaine said, 'that a place like this has a murder to talk about. You'd expect people to make the most of it.'

Exenley stooped to throw her ball back to a small girl who had been on the point of running into the roadway after it. He was not wearing a jacket, but was dressed in an old pair of flannel trousers, obviously used for odd jobs about the village, sandals, and open-necked shirt. As he retrieved his shopping basket, which he had temporarily set down upon the path, Tremaine thought what a homely, reassuring figure he made, with his stocky form and broad, kindly features.

There was something solid about Ralph. He was part of Moulin d'Or. He represented the decencies of the place. The simple decencies which had been outraged by murder and the subsequent invasion by its camp followers.

'Whether there's any solid reason for it I wouldn't like to say,' Exenley remarked, 'but there's one person who's an odds-on favourite as the murderer.'

'Le Mazon?'

'Yes. I suppose he'd have been a natural choice in any case on account of his reputation, and with all the other things added the opinion locally is that he's the fellow the police are after.'

'The other things?'

'Well, he's known to have had dealings with Latinam. And then there's the way in which Inspector Marchant's been working. Looking for people who might have seen him on the night of the murder and so on. It didn't take long for *that* news to get around.'

'What about you, Ralph. Do *you* think he might have done it?'

Exenley chuckled.

'*You're* the detective! But for what it's worth my opinion is that it would be a very satisfactory solution if it turned out to be Le Mazon who killed Latinam. He's been making himself a nuisance hereabouts for far too long.'

'You mean getting the place a bad name by his activities?'

'Not only that. You've had a chance to see Moulin d'Or now and you know what it's like—a quiet little place, reasonably prosperous and everybody trying to live in the way they want. Some people making a living out of growing tomatoes, some by taking visitors, by a little fishing, one or two cottagers engaged on building or quarrying—it's a sound little community. And Le Mazon's been like a sort of maggot eating at the heart of it.'

'You're very attached to it, aren't you, Ralph?'

'Yes, I am,' Exenley admitted frankly. 'I've made it my home and I've enjoyed watching it tick over. That's why I've resented Le Mazon. Everybody knows that he plays the bully when he thinks he can get away with it and that the village is under his thumb. The trouble has been that he's taken care not to come up against the law; the shopkeepers and the other people he's terrorized have been scared to say anything against him and without putting oneself in the wrong and being the aggressor it hasn't been possible to do much about it.'

'So Le Mazon,' Tremaine said, 'wouldn't be missed?'

'I don't think anybody would be sorry if the police took him off. Not that there's a general desire to wish a murder on to his shoulders, but if somebody has to be guilty we'd prefer it to be Le Mazon. But there,' Exenley finished, with a rueful grimace, 'I've said enough to show you that I'm prejudiced. You'd better not attach too much weight to my opinion.'

'It's possible,' Tremaine observed, 'that your prejudice may turn out to be justice.'

'You've found out something?' Exenley put the question quickly and then looked a little embarrassed. 'Sorry. I'm taking too much for granted. I don't suppose you'll want to give away any secrets.'

'Judging by the way news seems to travel in this district, Ralph, I hardly imagine it will remain a secret for long! It's just that Gaston Le Mazon is a very frightened man—or at least he's giving the impression of being one.'

'And a frightened man,' Exenley said shrewdly, 'is likely to do something rash. Is that it?'

'Yes,' Tremaine said, 'that's it.'

'Well, I dare say Colinet will keep a close eye on him. Once the police have begun to suspect that they've got the right man they don't let him out of their sight for long.'

Tremaine parted from his companion a few moments later—Exenley had several more purchases to make—and went on towards Janet's and Mark's bungalow.

Could it have been Le Mazon? It seemed that it was a solution which would satisfy all parties—except, of course, the man himself.

It would lift the shadow of suspicion from the other people concerned—people who must now be wondering uncomfortably whether the police had developed any ideas about them. It would dispose, for instance, of the unpleasant question mark which was now poised above Geoffrey Bendall following Le Mazon's interview with the Chief Officer.

But even as the thought came to him he realized that it was not Bendall who was in the forefront of his mind but Ivan Holt.

THE LADY WALKS AT NIGHT

IT HAD been intended to make Hedley Latinam's funeral a simple affair, but the newspaper publicity given to his death made that particular wish impossible of fulfilment. The route from the hotel to the church and the little cemetery behind it was thronged with spectators; in the cemetery, indeed, the cortege had difficulty in making its way to the graveside.

For Ruth Latinam it must have been a painful ordeal. It was inevitable that the main interest should centre upon her as the dead man's sister. She bore it composedly enough, however; she looked pale but she did not give way to any elaborate grief.

Everybody from the Rohane hotel was present, including the staff. Crevicher, the barman, looked self-conscious when Tremaine unwittingly caught his eye, but Ena Geffard seemed to have recovered her composure. She gave the impression that she was enjoying her brief moment of borrowed notoriety; Tremaine was inclined to think that her parents had troubled days lying ahead of them.

He had purposely chosen to mingle with the crowd rather than attend as a member of the funeral procession. He did not want to draw the attention of the reporters. He had recognized one Fleet Street man with whom he had had dealings; he did not desire to embarrass Colinet by having his presence made the subject of prominent comment. Already one or two newspapers had mentioned him by name.

When the brief ceremony was over he made his way unobtrusively to the Rohane hotel. As he had expected, Colinet was already there, occupying his usual seat at the desk in the office.

'Everything go off all right?' the Chief Officer asked.

'Apart from the crowds. There were no awkward moments from our point of view.'

'Miss Latinam take it well?'

'Yes,' Tremaine said. 'Yes, she took it well.'

'H'm.' It was a sound difficult of analysis. Colinet was silent for a moment or two and then he glanced up suddenly from under his brows. 'Did you know that Mrs. Burres and Major Ayres were leaving the hotel?' he asked.

Tremaine shook his head.

'No, I didn't know. But I'm not surprised. I imagine that now the funeral's over—and if *you* don't take a hand—all the guests will be leaving. In fact, I should think it quite likely that Miss Latinam will close the place down and try and get rid of it.'

'I'm not talking in that sense,' Colinet said. 'This arrangement was made *before* Latinam was murdered. Do you recall hearing anything about it?'

'Well, I don't know about the major but I remember Mrs. Burres being mentioned. Bendall said one day on the beach that he'd heard that she was leaving and he asked Latinam to do what he could to make her change her mind.'

'What did Latinam say to that?'

'Oh, something about it not being up to him to tell his guests what to do. Something quite casual.'

'I wonder?' Colinet observed, and Tremaine gave him a shrewd glance.

'You don't think it's quite as simple?'

'I've heard,' the Chief Officer said, 'that Mrs. Burres and the major were leaving the hotel because they were under notice to go.'

'Under notice? Latinam wanted to get rid of them?'

'So my information suggests?'

'But why? They've been here longer than any of the others. They were here when Latinam bought the hotel and I understood that it was part of his agreement at the time that they should stay on. What reason could he have had to give them notice?'

'There,' Colinet admitted, 'the ground is less firm. I don't know that the reason given to me is the correct one.'

'May I ask,' Tremaine said, 'who told you of this?'

'The best of all possible informants. Mrs. Burres herself. My impression,' the big man added, 'was that she was afraid I would find out anyway and wanted to make sure I found out from the right quarter.'

'She spoke for the major as well?'

'Yes. Does that surprise you?'

'No. I've always linked them in my mind.'

The Chief Officer's fingertips were drumming idly on the desk.

'Murders take place for all kinds of strange motives,' he said ruminatively. 'I suppose it *is* possible that a middle-aged woman might develop a homicidal dislike for a man who was trying to force her out of the place she had come to regard as her home.'

Tremaine thought of Mrs. Burres, knitting steadily, her stolid form in its shapeless costume giving her the appearance of a stubborn rock that had refused to allow its contours to be rounded by the action of the weather and the sea. There was something implacable about her.

'It's rather a dreadful idea,' he said slowly.

'Murder is a dreadful thing,' Colinet returned. 'There's no doubt,' he added, 'as to the dominant partner where those two are concerned. The major's just clay.'

'To opportunity then we can add a possible motive. Not a particularly obvious one, but who knows what goes on in a woman's mind?' Tremaine was looking troubled. 'Did she offer you any explanation for Latinam's attitude?'

'Said that he was a bad man who was up to no good and that he was afraid they might find out too much. Maybe that *was* the case. They'd been snooping on Latinam and Latinam didn't like it. Might even be that they were following him on the night he was murdered to see what he was up to. If he'd realized what they were doing anything could have happened.'

Colinet made it clear what was in his mind. Tremaine nodded. It fitted. It couldn't be ignored. It had to be set alongside the other things like Ruth Latinam's lying about going to her room, like Alan Creed talking furtively to Latinam and then pretending that he didn't have any dealings with him, and like Gaston Le Mazon's story about Bendall and Nicola Paston and the malevolence that had been in Hedley Latinam's face that day on the cliffs near Mortelet.

He left the big man in the office and went out to the headland. When you were faced with such a tangle of problems you needed solitude and a place in which to think. Maybe, in the air and the sunshine, the solution would be easier to find.

He spent some time lying on the springy turf near the crumbling edge of the cliff, endeavouring to set his thoughts in order, and when he went back towards the hotel he saw that two deck-chairs had been placed together at one end of the terrace outside the lounge. He caught a glimpse of Ruth Latinam's dark frock, acquired for her brother's funeral. She did not notice him come soft-footed over the grass.

'Please, Ivan,' he heard her say. 'Please don't ask me again.'

'It's got to be settled, Ruth,' came Ivan Holt's urgent tones. 'I'm not blaming *you*. I can understand how it happened.'

'You don't know the whole story,' she told him desperately.

'I'm not going to lose you now, Ruth. If necessary I'll take things into my own hands.'

There was a sudden shrill note of terror in her voice.

'No, you mustn't! Ivan, you mustn't—please!'

It was in that moment that Holt sensed that they were no longer alone. It was too late for concealment. Tremaine came on as if he was deep in thought, unaware of their presence. A moment later he looked up and gave what he hoped was a convincing start.

'Oh, hullo,' he said, feeling that he must sound rather too bright. 'Enjoying the sun? I think you're very wise. No good spending the time moping indoors. Can't do any good, you know.'

'No,' Ivan Holt said, through tight lips. 'No, it can't.'

He made no move to continue the conversation, nor did Ruth Latinam. Regretfully Tremaine went into the building.

Chief Officer Colinet was still in the office and he had been joined by Inspector Marchant. Tremaine eyed the tall, slow-moving but capable inspector with suddenly awakened interest; he had begun to associate Marchant's appearances with fresh items of information.

He was not disappointed.

'Marchant's been digging again,' Colinet said. 'It seems that he's managed to dig up another witness.'

The inspector shrugged deprecatingly.

'It was easy enough,' he commented. 'Now that they think Le Mazon is on his way out everybody in Moulin d'Or is anxious to put another nail in his coffin. At one time you could hardly get a word out of them; now it's a job to stop them talking.'

'Somebody else who saw him on the night of the murder?' Tremaine asked, but the inspector shook his head.

'No, this happened a day or two beforehand. Chap named Lenglois was taking a short cut home from the quarry where he's working and saw Latinam and Le Mazon together near the old mill. According to Lenglois they were having an argument. He didn't get too close—he wasn't anxious for them to see him—but he says he was near enough to be certain that Latinam was threatening Le Mazon and shaking his fist at him. Lenglois isn't prepared to swear definitely to this but he says he thinks he heard Latinam say something about Le Mazon's keeping his mouth shut or it would be the worse for him.'

'Maybe not much by itself,' Colinet said, 'but it goes with the rest. He had dealings with Latinam that won't stand too close an investigation, they quarrelled, and he wasn't where he says he was on the night of the murder.'

Tremaine looked at the inspector.

'Where is he now?'

'He's been spending most of his time mooning around the old gun emplacements up near the beach. Hasn't had much to do with anybody. We'll know where to find him—when we're ready.'

Colinet was on the point of leaving the hotel to go back to St. Julian Harbour, and Tremaine, too, took his departure. The atmosphere of the Rohane was still like that of a mausoleum although Hedley Latinam's body was no longer in one of the upper rooms. There was little conversation between the guests and such as there was did not go beyond the stilted and the formal. An instinctive agreement seemed to have been reached to keep a silence on the subject of the murder.

He could not blame them. When there was no knowing what damage a chance word might do it was clearly a matter of mutual benefit to keep a guard on one's tongue.

The net might be closing around Gaston Le Mazon, but there were other things that had yet to know the light of day; there was not one of the Rohane's occupants who was not nursing a secret of some kind.

It was disturbing. It made him wonder how much that was unpleasant might be still awaiting the moment of discovery.

That evening Ruth Latinam was very much on his mind. Janet noticed his preoccupation.

'Worried, Mordecai?' she asked, and he nodded.

'Yes. About Miss Latinam.'

'Ruth?' Janet sounded surprised. 'I thought it might have been Nicola Paston.'

It occurred to Tremaine then that he had seen very little of Nicola Paston. She had been present at the funeral and at the hotel but she had been self-effacing.

'Why Mrs. Paston?'

Janet shrugged.

'She rather intrigues me, that's all. I wonder why she's been on the island all this time?'

'Isn't the answer obvious?' Mark said. 'She's over here on holiday.'

'Is she?' Janet pursed her lips. 'She seems to be in the wrong place for a stay of the length she's been making. As a fair young widow she's missing her opportunities. They won't last for ever and a woman needs to be practical.'

Mark Belmore gave his wife an amused glance.

'You're the expert in that line of country, my dear. But what about young Bendall. Isn't *he* the answer to the young lady's long stay in the otherwise arid wastes of Moulin d'Or?'

For answer Janet looked at her visitor.

'All right, Mordecai, *is* he?'

'I'm interested in love's young dream,' he told her. 'I admit it. But I don't profess to be able to recognize it every time I see it, you know.'

His tone was casual but Janet's words had started a new line of thought. Momentarily his attention had switched from Ruth Latinam to her fair-haired companion. He recalled Bendall's words on the cliff, recalled his significant glance in Latinam's direction.

'Behold a fair woman!'

Tremaine frowned. Was he missing something? Was there some further mystery in which Nicola Paston had been involved and which had so far escaped him?

After supper he announced that he would take his usual stroll before going to bed. Mark did not offer to accompany him. He knew now that this was one of the occasions when his visitor liked to deal with his thoughts in silence.

'You know the ropes,' he remarked. 'If Janet and I have turned in when you get back, lock the door behind you.'

Once outside the bungalow Tremaine turned instinctively in the direction of the Rohane hotel. It was quite dark but he knew his way well enough by now.

He had almost reached the incongruous building on the headland with its two or three lighted windows when he saw a figure move away from it. Instead of continuing down the roadway it went towards the cliffs, taking the well-trodden path over the short turf.

There was something furtive about its movements; once clear of the hotel it stopped and waited, as if making sure that no one was following.

Tremaine did not think that he could be observed, for the roadway was in deep shadow at this point, but to make sure he went down upon one knee, crouching in the shelter of the low boundary wall. When it seemed that the figure had satisfied itself and was going on he struck across the rough ground in pursuit.

The way in which the coast sloped away from the headland on which the Rohane hotel was built favoured his purpose; he was able to keep the figure in view without exposing himself.

He saw that it was a woman. He thought that she was wearing a waterproof over a dress of some dark material. She was carrying something in her arms.

Nicola Paston had been occupying his mind so recently that his first impression was that it was she whom he was following, but when the hood of her waterproof fell back as she shifted the burden in her arms there was no glint of fair hair and he knew that it was Ruth Latinam.

As they moved away from the cliff towards the sand dunes it became less easy to keep her in sight and yet not allow her to suspect his presence, for she was evidently fearful and she stopped at intervals to look around her. Several times he was forced to drop hastily upon his face and lie motionless, trusting that she had not seen him.

Rising to his feet again after one such incident he realized that there was someone else approaching. He was aware that his behaviour must look suspicious and he crouched to the ground again until the newcomer should have passed.

It was a man. Peering cautiously towards the roadway he saw that it was Gaston Le Mazon. A brief gleam of moonlight escaping from the cloud barrier showed him the other's face, set and menacing.

What was *he* doing at such a time and place? It was true that Inspector Marchant had described him as wandering morosely in the neighbourhood of the beach, but that had been during the hours of daylight. By now he should have been safely indoors, particularly in view of the suspicion he knew attached to him.

Had he given the police watchers the slip in order to embark upon some nefarious errand?

Fortunately the man did not appear to have seen him but continued on in the direction of the hotel. Tremaine hesitated. Le Mazon was by way of being the suspect-in-chief; would it not be wiser to go after him and see what he was about?

His hesitation was, however, only momentary. It was Ruth Latinam whom he had set out to follow; he would abide by his original plan. He was not to know until later just how fateful that decision was to be.

The girl had left the headland and was traversing the bay. At first he thought that his delay had caused him to lose her, but then he caught sight of her figure in the darkness ahead and hurried after her. No doubt she, too, had seen Le Mazon and had waited for him to go by.

They passed the kiosk where Latinam had once stood waiting and skirted the deserted beach. There was less cover here and he had to allow his quarry to increase the distance between them. She began to climb the rising ground on the far side of the bay and he toiled after her.

It was an area of overgrown fortifications. The weapons had long since been dismantled but the thick concrete had been allowed to remain, and the surface was broken by the mounds marking the gun emplacements, covered now with turf and looking like natural hillocks.

Trying to climb the rough path without noise he lost sight of her again. He waited, and, thinking he heard the faint whisper of voices somewhere near, he dropped to the ground.

At last he risked going on, doubtful now whether he would be able to catch sight of her, but she had not gone far and he saw her standing under the massive concrete lintel of the entrance to one of the emplacements.

She was no longer hugging the parcel against her body; she was holding it by some kind of handle in her left hand. Relieved, Tremaine edged around the grassy mound so that he could see her more clearly.

He caught the rustle of movement behind him but he was too late to do anything about it. Ruth Latinam's motionless figure, the night sky, and the turf about him, rushed together in a remorseless flood of pain and darkness.

18

DEATH OFFERS A SOLUTION

THE noise was the swish of the sea and he was lying on a boat that was swaying gently on the water. But when he stretched out his hand to touch the gunwale his fingers closed upon grass and his aching brain tried desperately to find an explanation for the mystery.

Gradually the swaying died away. He opened his eyes to look up at a grassy bank and beyond the bank the stars. Surprised, he moved, and the ache he had been trying to trace swelled enormously and rapidly into a nauseating pain that was located in his head.

He swallowed and lay still. There was no mystery now. He had been following Ruth Latinam. He had thought that he had not been seen, but in this he had been mistaken. That was why he was now lying here upon the grass with a head that seemed to be alternately expanding and contracting.

He had been careless and he had only himself to blame. But it was a pity about Ruth Latinam. The situation didn't look at all promising.

He propped himself on one elbow and cautiously explored the site of the pain. There didn't seem to be any blood; he had been dealt an unpleasant blow but the damage wasn't serious. The night air would soon revive him completely.

In a few minutes he was able to stand. He was, however, decidedly shaky. Clearly, the sooner he got back to the bungalow the better.

He looked at his watch. It was past midnight. Janet and Mark might be wondering what had happened to him and thinking all kinds of things. Mark had said that they'd probably be gone to bed when he got back but there was nothing certain about it; they might still be sitting up for him, trying to make up their minds whether they should send for the police.

He walked briskly along the road at the side of the bay. He was feeling much better now, but he was in no condition to face a second encounter with whoever had delivered the blow which had knocked him out. He kept a sharp watch for Gaston Le Mazon or any other nocturnal prowler.

The bungalow was in darkness when he reached it. He was relieved that Janet and Mark did not seem to have been disturbed by his long absence.

He let himself in quietly and bathed the side of his head in the bathroom. The skin was scraped and there were the discoloured beginnings of a promising bruise.

He and Ivan Holt would make a pair . . .

His brain worked busily upon the sudden thought. That story about slipping on the rocks had been very thin. Could it be that Holt's bruise and his own possessed a common origin?

He knew now what it was Ruth Latinam had been carrying. A picnic basket. A basket which was probably the identical article he had seen on the desk in Latinam's office on the night of the dance at the hotel.

Holt might well have been on the track of some mystery in which Latinam had been implicated and have been surprised and knocked out just as he himself had been. And Ruth Latinam might be continuing the task upon which her brother had been engaged.

Was that the reason for her strained relationship with Holt? Was that what had lain behind the impassioned appeal he had heard Holt making to her?

When he went into breakfast the next morning Mark Belmore gave him a thoughtful stare.

'Investigations?' he asked.

Tremaine endeavoured to look puzzled and Belmore elaborated.

'The bruise,' he explained. 'And your belated return last night.'

'Oh.' Tremaine dealt carefully with one of the tomatoes on his plate. 'So you weren't asleep?'

'We couldn't settle down until we knew you were safely indoors,' Janet put in. 'Especially after some of the things that have been going on around here lately.'

'You don't have to tell us, of course,' Mark said. 'But we're interested, you know. Can't help it. We feel it's partly *our* murder, so naturally we want to keep abreast with what's taking place.'

'There isn't much to tell. Just that somebody seemed to take exception to my going up to look at the old gun emplacements on one side of the bay. Well, maybe not merely the gun emplacements.'

Tremaine recounted his night's adventure. Mark looked grave.

'I don't like the sound of it. You might have been lying out there all night. Have you any idea who hit you?'

'No. It happened too quickly.'

'There's someone who knows, anyway,' Janet observed. 'Unless Ruth Latinam didn't see what happened.'

'I think she did,' Tremaine returned soberly. 'In fact, I can't see how she could have failed to do so.'

Immediately after breakfast he walked up towards the Rohane hotel. He did not anticipate that the Chief Officer would be there so early—the murder investigation, although obviously of particular importance, was only one of the matters with which he was called upon to deal, and he was tending to leave the affair more and more in Inspector Marchant's hands—but to his surprise Colinet's car was already in the drive.

A great deal of activity seemed to be going on. There were more policemen in evidence than he had noticed the previous day.

He found the Chief Officer standing in the entrance to the hotel in conversation with Inspector Marchant. Colinet saw him approaching and nodded.

'Good morning. Let's go inside, shall we?'

The big man led the way into the office. Tremaine thought that he seemed tense; Inspector Marchant, too, seemed to have something on his mind.

When the three of them were seated Colinet gave his visitor a thoughtful glance.

'That's an expressive-looking bruise,' he commented. 'Mind telling me how you came to collect it?'

'Suppose,' Tremaine countered, 'I said that I'd slipped and banged my head on a rock—just like Ivan Holt?'

'I'd be interested. So interested that I'd like to hear who was holding the rock!'

There was a sudden twinkle in the big man's eyes. He settled his big frame more comfortably in his chair.

Tremaine recounted his story, feeling that the repetition was becoming monotonous.

'H'm.' Colinet placed the tips of his fingers together. He was looking graver again. 'Are you sure it was Miss Latinam?'

'Quite sure.'

'H'm,' said the big man again. 'What do you want me to do?' he added surprisingly. 'Arrest her? Bring her in and ask her all about it? Or what?'

'I certainly don't want you to arrest her. She could say that she didn't have anything to do with the attack on me; that whoever knocked me out, in fact, scared her away from the place immediately afterwards.'

'*And* scared her from telling anybody about it, although you might have been dead for all she knew?'

'Yes, it looks bad. But I'm not sure that it would be a good thing to make an open accusation against her. Not at this stage.'

Tremaine regarded the Chief Officer dubiously, wondering how he would take it. Colinet had to be practical. He couldn't afford to allow himself to be swayed in his duty by any sentimental considerations.

But the big man seemed in no hurry to challenge Ruth Latinam. He remained silent for a few moments, and when at length he did speak it was apparently not the girl who had been on his mind at all.

'About how long was it,' he asked, 'between the time you saw Gaston Le Mazon and the time you were attacked?'

'At a guess,' Tremaine said, 'about twenty minutes.'

'You say that Le Mazon didn't see you and that he went on in this direction?'

'That's right.'

'Suppose,' Colinet said slowly, as though he was trying to convince himself as he spoke, 'that he *did* see you and only pretended he was going towards the hotel. Suppose he turned back on his tracks and followed you to the gun emplacement and that it was Le Mazon who gave you that knock on the head.'

So that was what Colinet was after. Well, it wasn't so wild a possibility. After all, Latinam and Le Mazon had been hand-in-glove, and it looked as though Ruth Latinam was carrying on with what her brother had begun.

Tremaine frowned, thinking back over the previous night's events.

'It could have happened like that, although I didn't see any sign of Le Mazon following me. Maybe I was too busy trying to keep Miss Latinam in sight.'

'Le Mazon wouldn't have had any difficulty in trailing you unobserved,' Inspector Marchant said. 'Not with his experience of moving about at night.'

Tremaine nodded.

'Well, it won't take long to get at the truth. All you need do is to bring him in for questioning.'

'That,' Colinet said, 'is just what we *can't* do.'

Tremaine stared at him.

'He's given you the slip?'

'He's given us the slip all right. But not in the way I think you mean.'

There was an odd note in his voice that brought a sudden suspicion into Tremaine's mind. In an intuitive moment of awareness he knew what was coming.

'Le Mazon,' he said. 'Something's—happened to him?'

'Something's happened all right,' Colinet said grimly. 'Early this morning he was found lying dead at the foot of the cliffs in front of the hotel.'

'Dead!' Tremaine echoed the word. Only a few hours before he had passed Le Mazon near this very place; it was not easy to assimilate the knowledge that the burly figure which had given him a sense of uneasiness with its almost animal menace was now no more than an inanimate shell. He returned the Chief Officer's steady gaze. 'What was the cause?'

'Broken neck, head injuries,' the big man returned briefly. 'Looked as though he'd jumped over.'

'Who found the body?'

'Crevicher. He's in the habit of going for an early swim when the tide's right. When he got down to the beach this morning just after six he found Le Mazon lying among the rocks. He was sensible enough to get in touch with us right away without saying anything to anybody else.'

'There's no question of Crevicher knowing anything about it?'

'None,' Colinet said decisively. 'I've talked to him myself, and I haven't any doubts on that point. He was badly scared over that little episode with the girl a few days ago and he's anxious to get in our good books. Couldn't hand over enough information.'

'Didn't you have a man watching Le Mazon?'

'It isn't easy to keep an eye on a man in the dark and Le Mazon knew this district better than most people. He managed to slip away from his cottage after the light had gone out and he was supposed to have been safely in bed. Our man was still there this morning waiting for him to get up when Crevicher contacted us.'

'It looks,' Tremaine said quietly, 'as though I was the last known person to see Le Mazon alive.'

'You seem to have a flair for it,' Colinet agreed. 'First Latinam and now Le Mazon. Unless, of course, it was Le Mazon who gave you that bruise. In which case it puts Miss Latinam in the limelight.'

'You said that it appeared that Le Mazon had jumped. Does that mean it was suicide?'

'Not necessarily. But the signs certainly point that way.'

Colinet opened the drawer of the desk. Carefully he took out an object which had been inside it and passed it to Tremaine.

'This was found on him. It didn't seem to be the kind of thing I'd have expected him to carry around so I took charge of it. I'm wondering whether you can tell me anything about it.'

With a look of surprise Tremaine took the object from the edge of the desk. It was a cardboard box. Inside it, lying on cotton wool, was a cigarette-lighter. It was a flamboyant piece of work in silver, intricately designed and with an elaborate cap in the shape of a standing lion.

Memory stirred as he gazed at it.

'Mean anything to you?' Colinet asked.

'This was found on Le Mazon's body?'

'Yes.'

'But I'm sure I've seen it before. It was Latinam's.'

The Chief Officer stirred. He gave Inspector Marchant a glance in which there was something of triumph.

'I rather thought it might have been. We've tested it but his prints aren't on it. That's why I tried it out on you. If it belonged to Latinam it makes the whole thing hang together.'

'I see.' Tremaine pushed back his pince-nez. 'Le Mazon killed Latinam, realized that you were after him and that the game was up, and committed suicide by jumping over the cliff. That's the theory?'

'It's *a* theory. We're not banking on it—yet. But it looks reasonable. You saw him for yourself. You know what kind of state he was in. And if we can prove that Latinam had his lighter in his possession when he left here on the night he was murdered we'll be that much nearer home.'

Colinet sounded confident but not triumphant. He also seemed a little relieved, as though an unpleasant duty he had been expecting had not fallen to his lot after all.

'There's still the motive,' Tremaine said. 'For the murder if not for the suicide. Just why should Le Mazon have killed Latinam?'

The big man shrugged.

'Finding the solution is just the beginning. Now we've got the job of making all the pieces match up. There's a long way to go yet but once we know *where* we're going the rest is just plodding routine. We'll get the answers in good time. Is that bruise of yours troubling you?' he added, apparently going off at a tangent.

'No, I hardly know it's there.'

'That's fine. Because I don't want to see the cat among the pigeons. I've put through several enquiries and until the reactions come in and I'm in a better position to know what I'm talking about I'd like the atmosphere to stay as tranquil as possible. If you see what I mean.'

'Yes,' Tremaine said, 'I see what you mean.'

Colinet might feel that he had a pretty shrewd idea about who had killed Hedley Latinam but he wasn't going to allow matters to rest there. If he hadn't had a great deal to say to Geoffrey Bendall and Ruth Latinam it didn't mean that he wasn't bothering about them. He intended to get the whole picture.

Tremaine eyed the Chief Officer with respect. Despite his great bulk that sometimes gave him a deceptive air of lethargy there wasn't much he allowed to escape him.

THE TRUTH IS PLAIN

'AND what,' Ralph Exenley said curiously, 'have *you* been up to?'

Passing the bungalow Tremaine had seen Exenley coming out of his greenhouses and had waited for him to walk over to the entrance gate. Self-consciously he put up a hand to the side of his head.

'You mean this?'

'Of course that's what I mean,' Exenley said with a smile 'What is it? One of the penalties of detection?'

'Well, I suppose that's a fair description, Ralph.'

Tremaine told his story. Exenley set down the basket of tomatoes he had been carrying, his face serious.

'There's no doubt that Ruth Latinam must have known about your being attacked?'

'No doubt at all.'

The accustomed twinkle was missing from Exenley's eyes. He rubbed his dark chin, obviously troubled.

'Have you seen her since?'

'Not to speak to, but I caught a glimpse of her when I was at the hotel just now and I think she must have noticed me.'

'She didn't say anything? About last night?'

'No, I'm afraid she didn't, Ralph.'

'You've told the police, of course?'

'Yes. I was talking to the Chief Officer a few moments ago.'

'What's he going to do?'

'About Ruth Latinam? At the moment he doesn't appear to be going to do anything. But I don't think it's a state of affairs which is likely to last.'

'I see.'

Exenley frowned. Tremaine eyed him understandingly.

'You're concerned about her, are you, Ralph?'

'Concerned?' His companion shook his head. 'I don't know her well enough to go that far. But she strikes me as being a nice girl. I don't like to think of her being mixed up in a bad business of this kind. I wonder where Le Mazon comes into it? You say *he* was about at the time?'

'I rather gathered,' Tremaine said, 'that you hadn't heard the news.'

'What news?'

'Gaston Le Mazon is dead.'

'Dead!' Exenley looked at him incredulously. 'Le Mazon? But if you saw him last night—'

'It must have happened not long afterwards. Crevicher, the barman at the hotel, found his body lying at the foot of the cliffs early this morning.'

Exenley rubbed his chin again.

'That's a new development if you like! I don't mind telling you that Le Mazon was my bet for Latinam's murderer, but who on earth could have wanted to kill Le Mazon?'

'Maybe no one,' Tremaine said. 'Colinet said it looked like suicide.'

'Suicide?' Exenley repeated the word doubtfully. 'Le Mazon wasn't the type I would have expected to commit suicide. Are the police sure about it?'

'Reasonably so. They know that he was in a bad state of nerves.'

'I dare say. But there's a long way to go from that to killing himself by jumping over a cliff!'

'Witnesses were coming forward to say they'd seen him out on the night of the murder and that he'd had an argument with Latinam. He must have felt that the game was up.'

'Even so, the police must have something else to go on.'

'They have,' Tremaine said quietly. 'A cigarette-lighter that's known to have belonged to Latinam was found on Le Mazon's body.'

'Well, that makes the whole thing sound a lot better,' Exenley said, his face clearing. 'Le Mazon *did* kill Latinam. It was a stupid thing to carry that lighter around with him but then he wasn't particularly intelligent. He finished himself off because he knew he was guilty and that the police were catching up with him, If he'd been innocent he'd have stayed and faced things out.'

'That's the line Colinet seems to be taking,' Tremaine agreed.

He left Exenley to his tasks—the constable who had been posted at the bungalow after the discovery of Latinam's body had now been withdrawn and the flood of sightseers had subsided to a spasmodic trickle—and strolled towards the beach. On the way he saw Mrs. Burres. He would have passed her with no more than a nod of recognition, since she had shown no disposition to engage him in conversation on his visits to the hotel, but she stopped when she saw him approaching, barring his path with an air of challenge.

'I suppose you know all about it?' she said.

'About what, Mrs. Burres?'

'He's up there again this morning,' she went on, with a gesture in the direction of the hotel. 'The Chief Officer, I mean.'

He did not think that it was Gaston Le Mazon who was in her mind although she must be aware what had happened. There was a more personal note in her voice.

'It's natural that he should be there this morning. In view of what has taken place,' he told her.

'Because of that man Le Mazon? He was a bad lot by all accounts and that kind come to a bad end sooner or later.' There was no vehemence in her voice; she sounded, in fact, quite disinterested. Tremaine wondered whether she would have been quite so detached about it if she had known of Colinet's murder and suicide theory, and her next words gave him the answer. 'You've been told that Latinam was trying to get rid of me?'

'I've heard that Mr. Latinam asked you if you would find other accommodation,' he said. 'The major, too, I understand.'

'Yes, the major, too. Now you know why I had no room for Latinam. Why neither of us had any room for him,' she added. 'After all this time, to turn us out like that. He got what he deserved and I don't mind who hears me say it.'

She wasn't disinterested now. There was a rasping note of hatred in her voice.

'You'll still be leaving?' he asked, pretending he had not noticed it.

'I wouldn't stay here now,' she said. 'Not for all the pleading. I'm sorry for that girl. I don't think she could do much about it. But it's no good her asking me now. My nephew's told me I can stay with him. I'm going at the end of the week. The police won't want us any more, will they?'

There was a sudden note of doubt in her voice. She clutched Tremaine by the arm.

'They won't want us to stay?' she repeated.

'That's a question I can't answer, Mrs. Burres. This morning's discovery may have changed the Chief Officer's plans.'

He was deliberately non-committal. He knew that she had spoken to him because she was anxious to find out what the police were doing; it would be as well not to enlighten her.

He watched her go toiling up the hill in the direction of the hotel, thinking how masculine she looked; and then he made his way on slowly towards the beach.

It was a clear, still morning. It was the kind of day when it would have been pleasant to sit and laze upon the shore, watching the boats move across the water and the small boys paddling among the pools. It was all wrong that the shadow of murder should lie over such a scene.

Two people were coming up from the rocks. He waited for them to approach.

'Still taking your daily swim, I see,' he remarked as they drew near him.

'The world still goes on,' Alan Creed said, 'though kings and emperors die.'

His manner was casual. Tremaine regarded him thoughtfully.

'I haven't seen anything of you lately. Not since the night of the dance, in fact. It was terrible news about Mr. Latinam!'

'Terrible,' Valerie Creed said. She drew her bathing wrap tighter about her and moved closer to her husband. 'The police—the police haven't found out yet who did it?'

'I think they're very satisfied with the progress they're making.'

They did not seem to have heard about Le Mazon. It had happened very early, of course, and Colinet had obviously handled the affair circumspectly.

'They're behaving as though they're busy enough, anyway,' Alan Creed put in. 'Thought I saw some activity going on up at the hotel this morning. But I can't say that I'm very much concerned. It isn't exactly a pleasant thing, of course, to have one's neighbours getting murdered. Not in the ordinary way. But from what I've heard about Latinam he wasn't altogether a worthy character. No ill of the dead and all that, but you can't help learning things.'

'Things?'

'That's right. Things. Moulin d'Or's quite a place for gossip. I'd have thought you'd have discovered that!'

Creed's smile removed any malice that might have sounded in his words. He did not, however, offer to continue the conversation. He walked on, his arm around his wife's waist, and in a few moments they had passed out of sight along the lane leading to their cottage.

For some time after they had gone Tremaine sat on the rocks staring out over the beach. Queer doubts had begun to rise in his mind. His encounters with Mrs. Burres and with the Creeds had set all kinds of thoughts in motion.

Was it all going to be as simple as Colinet had implied? There were too many loose ends; too many people were unexplained. He was aware of a vague feeling of dissatisfaction with the way in which things were travelling.

When he returned to the Rohane hotel after lunch the feeling had intensified. It might have been due to the way in which Mark and Janet Belmore had taken the news about Le

Mazon. They had been so ready to accept Colinet's theory; so willing to fall in with the solution it provided.

That was the trouble. They'd been too relieved; they'd shown how much they'd been fearing something worse. You couldn't help thinking there might have been reason behind their fears.

The Chief Officer's car wasn't in the drive but automatically Tremaine made his way to the office. The constable outside recognized him and saluted.

'Inspector Marchant's inside, sir.'

The implication in the man's tone was that the inspector wished him to enter. Tentatively Tremaine knocked upon the door. As he pushed it open, however, he caught the murmur of voices from the room. He would have withdrawn but Marchant caught sight of him and called out quickly.

'It's all right, Mr. Tremaine. Come inside. I'm glad you're here.'

The inspector was a well-built man but seeing him in the chair usually occupied by Colinet's massive frame gave him an air that was almost delicate. There was a woman facing him. She had no claims to beauty; her face was weather-beaten and traversed by lines of care; her hands were the coarse, worn, and disfigured hands of a woman bred to toil. She was wearing a patched blouse and a skirt of some rough material that classed her among the under-privileged.

'This is Mrs. Le Mazon,' Marchant explained. 'She came to see the Chief Officer. I've told her that I do not expect he will be here again today but I've telephoned to St. Julian Harbour and arranged an appointment for her in an hour's time. You might like to come along with us.'

The inspector's tone was quite level but the significance of his expression gave Tremaine his clue. Besides, Marchant would not have contacted his superior at St. Julian Harbour for nothing.

'Mrs. Le Mazon has brought fresh information?' he asked.

'Yes,' Marchant said. 'Rather important information.' He saw the woman's eyes go to the newcomer. 'This is Mr. Tremaine,' he added, for her benefit. 'You may speak quite freely in front of him.'

She nodded. It was a heavy gesture in which weariness, sorrow, and resignation all had a part.

'I have heard of Mr. Tremaine,' she said.

'Mrs. Le Mazon has come to tell us,' Marchant went on, 'that she is not satisfied that her husband's death was due to his suicide.'

Her thick, drooping body straightened.

'He would not have killed himself. Not Gaston. That would not have been his way. I was his wife. I *know*.'

There was a quiet emphasis behind the last word that came from a deep, unshakable certainty. Mordecai Tremaine pushed his pince-nez firmly into place. All the doubts which had been vague, disturbing shadows on the mirror of his mind rushed suddenly into solid shape; his own voice seemed to be projected from a stranger whom he was watching with breathless interest.

'I appreciate how you must feel, Mrs. Le Mazon. But there are many things to suggest that it *was* suicide.'

'The inspector has told me. You think that it was Gaston who killed the Mr. Latinam who was here and that when he knew that he had been discovered he threw himself from the cliff. But it is not so. Gaston was my man. I know what he would do. There were many bad things to bring sorrow upon us. But he would not kill.'

'You knew that he and Mr. Latinam were working together? That they were even seen to quarrel on one occasion?'

'But it was not Gaston who killed him,' she said doggedly. 'He wanted to prove that it was not so. That was why he went out last night. He was going to show the police that he had nothing to do with what happened.'

Tremaine leaned forward. 'He went out to meet someone?'

'That is what I understood. He wanted to be cleared. He wanted it to be known that he was not guilty.'

'Yet he was frightened. He acted like a man who knew that he *was* guilty.'

'It is true,' she said. 'He was frightened.' Her voice became softer; briefly the lines were smoothed from her face and she spoke as a mother might have spoken of a troublesome but still beloved child. 'Gaston was not a brave man. He was big and rough, and sometimes he did cruel things. But he was not brave. He was afraid when he knew the police did not believe what he had said. He wanted so much to show them they were wrong. Before he went out,' she said, the tenderness of memory in her eyes, 'he cried in my arms. He called me Marieque. It is the fond name he had for me when we were young. It is many years since I have heard that.'

'But he did not kill himself.'

'No,' she said simply, 'he did not kill himself. He would have been afraid.'

Tremaine was silent. There would be no swaying this woman who was constant in her grief. She had known many bitter years with a man who had been a rogue and who had no doubt ill-treated her when the mood was on him but she could regard him still with a tenderness and a candour that were both unafraid. Truth was in the room, irresistible in its simple force.

'On the night of Mr. Latinam's murder,' he said at last, 'your husband was not at home with you, although he told the police that he was. Do you know why he lied about what was, after all, a very important thing?'

'Yes, I can tell you that. Now that Gaston is dead it does not matter. He said that he was at home because he went that night to St. Jean's. There was a house he knew where the people would not be living because they had gone to the mainland for several days.'

St. Jean's was the adjoining district to Moulin d'Or. Tremaine had noticed a number of fairly large houses in the area.

'He went there to steal?'

'He went to steal,' she said, and bowed her head.

At that moment the constable whom Tremaine had noticed outside knocked at the door and looked into the room.

'The car's here now, sir.'

Marchant nodded and rose to his feet.

'Thank you, Constable.' He glanced commiseratively at the woman. 'Shall we go, Mrs. Le Mazon?'

'One last question,' Tremaine said. 'If you don't mind, Inspector. Did you ever see your husband use a silver cigarette-lighter? Rather a large one, with a cap shaped like a lion?'

She shook her head.

'No, I did not see it. I am sure he did not have such a thing.'

Tremaine glanced at Marchant. It was a significant glance. It was a glance which asked whether Chief Officer Colinet had any inkling of the surprise which was awaiting him.

20

MEMORY PROVIDES THE ANSWER

THE journey to St. Julian Harbour took them half an hour. They drove through the narrow streets to the grey building set on the hill where police headquarters was located. Colinet had just finished a conference with a number of the island's officials and they were conducted to his room without delay.

He took the news surprisingly philosophically. It was impossible to tell from his placid face that a theory he had apparently regarded as established had been swept utterly away.

Clearly he was impressed with the sad-faced woman's testimony. He made no attempt to shake it or to cross-examine her. Only on one point did he ask questions.

'We're still trying to discover, Mrs. Le Mazon,' he said, 'just what your husband's connection was with Latinam. Can you give us any help at all?'

'I am sorry,' she said. 'I do not know it. Most things Gaston would tell me but not this. I think it was because it was something he had not done before and he was afraid of being found out. When he spoke it was just about the man.'

'The man?' Colinet said quickly.

'Yes. There was a man he was to meet.'

'Where was the meeting to take place?'

'Gaston would not say. He was to take his boat. That is all I know of it.'

'It was a meeting arranged by Latinam?'

'Yes. Gaston did not like it. That is why they quarrelled.'

She stopped, patiently awaiting the next question. Colinet sat regarding her thoughtfully.

'There is nothing else?'

'I am sorry,' she said. 'There is nothing else.'

The big man nodded, apparently satisfied.

'I am glad you came to see me, Mrs. Le Mazon. In an affair like this we are glad when people give us help. The police are not your enemies. It is our duty to find out the truth.'

'It is right that you should know about Gaston,' she told him.

Colinet held her eyes. His voice was grave but there was a kindly note in it.

'I would prefer it, Mrs. Le Mazon, if you did not go back to your home. I will arrange for you to stay here in St. Julian Harbour. You have heard of the big house called Le Bel Abri, where elderly and lonely people and those who have no one to look after them may live?'

'Yes, I have heard of it. Le Bel Abri is a good place.'

'They will look after you well and you will have nothing to worry you. I will see that everything that has to be done with regard to your husband is carried out. Later on if you should wish to return to Moulin d'Or there will be no difficulty. Will you do this for me?'

She accepted what he had said without resistance; it seemed that she was without personal desire and prepared to resign herself to whatever might be planned for her.

'I will do it,' she said tonelessly.

When she had gone out with Inspector Marchant Tremaine glanced questioningly at the Chief Officer.

'You think she may be in danger?'

'Two men have been murdered,' Colinet said. 'I'm not running any risks. Whoever killed Le Mazon to keep him from talking may be reasoning that he could have passed on something to his wife, making *her* a potential source of danger as well. And it won't do her any harm to have a spell at Le Bel Abri. Poor creature, I don't suppose she had much of a time of it with that husband of hers!'

'I thought,' Tremaine observed, 'that you were more or less satisfied that the case was closed. You don't appear disturbed at the thought that it may be wide open again.'

Colinet smiled.

'I've been in this game too long to be disturbed easily. Certainly I said that it was a reasonable theory that Le Mazon had first murdered Latinam and then committed suicide. But it was no more than a *theory*. There were still plenty of things waiting to be cleared up. I believe I made that point. Anyway, it was a theory that *you* never did have much faith in, wasn't it?' he finished.

'That's true,' Tremaine admitted. 'I didn't feel happy about it. Somehow it didn't seem good enough. I met Mrs. Burres this morning,' he added. 'She told me that she was planning to leave at the end of the week. She was wondering whether you'd allow her to go.'

'I'll have to speak to Mrs. Burres,' Colinet said. 'Maybe I wouldn't have minded but under the latest circumstances I'll have to explain to her how much I'll appreciate her changing her plans and staying a while longer. I'll point out to her that nobody will be leaving,' he added grimly. 'Not just yet.'

By the time Tremaine got back to Moulin d'Or it was clear from the air of the little groups of villagers talking in the streets that the news of Gaston Le Mazon's death was now generally known. He didn't doubt that the visit the dead man's wife had paid to Colinet was also common knowledge. It wouldn't be long before the tide of sightseers poured in again; two murders in the same locality offered an opportunity that couldn't be ignored.

Inevitably the conversation in the bungalow that evening turned upon the topic that was doubtless by now spreading gossip and conjecture throughout the island. Mark and Janet Belmore had invited Ralph Exenley over and the four of them were sitting in the lounge with the evening shadows beginning to fall.

'The Chief Officer's certain that it *was* murder in Le Mazon's case?' Mark asked.

'His wife's quite definite that when he went out last night it was to do something about clearing himself of the murder charge. She swears that he wouldn't have killed himself and if you'd heard her, Mark, you'd be as convinced as I am that she's telling the truth.'

'The inference in that,' Exenley commented, 'is that he went out to meet somebody, and that that somebody threw him over the cliff because he was afraid his own neck would be in danger if Le Mazon talked. Right?'

Tremaine nodded agreement.

'That's it, Ralph.'

'I must say it seems much more likely to me than that Le Mazon lost his nerve and committed suicide. It never did strike me as being much of a solution. Le Mazon wasn't the suicide type.'

There was a faintly inviting note in his voice, as though he was diffident to express himself unasked but would respond to any request that he should reveal what was in his mind.

'You've thought of something, Ralph?'

'Yes,' Exenley said seriously, heaving himself upright in his chair. 'Yes, I have. After you'd gone this morning, Mordecai, I started thinking about your adventure last night when you collected that bruise of yours. You said that when you saw Ruth Latinam, she was carrying a picnic basket, didn't you?'

'Yes, she was.'

'And the other day,' Exenley pursued, 'you happened to mention that you'd been looking at the old windmill and you asked me if anybody used it. You said you'd seen crumbs on the floor as if somebody'd been having a picnic meal.'

'That's right.'

'Suppose Latinam had been taking food to the mill? Suppose, now that he's dead, that his sister is going on for some reason with what he was doing?'

'It's possible,' Tremaine said slowly. 'On the night of the dance at the hotel I got into Latinam's office by mistake. There was a picnic basket on his desk, and I'm pretty certain that it was the same basket that Ruth Latinam had last night. But last night's affair didn't take place anywhere near the mill.'

'In any case,' Janet interposed, 'why on earth should either of them want to carry picnic baskets around?'

'It's a long shot,' Exenley said diffidently, 'but I've a feeling there's something in it. What about that fellow who broke out of Parkhurst prison a short time back?'

Tremaine gave him an intent glance.

'You mean Marfield?'

'Yes, that was his name. He hasn't been laid by the heels yet, has he?'

'No, I don't think he's been recaptured. I haven't noticed any report of it.'

'He seems to have thrown the police off the scent pretty thoroughly. There've been all kinds of rumours about what's happened to him. He could have gone to earth anywhere—even here.'

'In other words, Ralph,' Tremaine said quietly, 'you're suggesting that Marfield's been hiding in the mill—here under our noses? That until Latinam was murdered he was keeping an escaped convict supplied with food?'

'Well, I'm suggesting that he used the mill until you and young Holt started taking too close an interest in it. After that he decided it would be safer if he found a new hiding-place. That's why Ruth Latinam was taking a picnic basket to the gun emplacement.'

'It fits all right, but it's certainly a long shot. Just because Marfield's prison-break on the Isle of Wight seems to have coincided with Hedley Latinam's habit of carrying picnic baskets around it doesn't follow that the two things are connected.

There may be all kinds of other explanations for Latinam's behaviour.'

'And for his sister's keeping it up now? I know it *sounds* like a long shot but is it really so wide of the mark? Latinam was a queer type. Where did he come from? Why wasn't he very concerned about making his hotel a paying proposition? Why did he want to get rid of the major and Mrs. Burres? If he was such an odd customer, why *shouldn't* he have been mixed up with Marfield's getting out of prison?'

'It was a tremendous risk to take. Suppose Marfield had been traced?'

'I dare say he thought of that and took care to cover his tracks. If the police had managed to catch up with Marfield there wouldn't have been any evidence to connect him with Latinam, even if there'd been a good deal of suspicion. Besides, if Latinam was used to being on the shady side of the law I don't suppose he'd have looked upon it as being such a risk.'

'You're putting up a good case.' Tremaine settled his pince-nez firmly into position. 'But what about the murder? How does *that* fit into the picture?'

Exenley shrugged.

'I wouldn't know,' he admitted. 'The only thing that occurs to me off-hand is that Marfield and Latinam quarrelled—it was a case of thieves falling out. Maybe Marfield didn't think matters were moving quickly enough and was tired of having to keep under cover; maybe Latinam thought he wasn't getting a big enough rake-off for what he was doing. It came to blows. Probably Marfield didn't mean to strike to kill—that's why he dumped the body in the water tank while he thought things out.'

There was an atmosphere of excitement in the lounge. Janet and Mark had caught something of Exenley's enthusiasm as he had been developing his theory and were leaning forward eagerly.

'It explains Gaston Le Mazon,' Mark said. 'His job was getting Marfield on the island. That's what was behind those lights you saw off-shore and it's why he had to use his boat.

He rowed out to the ship that had brought Marfield down-Channel and took him to the old mill. *That* was the tie-up with Latinam. He was the obvious man for Latinam to use.'

Janet took up her husband's account.

'But it was too big for Le Mazon. He was a crook in a small way—just a local smuggler—and he got scared. He tried to back out and Latinam wouldn't let him. And then, after the murder, he was afraid to say anything about Marfield because of the part he'd played; that's why you frightened him when you talked about the mill and the lights. He tried to put suspicion on to Bendall at first, and then, when he realized that the police didn't think his story was good enough he saw that there was nothing else for it and he did go out to try and find Marfield.'

'Only Marfield got in first,' Mark finished, 'and made sure that Le Mazon wasn't going to talk.'

Tremaine looked from one to the other of them with a smile.

'You've thought up a plausible theory. But what about the lighter?'

Mark looked puzzled.

'The lighter?'

'Latinam's cigarette-lighter that was found on Le Mazon's body.'

'Obviously,' Exenley said, 'it was put there by Marfield to send everybody off the scent. He took it from Latinam when he killed him and left it with Le Mazon so that it would support the theory that Le Mazon was the murderer and that he'd thrown himself off the cliff when he'd realized the game was up.'

'The trouble is,' Tremaine said, 'it puts Ruth Latinam in a very awkward position. The implication is that she's now aiding her brother's murderer.'

'That's true enough,' Exenley said, with less enthusiasm. 'That's the part I don't like. But I never had the impression that there was much love lost between Latinam and his sister and perhaps Marfield has some kind of hold over her.'

Tremaine leaned back in his chair.

'So it goes back to the Armitage affair,' he said slowly.'
'That's where the roots of this thing lie. It's—'

He broke off. Suddenly his mind was vibrating with the
exhilaration of the knowledge he had been vainly seeking for
many days and which had now come to him unexpectedly
out of the buried depths of his memory.

'I believe that's it, Ralph!' he breathed. 'I believe you've
hit it!'

For he knew at last where he had seen Valerie Creed before.

21

BACKGROUND PICTURE

THERE was a neat pile of papers on the desk in front of Chief
Officer Colinet.

'The results are beginning to come in,' he observed with
satisfaction, as Tremaine entered the office at the Rohane hotel.
'Trouble is in this business you have to do so much routine
work that takes valuable time and doesn't look spectacular.
Gives the newspapers a chance to ask questions—especially
when there are *two* corpses lying around. But when you
have done it the dividends are worth waiting for.' His plump
forefinger tapped the pile of papers. 'We've been putting the
background to our friend Latinam.'

'Anything—promising?'

Tremaine wasn't quite sure how far Colinet would go in
handing out information; it was natural that the police should
wish to keep some things back. But the big man seemed to
have taken him fully into his confidence.

'Latinam came over here from London with his sister,' he
went on. 'But before that he was in Yorkshire—at a little town
called Milverdale. He was on very good terms with a retired

woollen merchant whose name was Summerfold. Such very good terms, in fact, that when the old man died he left all his money to Latinam. According to this report I've just received, his fortune, after paying death duties and other expenses, came to about thirty thousand pounds.'

Something was stirring in Tremaine's memory. Something that was connected with a sunlit day on a beach and a vague impression of watching the cut and thrust of a duel in which the adversaries seemed to be at pains to conceal their contest.

'Did Summerfold die—naturally?'

Colinet's eyes narrowed slightly. He flicked the papers idly.

'You think he might have been—helped? And by Latinam in particular? It appears unlikely. The report says he died of heart failure and there's no suggestion anywhere that there was any funny business attached to it. The old man had been ailing for a long while.'

'What made him leave his money to Latinam?'

'You had a chance of seeing Latinam for yourself,' Colinet said, 'so you can correct me if I've been misinformed. But from what I've been able to gather he was one of these people who always look cheerful even if they're not. When he gave his mind to it he could be what you might call the perfect host and companion. Just the type, in fact, to appeal to a bitter and lonely old man who'd probably reached the stage when he was ready to react to a friendly word.'

'And that described Summerfold?'

'Before Latinam turned up he'd been living on his own for years. He had a housekeeper but didn't have anything to do with anyone else. He was almost a recluse.'

'He was a bachelor?'

'No—widower. There was apparently some tragedy or other connected with his marriage. His wife died about twenty years ago, but she hadn't been living with him for some while before that. She's supposed to have gone off with another man. That was what made Summerfold shut himself up. He didn't have a good word to say for a woman after that—became a thorough-going misogynist. He was more or less compelled to have a housekeeper, but she seems to have been the vinegary, spinster type and not a real woman, anyway.'

'He must have been a very unhappy man,' Tremaine said quietly. 'And he must have been very much in love with his wife.'

'Rather looks that way,' Colinet agreed. 'To become so bitter about it. You don't usually get reactions of that kind without real feeling.'

'He had no relatives?'

'No very near relatives.' The Chief Officer glanced down at the papers in front of him. 'There was a much younger sister who died some years ago, and a cousin of about his own age. They were both married, and apparently there are children or grandchildren living. They haven't been traced yet, but that shouldn't be a difficult job.'

'I suppose that if it hadn't been for Latinam they would have benefited under the will?'

'They would have taken everything. Summerfold's original will left his money to be divided equally between any of his next-of-kin still living. It was revoked, of course, by his will leaving the whole lot to Latinam.'

'Latinam must have worked very hard on the old man,' Tremaine commented. 'How did he get in touch with him?'

'Saved his life by preventing him from being run over by a car. The story isn't very clear but it was something of the sort. It made Summerfold feel that he owed Latinam a debt, and after that I imagine it was just a case of Latinam playing up to him—sympathy, flattery, pretending to understand him. You know how these things can be done. Especially by an expert in the confidence line of business.'

Tremaine's eyes opened wider.

'Latinam?'

'Yes. He wasn't really the kind of permanent inhabitant we like to have over here. He knew too many of the wrong people. But enquiries are still going ahead about that. It may be a day or two before I've got the whole story.'

'At least we know where he got the money from to buy this hotel,' Tremaine observed. 'And it looks as though we can make a guess at why he wasn't in a hurry to try and make it pay. He wasn't in an ordinary line of hotel keeping.'

'I'd be inclined to set that down as a slight understatement,' Colinet said dryly, 'but I see what you mean!'

'Was Ruth Latinam in Milverdale with her brother when this wooing of Summerfold was going on?'

'The report doesn't say much about her. She seems to have accompanied Latinam to most places, but with Summerfold being a woman-hater I dare say she was kept well in the background at Milervdale until the old man died.' The Chief Officer glanced at his visitor with raised eyebrows. 'You seem very interested in the young lady!'

'Not without reason,' Tremaine said pointedly, and he fingered the bruise on the side of his head.

Colinet's smile was a little grim.

'I rather gather she hasn't had much to say to you about *that?*'

'No,' Tremaine said, 'she hasn't. Do you happen to know,' he added casually, 'what's happening about that man Marfield who escaped from Parkhurst prison not long ago?'

Colinet did not reply for a moment or two. His grey eyes were steady and probing.

'We've been asked to keep a look-out for him,' he returned carefully. 'As a matter of routine. Any particular reason for asking?'

'It's been suggested that he might be over here.'

'In other words,' Colinet said, 'that he might have known Latinam and that Latinam might have had something to do with his escape?'

No, Colinet wasn't asleep. He wouldn't have ignored Ruth Latinam's nocturnal wanderings, nor would he have missed what Gaston Le Mazon's wife had said about the man her husband was to meet.

'It isn't unknown for convicts to get in touch with people outside,' Tremaine said. 'There are various channels of communication—other prisoners being released and taking messages and so on. Maybe if you checked back you might find that among the casual visitors Latinam had in the two or three months prior to his being murdered there were men who'd just been released from Parkhurst—sprung, I believe, is the orthodox term.'

'Is it?' The Chief Officer smiled. 'I'm just a policeman. I don't know all these underworld expressions you criminologists get hold of! You might like to hear, though,' he added more seriously, 'that Ruth Latinam didn't leave the hotel last night. It might have been because she knows you must have told me about what happened the night before, and with her experience of these—er—activities—she might have guessed I'd set a man to watch her.'

'Did you take any other—precautions?'

'This island is honeycombed with fortifications of various kinds—gun emplacements, watch-towers and the like. I just haven't the men to cover them all, and even if I did set the whole place by the ears and order a general search it wouldn't be difficult for anyone using them as a hiding place to slip away somewhere else until the fuss died down. But that doesn't mean, of course, that I don't know what to look for.'

Tremaine recognized the implacable determination in his words. The machine would advance step by step and sooner or later it would achieve its relentless purpose. It wouldn't be spectacular, but it would be sure.

The Creeds were coming up from the water's edge as he left the headland and he came face to face with them as they reached the roadway behind the dunes. He did not think they were anxious for the encounter but there was no avoiding it and Alan Creed clearly tried to make the best of the situation.

'You're being kept busy. First Latinam, and now that fellow La Mazon. Moulin d'Or's getting itself a bad reputation!'

'Yes,' Tremaine said. 'Yes, I'm afraid it is.' He looked into the other's face, smiling and yet somehow hard. 'I'm glad I happened to meet you this morning. Do you mind if I ask you a question?'

Creed gave him a quizzical glance.

'You sound mysterious! But go ahead. I'll risk it.'

'I was wondering,' Tremaine said, 'whether you'd ever heard of a man called Armitage?'

There was a silence. Valerie Creed clutched her husband's arm. Her face looked suddenly haunted.

'That the question?' Creed asked, casually.

'Yes,' Tremaine said, 'that's the question.'

'Then the answer's no, I've never heard of anybody called Armitage. Why did you ask?'

'Because I think that Hedley Latinam knew all about him and I felt certain that *you'd* know all about him, too.'

'Then I'm afraid you're disappointed,' Creed returned coolly. 'Was it important?'

'It could be. As important, in fact, as the matter you were discussing so confidentially with Latinam one day in one of the bays at the other end of the island.'

Creed disengaged himself from his wife's grasp. His face was grim, smiling no longer. There was an expression on it which was reminiscent of the way he had looked when he had been talking to Latinam.

'Look,' he said, 'just take some friendly advice. Two men have been murdered here. It's plain that there are people around who aren't particular about what they do if they think someone's making himself a nuisance. I wouldn't care for anything to happen to *you*.'

Tremaine pushed back his pince-nez. He was glad that it was broad daylight and that there were other people in sight.

'You aren't threatening me?' he said quietly.

'Threatening you?' Creed laughed. It was an ugly sound. 'Why should you imagine I'd do a thing like that? I'm merely looking after your interests.'

He waited, his eyes on Tremaine's face. And then he took his wife's arm.

'Come along, my dear, it's time we got changed. And I'm sure Mr Tremaine must have a great deal to do.'

Tremaine watched them go. Valerie Creed's steps were dragging; he saw her husband's arm go around her for support.

The details of the Armitage affair were coming back to him now. Marfield had gone down for ten years, but Armitage, who had actually forged the cheques which had been the basis of the fraud, had got off with the comparatively light sentence of eighteen months. He had given evidence for the prosecution. But for him, indeed, the police might have been unable to bring the gang to court, and this had been taken into account when sentence had been passed.

There had been much speculation as to the reason for Armitage's behaviour; certain of the more sensational Sunday newspapers had written up the case with a good deal of embroidery, which was one cause of its having become so well known to the general public.

It had been stated that Armitage had fallen in love; that a woman had been responsible for his repentance, and that she had agreed to wait for him until he came out of prison.

Such a touch of romance, especially since Armitage had admittedly been unaware at first of the true nature of Marfield's activities, had naturally been news. There had been photographs of the woman concerned. And the woman of those photographs was Valerie Creed.

It was not the name by which she had been known in those days, but despite the blurring of memory Tremaine was certain that she was the same woman. Some of the press photographs had been extremely clear.

Armitage, then, was Alan Creed, released from prison and trying to settle down under another name with the woman who had stood by him and for whom he had betrayed his companions.

And Marfield, the ringleader of the gang, known to be a desperate man, and proving it by the fact of his escape from prison, was probably in the neighbourhood—leading the life of a fugitive and doubtless with the bitterness of hate and the desire for revenge in his heart.

It sharpened the drama to a point at which it seemed inevitable that there should be another grim climax.

If Marfield knew about Creed or Armitage; and Creed knew in turn of Marfield's presence on the island, then sooner or later the paths of the two would cross.

But there were still pieces of the puzzle lacking. *Why* had Latinam linked himself with Marfield? And why hadn't Marfield done anything about Creed? He must have had ample opportunities of taking his revenge undetected.

Tremaine wrinkled his brows, concentrating upon the problem. At the time of the trial there had been a mention of the large sum of money the gang had been known to have accumulated.

Was *that* the solution? Was it possible that Armitage's repentance had not been as genuine as it had seemed? Had the whole thing been engineered with the woman who was now known as Valerie Creed to enable them to make off with the spoils?

It would explain many things. It would explain, for instance, where Latinam came into the picture.

He had known about the affair from the beginning. He had discovered the whereabouts of Armitage and his wife and had promptly followed them and bought the Rohane hotel as a cover for his real intentions. Then he had managed to get in touch with Marfield and had had a hand in the man's escape from the moment of his breaking clear of the prison buildings. It was the help a man received outside the walls which was the most important in ensuring that he stayed at large.

But why had Latinam called in Marfield at all? Judging by that conversation among the rocks he had already been demanding blackmail from Creed. Why had he not kept matters in his own hands and gone on with his extortion as long as the money had been there to collect?

Creed would have paid. He would have paid for the sake of the woman if for no other reason.

Tremaine thought he knew the answer. Latinam had been afraid. He had known that one day Marfield would be released and that when that day came he would require his share of the money he had helped to accumulate.

Merely to have blackmailed Creed would have given Latinam a steady income, but it would have been an uneasy one, overshadowed by the fear of what would happen when Marfield found out. But with Marfield as an ally–with Marfield, in fact, in his debt because of his having connived at his escape–that fear would be removed.

Tremaine drew a deep breath. So far so good. The puzzle was involved, but at least it was possible to make some kind of coherent pattern out of it.

But what about the murders? Had it been Marfield who had killed Latinam? Either accidentally in the course of a quarrel, or deliberately because he had realized that it lay in Latinam's power to hand him back to the police and because Latinam had given him reason to think such a thing might happen? Or–had it been Creed, stung into fury by the realization that Latinam had launched Marfield into his paradise, who had struck the fatal blow?

In which case, where did Le Mazon come into it?

'Are you any nearer a solution?'

He looked up with a start to find himself facing Nicola Paston.

'You look as though you're up against it,' she went on, smiling. 'Can I help you out?'

The sight of her fair hair gleaming in the sunlight overthrew the careful edifice of supposition he had been erecting and left it scattered around him.

Behold a fair woman . . .

'Perhaps,' he said, trying to gather his thoughts. 'Perhaps. I was wondering who might have killed Mr. Latinam and Gaston Le Mazon.'

'Oh.' The monosyllable had a flat sound. 'Oh. I see. In that case I'm afraid there isn't anything I can do.'

'But I think there *is* something you can do,' he corrected her. 'In an affair of this kind there are always a great many loose ends. It's highly important to see that they're gathered up.'

'Loose ends?' she echoed. She was unsure of herself but trying not to let him see it. 'You mean they haven't really anything to do with the case at all?'

'Sometimes they haven't. Sometimes, though, things you thought were loose ends turn out to be very important indeed.' He hesitated. 'I don't want to touch on a subject which may be painful to you, but I've been wondering lately what your name was—before you became Mrs Paston.'

She stared at him for a long while, without speaking, and he prompted her.

'Was it, by any chance—Summerfold?'

The colour went slowly from her face.

'Yes,' she said reluctantly. 'Yes, it was.'

22

THE CLUE IN THE CHURCH

MORDECAI TREMAINE was aware of a sense of urgency. Matters were hurrying to a climax, and he did not want it to be a climax of the wrong kind.

The day was Sunday. He had made up his mind to go to church but it was too early yet for the morning service and he was walking along by the beach. It would help him to calm his thoughts before he entered the little grey church whose tower rose above Moulin d'Or.

Alan and Valerie Creed, Marfield—the dark, brooding Marfield whom he had never seen—and Nicola Paston were inextricably mixed in his mind. The pattern was alternately clear and clouded with mystery.

It was Ruth Latinam who was the cause. He was not sure of her. He was not sure of her motives or of what was going on behind her sombre, haunted eyes.

He did not want to meet any of the people from the Rohane hotel, but it was perhaps inevitable that on such a fine morning he should do so. Near the kiosk, the shutters of which were just being taken down, he encountered Ivan Holt.

The other's face still bore the expression of aggressive wariness that had marked him since Latinam's death. He eyed Tremaine morosely.

'Your police friends don't seem to be getting very far.'

'Sometimes it's necessary for the police to make a great many enquiries before they're in a position to make an open move,' Tremaine returned evenly. 'But when they do move they've made sure of their facts.' He saw the darkening of Holt's face and decided that there was an advantage that might be pressed. 'How did you get on with your own enquiries?'

'What enquiries?' Holt rejoined, so sharply that Tremaine knew that his ranging shot had reached its mark.

'You went to the mainland some days ago. A business trip, wasn't it?'

'Yes, that's right. A business trip.'

'Rather a pity you had to break into your holiday. But you've had quite a long holiday over here so I don't suppose it went too much against the grain.'

Holt's expression was grimmer than ever.

'You seem to be taking a great interest in my affairs.'

'No greater than the police are doing,' Tremaine returned. His air did not suggest that he found anything outrageous in the comment. 'Murder tends to produce an interest in the affairs of anybody who might possibly have been concerned in it.'

He did not wait for Holt to reply but went quickly on in the same conversational tone. He looked harmless and quite benevolent. So much so that it was clear that the younger man was undecided what attitude to adopt.

'The air services are so convenient in these days. It's remarkable how far one can travel even in a comparatively short time. It would be possible to get as far, say, as Yorkshire, do one's business and return here all in the space of a day or two.'

'What makes you mention Yorkshire?' Holt said.

The question appeared to be dragged from him. Tremaine faced him gravely, no longer either harmless or benevolent.

'Because that's where you went, isn't it, Mr. Holt? What did you find out?'

'Nothing,' Holt said, between his teeth. 'Nothing!'

Tremaine did not lower his gaze but he seemed abruptly to lose interest in that particular topic.

'How is Miss Latinam this morning?'

Holt shifted his feet. He leaned backwards slightly, like a boxer who had changed his stance to meet some new form of attack from his adversary.

'She buried her brother the other day. How should she be?'

'She hasn't been looking well, to me,' Tremaine said. 'Quite thin and pale in fact. I think she's been feeling the strain.'

The words sounded innocuous enough but it was clearly not the construction Holt put upon them. His fists clenched.

'Don't you worry about Ruth,' he said tensely. 'Just leave her alone. You hear me! Leave her alone!'

Tremaine stepped back a pace. He looked disconcerted.

'I've certainly no wish to cause her distress. I realize what a very difficult time she's been having. If there's anything I can do to help—'

Holt relaxed. He lost his air of menace.

'I'm sorry,' he said, making a visible effort to control himself. 'I don't know what's wrong with me lately. Feeling the strain a bit myself, I suppose. I've been talking like an ass, haven't I? Please forgive me.'

'Of course,' Tremaine said. 'I know how unpleasant the situation has been. I think we shall all be glad when the police take some definite step.'

'Yes,' Holt said. 'Yes, we shall.'

But the words were insincere. Tremaine watched him go off across the dunes. There was still something that didn't fit; something that lay behind Ivan Holt's jumpiness and the fear that was in his heart.

Holt was in love with Ruth Latinam and he had heard the girl confess that she was in love with him in return. Where, then, was the obstacle?

Had it been Latinam? Not on the surface at least. He had always seemed well disposed towards the prospect of such a union; if his sense of humour had been a little obvious and strained at times he had certainly shown no hostility towards Holt.

Unless that jovial attitude had been a cloak for something unpleasant; something, in fact, frankly antagonistic. Was *that* the reason for Ruth Latinam's reluctance to be drawn into any discussion and for her cool, distant air?

It was a possibility, but on the other hand if she was really in love with Holt she would surely have stood up to her brother over such an intimate matter?

And there was Holt himself to be considered. He wasn't a weak young man who would give up the girl he wanted without a struggle. It wasn't easy to imagine him giving way to Latinam.

Suppose he *had* stood up to Latinam? Suppose there'd been an argument and in the course of it Latinam had been killed?

No wonder Holt might now be showing signs of panic and Ruth Latinam carrying dread in her face!

Gaston Le Mazon might have suspected what had happened. He might have gone to the Rohane hotel with the idea of confronting Holt, and Holt, in desperation, might have become a murderer for the second time in order to avoid detection.

There was a certain plausibility about the theory and yet it didn't wholly meet the case. Surely it would have been quite sufficient for Holt to have taken Ruth Latinam away from the island and left her brother to snap his fingers in impotent rage! There had been no need for violence. Besides, it didn't explain what the girl had been doing near the gun emplacement.

Tremaine turned to retrace his steps in the direction of the church and found himself walking towards Geoffrey Bendall and Nicola Paston.

Since his meeting with her on the previous day Nicola had done her best to avoid him. He thought that she was nervous now; she was clinging to Bendall's arm as if for support.

'So the wires have been humming, eh?' Bendall said, as they approached. 'The tireless sleuths have been busy while the rest of us have been sleeping!'

It seemed, Tremaine reflected, that he was anxious to go straight for the point.

'You've seen the Chief Officer?'

'No. But *you* saw Nicola yesterday.' Bendall disengaged his arm from her hold and slipped it around her waist. It was clearly meant to indicate that they stood together. 'I'm afraid you rather upset her.'

'In what way?'

'By discovering our dark secret,' Bendall said boldly.

'I imagine,' Tremaine said, 'that what you're trying to tell me is that you also are one of the late Mr. Summerfold's relatives?'

'Nicola and I are the only two. My mother was Christopher Summerfold's younger sister. Nicola's father was the son of his cousin. We're the last limbs of the tree.' Bendall's lips twisted. 'War and natural causes have lopped the branches of what was never a particularly sturdy oak.'

'But for Hedley Latinam you and Mrs. Paston would have shared your uncle's fortune?'

'That's the answer,' Bendall agreed. 'I didn't see much of my uncle. He was a queer old bird in lots of ways. His ideas weren't mine and he didn't give my mother the help he might have done when she needed it. But he *was* my uncle. I didn't see why his money should go outside the family.'

'So in spite of the will you decided to try and do something about it?'

'I looked up Nicola and she agreed that the thing was worth trying. If we were cut out of the will, anyway, we could hardly lose.'

'I take it that you didn't embark on such a plan without believing there might be *something* you could do. What gave you such a thought?'

'Latinam,' Bendall said bluntly. 'I knew the whole thing was phoney. The way he got in touch with my uncle by making it look as though he'd saved his life—he probably hired the driver of the car to do it; I've never heard that he was ever traced—and the way he tried to keep on his right side. It seemed to me that anybody who was ready to play that kind of game had most likely been up to shady tricks before and that it would be worthwhile keeping a watch on him. Sooner or later he might put a foot wrong and then *we* might come in.'

Tremaine gave him a speculative glance.

'Do you think Latinam suspected you?'

'I'm not sure. Sometimes I think he may have done. I used to try and get him off his guard by referring to schemes like the one he'd carried out to see if he'd lose his temper and let something slip. I came pretty much into the open once or twice and Latinam wasn't a fool—even if he *was* a large-sized crook!'

'I could tell that there was some kind of duel going on between you and I used to wonder what was behind it. You were after your revenge and you amused yourself by trying to—well, twist Latinam's tail.'

'I suppose you could call it that. It didn't seem to get very far with him, though.'

'Didn't it? Thank you for being frank with me, anyway,' Tremaine said. 'I suppose you *are* being frank?'

'Of course,' Bendall said elaborately. 'What makes you think I'm not?'

'I dare say it's my suspicious mind. It leads me to all kinds of queer thoughts. Why didn't you speak of all this before? It would have made things so much easier.'

'Would it? Before Latinam was murdered,' Bendall said practically, 'there wasn't any point. Nicola and I were playing our own game in our own way; we didn't want to invite outsiders into it. And *after* he was murdered—well, it seemed to be asking for trouble to say anything then.'

'What you mean,' Tremaine observed, 'is that it might have provided you with a motive for having killed him and could therefore have made things awkward for you with the police.'

'I suppose I do,' Bendall admitted. 'But put yourself in our position. There was nothing to connect us with Latinam or with the old man called Summerfold who'd left him his money. My mother changed her name, of course, when she married, and Nicola is a widow; that's why we thought we were safe in the first place in coming after Latinam. He'd never have cause to suspect us from our names. There wasn't any purpose in starting up a lot of scandal that didn't have any bearing on the case.'

'Is it certain that it *wouldn't* have had any bearing?' Tremaine studied them both gravely. 'You *didn't* have anything to do with the murder?'

'Don't be absurd!' Bendall protested. 'What did we have to gain by killing Latinam. *That* wasn't likely to get us the money. Even if we could have been certain that he hadn't made a will it wouldn't have brought the money back in our direction.'

'You might have thought more of revenge than of the money.' Bendall's lips curled.

'I'm not such a fool,' he said curtly. 'Neither is Nicola. Anyway, Latinam wasn't the only one to get himself murdered. Why should either of us have wanted to kill Le Mazon?'

There was, Tremaine thought, quite a sound answer to that, even if Bendall wasn't going to admit that he knew it. Latinam had suspected enough and had been ruthless enough to have been prepared to dispose of both Bendall and his companion. Le Mazon was to have been his instrument; the operation could conceivably have gone into reverse if Bendall had been aware of the plan.

He held Bendall's gaze for a moment or two, and then glanced at his watch.

'Dear me, I must hurry. I've made up my mind to attend service this morning and I hadn't realized it was so late.'

'Time goes quickly,' Bendall said, with a sarcasm he could not restrain, 'when you're hot on the trail.'

Nicola Paston gave him a look of entreaty.

'I think we should be going, Geoffrey. We don't want to detain Mr. Tremaine.'

'No, that's right,' Bendall said. 'We don't.'

On his way to the church in the village Tremaine's thoughts, far from being suitably calm, were once more in a turmoil.

It was plain why Bendall had admitted his interest in Latinam. He had known that it was about to be discovered anyway and he had decided to get his confession in first.

But had he been as frank as he had claimed?

That was a very different matter. Tremaine was certain, in fact, that he hadn't been. Just what had he been planning? He had said something once about things not being as straightforward or working out as he had expected. He had talked about having to stop and think when you found that you couldn't have what you wanted without doing damage in another direction.

He hadn't taken the trouble to come to the island with Nicola Paston merely for the purpose of baiting Latinam. He was too intelligent to be satisfied with that kind of arid revenge; he had been after something more.

Behold a fair woman . . .

Once again the phrase came back to his mind and with it a memory of Nicola Paston walking over the cliffs. Why had Bendall used that expression? Where did it *belong*?

Colinet was undoubtedly being confronted with a wide choice of suspects now.

Mrs. Burres and Major Ayres; hating Latinam for what he had done to their security, and Mrs. Burres at least in a hurry to get away from the island and the police investigations.

Ivan Holt and Ruth Latinam; in love with each other and yet on uneasy terms, with Ruth Latinam making furtive journeys, perhaps to aid an escaped convict, and Ivan Holt labouring under some fear he would not disclose.

Geoffrey Bendall and Nicola Paston; robbed of their inheritance and joining forces to pursue the man who had been responsible, Bendall pretending frankness because he knew it was inescapable but still retaining a secret.

Valerie and Alan Creed; trying to build a new life away from the surroundings they had known and finding the past seeking them out, with Alan Creed grim and bitter under the threat of blackmail, maybe knowing that Latinam had brought the man whom he had betrayed out of the prison shadows to haunt him.

And Marfield himself; unseen and unpredictable, lurking somewhere in the background, unable to get away unaided, and maybe awaiting his chance to seize his revenge.

Yes, the choice was wide enough.

It was very cool in the church. It was a place of refuge, and it was a refuge now that he needed, for the time he dreaded was very near. The time when a human being was to be faced with judgment.

This was the fixed, immutable end, and it filled him always with despair since it was at odds with all that was sentimental in him. Sometimes it was in the open spaces that he found solace, with the sea and the sky or the still countryside around him; sometimes, as now, it was in the mellow sanctuary of a church.

The lesson was from the twelfth chapter of Genesis. It was the story of Abraham's going down into Egypt because of a famine in the land of Canaan. He sat listening to the deep, resonant voice reading the words.

'And it came to pass, when he was come near to enter into Egypt, that he said unto Sarai his wife, Behold now, I know that thou art a fair woman to look upon:

Therefore it shall come to pass, when the Egyptians shall see thee, that they shall say, This is his wife: and they will kill me, but they will save thee alive.

Say, I pray thee, thou art my sister: that it may be well with me for thy sake . . .'

One phrase detached itself from the rest to emblazon itself upon his mind.

Behold . . . a fair woman . . .

Truth blazed around him. Not Nicola Paston. Not Nicola, after all, but Ruth! That was what Bendall had meant. That was why he had looked at Latinam!

Not Nicola, whose fair hair had gleamed in the sunlight, but the dark, haunted Ruth, who was also fair to look upon.

The pieces were tumbling into place now. Summerfold, the woman-hater, leaving his fortune to the man of dubious character who had schemed and wormed his way into his confidence; Mark Belmore saying that when Hedley Latinam and his sister had arrived on the island there had been unsavoury rumours concerning them; Bendall taking such pains for such little apparent satisfaction and talking about doing damage where it had not been his intention.

Yes, it all fitted. It fitted too neatly to be anything other than the truth.

At first Ruth Latinam had been no more than a name to Bendall; now she was a person. A person whom he could not willingly harm, despite the villainy of the man to whom she had been married.

Unobtrusively Tremaine rose to his feet. He was glad he had chosen a seat near the back of the church. There were one or two curious glances at his strained face but he managed to reach the doorway and the open air without attracting too much attention.

He could not have stayed. For one thought was now clamouring at the gate of his awareness to the exclusion of all others.

Ivan Holt might have had little motive for killing Hedley Latinam in order to marry his sister. But how deadly a motive for murder he had possessed if she had instead been Latinam's wife!

23

THUNDER IN THE AIR

MARK BELMORE watched his guest stub out nearly a third of the cigarette he had been smoking at the conclusion of their evening meal.

'Things are beginning to stir, aren't they, Mordecai?' he remarked quietly.

'Yes, Mark, they are,' Tremaine returned heavily. 'It's always a bad business when it gets this far.'

'Colinet thinks he's nearly home?' queried Ralph Exenley.

He had been invited over for the evening and occupied the fourth place at the table.

'Surely that's a good thing rather than a bad one?' he went on. 'Nobody likes to think a murderer's running around loose!'

'That's true enough, Ralph. It's just that I'm not sufficiently hardened to it. I haven't been a professional who's had to learn to take such things for granted. When I know that a human being is coming to the end of the road—even a human being who's broken the law in a terrible way—I can't avoid feeling depressed.'

Exenley nodded sympathetically.

'I know what you mean. It tends to break down your belief in the ultimate goodness of things, but evil does exist and it's as well to face it in the end.'

'Are you going up to the hotel again?' Janet asked.

'Yes,' Tremaine told her. 'The Chief Officer asked me to come back. He's been there practically all day himself.'

'Then he *does* expect something to develop,' Mark said decisively. 'I say, Mordecai, you're looking as though you oughtn't to go too far on your own. You've been taking it too hard. Besides, after what's been happening lately I don't think it's altogether safe outside. Why not let Ralph go along with you for company?'

'A good suggestion,' Janet said enthusiastically. 'Ever since you were attacked the other night I've been scared every time you've gone out. And I'm sure Ralph won't mind.'

'No, of course not,' Exenley put in. 'I'd rather like the chance to look in on things—especially if the Chief Officer's expecting something to happen.'

They walked up the road together. The strength had gone out of the sun but there was still an hour of daylight left.

'You're sure this isn't putting you out, Ralph?' Tremaine said. 'I know you don't get around too much as a rule and there'll be quite a crowd at the hotel.'

Exenley grinned.

'Even a recluse like me doesn't turn down this kind of opportunity. You don't think I'll be in the way?'

'Of course you won't,' Tremaine returned confidently.

He was not as certain as he tried to sound, however. He wondered how Colinet would take it. Policemen didn't care to have the scene of their operations cluttered up with spectators.

The big man came through the main doorway to meet them as they reached the hotel; obviously he had seen their approach. His glance rested fleetingly but curiously upon Exenley.

'You know Mr Exenley, of course,' Tremaine said hastily, in an endeavour to forestall any objections. 'You don't mind his being here?'

The Chief Officer's hesitation was not pronounced enough to be uncomfortable.

'Not if he has your backing. Anyway, it was his water tank. I dare say he feels a personal interest!'

Tremaine felt relieved. Colinet wasn't going to be difficult. Perhaps it was a sign that he considered the situation to be well under control.

The big man evidently did not wish to go back into the building. They strolled with him across the turf at the side of the hotel.

'I don't think it will be long now,' he remarked.

'Miss Latinam?' Tremaine queried.

'She's showing signs of breaking. Some of the others aren't in much better shape.'

'She hasn't been out?'

'Not without one of my men very obviously in attendance. She hasn't been able to do—what she may have wanted to do.'

Colinet looked in Exenley's direction. He raised his eyebrows a fraction.

'It's all right,' Tremaine said. 'Ralph knows all about it. He couldn't help seeing what happened to me the other evening.'

He indicated the now faint bruise on his head. Colinet nodded, satisfied.

'It's that chap Marfield, isn't it?' Exenley said diffidently. 'The one who escaped from Parkhurst?'

'Well, it *might* be,' Colinet returned. 'We haven't set eyes on him yet, so officially we can't say. But there are often things we know but don't talk about officially because we haven't the necessary proof.'

Tremaine adjusted his recalcitrant pince-nez. They had reached the corner of the hotel now and were looking out over the cliffs towards the water.

'If it *is* Marfield,' he said slowly, 'he's been depending on Ruth Latinam for food and perhaps for aid of another kind. If he doesn't get it—or if he doesn't see anything of her—it's bound to bring him out of hiding. Even if he isn't in immediate danger of starving he'll be compelled to try and find out what's happening. He daren't risk letting too much time go by in ignorance.'

'That's the way *I* see it,' Colinet agreed. 'And when he *does* show up he'll find we've arranged a reception party for him.'

'You seem to have the whole thing well organized,' Exenley said admiringly. 'Force Marfield into the open and your murderer's in the bag.'

'If Marfield *is* the murderer,' Tremaine said, and the Chief Officer gave him a sharp glance.

'You don't sound too happy about it.'

'I'm not,' Tremaine admitted. 'I know it looks like the obvious answer, but it seems such a stupid thing for Marfield to have killed Latinam, the man he was depending on.'

'Crooks *are* stupid,' Colinet observed dryly. 'Most of them, anyway.'

Tremaine was still staring across the cliff, his thoughts plainly unresolved.

'Did you discover anything about the will?'

'You were right there,' Colinet said. 'There was a clause in it in which Summerfold wrote down what he thought about women and said that he wanted nobody who'd been foolish enough to get married to benefit from his estate. He certainly had a bee in his bonnet over it; his wife going off as she did seems to have sent him properly off his balance in that respect. He laid down that Latinam was to come into the money provided that he wasn't married—as he understood was the case—and provided that he didn't get married within two years of his becoming entitled to the legacy. If Latinam broke the conditions the money was to go to Summerfold's nephew, the son of his late sister, Mary Summerfold. Bendall wasn't actually mentioned by name. If *he* was married everything was to go to charity.'

'So *that's* what brought Bendall here.' Tremaine gave up his unseeing stare over the cliff and turned to Colinet. 'He may not have known definitely that Latinam was married to the woman he was passing off as his sister but he suspected something of the kind. It wasn't just the desire to revenge himself on Latinam that was in his mind; there really was a chance of getting hold of his uncle's fortune.'

'But couldn't a will like that be challenged as unreasonable?' Exenley asked, frowning.

'I dare say it could,' the Chief Officer agreed. 'I'm not competent to express a legal opinion on it, but the conditions sound drastic enough to have given Latinam grounds for disputing them, even if Bendall did manage to prove that he'd been married all along. In view of the other circumstances, though, Latinam couldn't have felt very sure of himself. Bendall must have given him a bad time.'

'Where does Mrs. Paston come into it?' Exenley said. 'She didn't stand to benefit in any case. It looks as though Bendall was prepared to go shares with her although he didn't need to do so. Surely that's a point in his favour?'

'Another point in his favour,' Tremaine observed, 'is that when he came to know Ruth Latinam he tried not to hurt her. He knows that she and Ivan Holt are in love and he's been keeping quiet about the marriage to avoid throwing suspicion on Holt.'

'He's been keeping quiet about several things,' Colinet remarked significantly.

'What about Mrs. Burres?' Tremaine said, changing the subject a shade too obviously. 'Any reaction there?'

'You don't get much reaction from a piece of granite,' Colinet said. 'She sits there knitting like the figure of doom. But let's go inside. The light's fading and you're making things sound too complicated. I hate complications!'

They went into the hotel and walked through into the lounge. All the others were there, sitting about the room in the increasing shadows, apart from each other, not speaking, and yet linked by an atmosphere of tension that was frighteningly palpable.

There was a stir of movement as Colinet's massive form loomed in the doorway. Suspicion, fear, hostility—they were all there in the glances that met them as they entered.

Tremaine looked around. At Mrs. Burres, shapeless, incalculable, the knitting in her lap. At the major, his appearance gaunt and haggard in this light, clearing his throat with nervous uncertainty.

At Geoffrey Bendall, nothing cynical in his attitude now, his features sharply outlined, his head thrust forward. At Nicola Paston, more composed than any of the others, her fair hair set against the windows leading to the terrace behind her.

At Ruth Latinam, pale, nervously twisting a handkerchief in her lap. She did not meet his eyes. Not by a single word had she referred to that incident on the cliff, but that she was well aware of what had happened was plain enough.

And he looked at Ivan Holt, sullen and removed, an unspoken aggression in his face.

Colinet was right. This was the brooding before the storm.

There were other players in the drama who were not yet present. There was Marfield. There was Valerie Creed, and there was her husband, Alan Creed, who had revealed once already the desperation in his mind.

Ivan Holt thrust himself suddenly from his chair.

'Think I'll go out,' he said shortly, addressing no one and everyone.

Ruth Latinam's eyes widened. They were dark with terror.

'No, Ivan. No, don't go out—please!'

Holt disregarded her.

'Can't stay here,' he muttered. 'Atmosphere's stifling.'

He pushed open the windows to the terrace and they watched him pass out of sight along the building. Ruth Latinam made a movement as though to follow him and then relaxed again. There was despair in her attitude. She was, Tremaine thought, waiting for something.

The light was going quickly now. Colinet had said nothing since he had entered the room; he, too, seemed to be waiting.

It was not necessary for him to wait for long.

24

THE PATTERN LOOKS NEAT AND TIDY

FROM somewhere in the building there came a sudden cry and the crash of glass. It was followed by the sound of a piece of furniture thudding to the ground.

As though a tableau which had been becoming impossible to maintain had dissolved at the peremptory wave of a producer's hand, the room filled with movement. Tremaine thought that his own reaction had been swift but he was behind Ruth Latinam as she rushed in panic through the door.

The room Hedley Latinam had used as an office was in disorder. The desk had been overturned and the window had been broken. Ivan Holt lay crumpled in one corner.

Ruth Latinam went to her knees at his side. She heard Tremaine behind her and twisted to face him, wildness in her eyes.

'He isn't dead?' she cried, clutching at him. 'Say he isn't dead!'

He looked down at the man on the floor.

'No,' he said reassuringly, 'he's a long way from dead. Just knocked out for a moment or two, that's all.'

Holt opened his eyes. He saw Ruth Latinam and instinctively he reached up to her. And then he saw the big form of Colinet and the guarded look settled in his face.

'What was it?' the Chief Officer said. 'What happened?'

Holt's lips tightened.

'I don't know,' he said. 'I didn't get a chance to see.'

'It was Marfield,' Ruth Latinam said desperately. 'I know it was Marfield. Tell them, Ivan, tell them!'

The expression on Holt's face changed; they saw the bewilderment there as he stared up at her.

'He swore he'd kill you if I said anything,' she went on. 'That's why I couldn't go to the police. I knew he meant it. I was afraid for you, darling—so very afraid!'

Holt struggled up. His arm went around her.

'I caught him in here,' he said crisply to Colinet. 'He knocked me down and made a bolt for it. He can't have got far.'

The Chief Officer was already turning towards the doorway, his bulk thrusting a way through the people blocking it and the passage beyond. Tremaine was aware of an upsurge of relief. It had been fear for her lover and no sinister motive which had lain behind Ruth Latinam's behaviour. She had known Marfield to be a man who might shrink from no crime and she had not dared to ignore his threats.

He did not think that she had suspected the escaped convict of having killed her husband; her first reaction had been that it had been Holt who had been responsible for she had known that he suspected Latinam of menacing her in some way.

That was the reason for the dread she had shown on that morning when she had heard of Latinam's death. She had known instinctively that it was murder, although the word had not been used, and at once her mind had gone to Ivan Holt. It had been the knowledge that Holt was intent on probing the mystery in which she was involved and might be in danger that had taken her out in search of him on the night of the murder.

But she had said nothing that might have betrayed him, and rather than expose him to Marfield's threats she had run the risk of bringing herself under suspicion. No doubt it was for the sake of Ivan Holt, too, that she had kept silent about the incident at the gun emplacement and had not revealed to the police that the dead man had been not her brother but her husband.

Looking at them now, Holt still with his arm about her waist, Tremaine thought that the doubts had gone and that from this moment they had a chance to make their own way together. His sentimental soul expanded. He left them and went after Colinet.

He found the big man outside, issuing crisp orders. It was clear that the machine was going into prearranged action; Marfield might have emerged undetected from his hiding place but he was going to need more than a little luck to get back to it.

'Where is he? Which way did he go?'

He turned, thinking that the question had been addressed to him, and found himself staring into Alan Creed's set face. His wife was with him, pale and alarmed, clinging to his arm.

Creed was not looking at him and he realized then that the question had been meant for Exenley who had gone out at the same time as the Chief Officer.

'Not sure,' Exenley said. 'Over that way, I think,' he added, with a gesture. 'But look here, this is no place for you. Go back, both of you.'

Before Creed could reply there was a shout from the direction of the roadway. A wildly running figure broke out of the semigloom, making for the headland.

'We've headed him away from the road,' Colinet said exultantly. 'We've got him now!'

Both Exenley and Creed automatically followed his pointing finger, Creed turning away from his wife. Tremaine stepped quickly to her side.

'What happened to the money, Mrs. Creed?' he said urgently. 'The money from the Armitage affair that Marfield came here to get!'

'It went back,' she said tremulously. 'Every penny of it. I told that man Latinam but he wouldn't listen. He was trying to blackmail Alan.'

She realized then that she had betrayed herself. She gave a gasp and her hand went to her lips. Tremaine touched her arm with a gentle pressure.

'It's all right,' he said. 'There's no need to worry. I don't think anyone will want to call back the past—at least, not as far as *you* are concerned.'

Another section of the puzzle had been completed. It *had* been the prospect of the loot from the Armitage affair which had lured Latinam to the island and later caused him to aid in Marfield's escape.

The purchase of the Rohane hotel had been merely a blind. He had had no interest in it as a going concern; that was why he had tried to get rid of Mrs. Burres and Major Ayres, first by freezing them out of the circle of the other guests and then by giving them official notice to go.

Resenting it, and suspicious of Latinam, they had spied upon him, no doubt in the hope of discovering something which would enable them to turn the tables. It had been the realization that their actions were in turn likely to arouse suspicion which had accounted for their strained behaviour since the murder.

If Latinam had known what they were doing it had doubt-less caused him no more than a cynical amusement. He had been a callous and cunning rogue. The manner in which he had publicly tried to throw Ivan Holt and his wife into each other's arms when he had been aware of the agony he was causing was sufficient proof of that.

Tremaine realized that Ralph Exenley was trying to attract his attention.

'There you are, Mordecai! There's your murderer!' Exenley pointed across the headland where they could see the running figure making for the edge of the cliff. 'Marfield, after all! Everything neat and tidy. Couldn't wish for anything better!'

Creed moved forward.

'I'll get him—'

Exenley caught him by the shoulder and pulled him back. 'No, he's armed! Look to Valerie. I'll see to this!'

He began to run across the headland. Colinet's big form stirred into protesting action.

'Come back!' he bellowed angrily. 'Leave him alone! It's a job for my men to do!'

Already the policemen who had been posted in a cordon that had pinned the hotel and its grounds against the sea had closed in, and now they were slowly but systematically narrowing the space left to the fugitive. Exenley paid no heed, and Tremaine put a hand on the big man's arm.

'Let him go,' he said quietly. 'He knows what he's doing.'

Marfield's blind flight had brought him now to the very edge of the cliff. He stopped, realizing that he was trapped. With his back against the sky he stood waiting; they were not close enough to see him clearly but they knew he must be panting from the effort he had made, drawing desperate, sobbing breaths into his lungs.

Exenley caught up with him. They saw Marfield's right fist swing out in a lunging blow and then he turned and ran once more.

This time it was along the crumbling surface of a narrow strip of the headland where erosion had gouged a great gash in the rock so that they could look across at a thin sliver of cliff which was almost detached from the rest.

Then he turned at bay and Exenley ran at him.

'Oh, take care!' Valerie Creed cried out.

The two figures swayed and struggled. A sudden sharp report lashed across the gap. One of the figures detached itself in a queer, crumpling movement and fell outwards.

'Marfield pulled his gun!' Alan Creed exclaimed. 'Ralph managed to turn it back on him and the bullet went into Marfield's own body!'

Valerie Creed was peering through the gloom, her eyes fixed with strain. Tremaine looked at her, at the line of the chin, the urgent upthrust of the head. He was sure now. The last doubt had been removed.

'Look out!' Colinet called sharply. 'Watch the edge, man!'

Even as he spoke, Exenley, moving along the narrow path, missed his footing and slipped helplessly over.

Valerie Creed screamed. They saw Exenley reach out desperately as he fell for an overhanging lip of rock. He hung there, his whole weight supported only by one hand.

Many things were in Mordecai Tremaine's mind in that moment which was the climax of the drama.

Hedley Latinam setting that drama in motion by following Alan Creed and his wife to the island. The Creeds choosing it as their retreat because Ralph Exenley—whom they knew by another name—had gone there before them and for the same purpose.

Latinam referring to Smooth Jonathan because he had known that what he had said would certainly go back to Exenley. Smooth Jonathan who had always avoided falling into the hands of the police and who had had a daughter.

Latinam bringing fear and blackmail into what had once seemed a secluded haven where the past could be forgotten . . .

Probably Exenley had paid until he had realized that Marfield had been brought to the island. And then he had decided that he must deal with the menace once and for all.

He had declined the invitation Janet had sent him for the night of the murder, not because his appointment in St. Julian Harbour had been so important but so that there should be no difficulty about his meeting Latinam. It had been Exenley for whom Latinam had been waiting at the kiosk.

Tremaine recalled the words the man had used.

'*You're early. She must mean a lot—*'

Smooth Jonathan's daughter meant a lot to him. So much that he was ready to submit apparently without protest to blackmail in order to protect her from unhappiness. That was what Latinam had been going to say.

There had no doubt been other secret meetings before. Tremaine was certain that it was Latinam whom he had encountered on that first night on the island, engaged upon one of his nocturnal excursions to meet someone with whom he had dealings he did not wish to become known—perhaps Le Mazon on that occasion, but possibly even Exenley.

He was satisfied now about the familiar and yet puzzling sound he had heard in the distance on the night Latinam had died. It had been the sound of Exenley's pump working to fill his water tank.

Exenley had departed from his usual practice and had not filled the tank immediately after watering that day. He had not done so because of the plans he had made. He had reasoned that it would be easier to thrust a dead body beneath the bars of an empty tank than a tank almost filled with water which would give that body a buoyancy which would make his task a troublesome one, and at a time when he dared not risk delay.

And the tank had been chosen, not to hide the body but to make sure of its early discovery before too many enquiries were set on foot, and to be certain that if Latinam had not been killed already by the blow on the head he had been given then he would very quickly drown.

Exenley had known by then, Tremaine realized, of his own desire to climb the ladder and look into the tank. It had been Exenley's suggestion, in fact, that he should come across for just that purpose on what the man had planned to be the morning after the crime.

Why his own tank? Why draw attention to himself in such a potentially dangerous manner?

It had not been that he wanted to put himself deliberately in peril. He had at any rate hidden the weapon he had used to strike Latinam down, in so successful a fashion that the police had not yet discovered it. He had placed himself in the limelight so that, paradoxically, he should escape it.

He had had too much to risk from a systematic investigation into the antecedents of all the inhabitants of Moulin d'Or. He had planned to put himself so obviously in the foreground that the police would take him for granted, and he had intended, at the same time, to divert suspicion in the wrong direction.

He had been swift to appreciate how useful a friend who had the confidence of the police could be; that was why he had told Chief Officer Colinet all about Mordecai Tremaine. He had estimated the reaction and had foreseen how he might profit by it.

Without making himself too obvious he had suggested that Gaston Le Mazon might be the murderer. Probably he had never anticipated that Le Mazon would be in serious danger; he had been concerned merely with making the trail as confused as possible.

But when Le Mazon, badly frightened, had shown signs of telling the police all he knew—perhaps more than Exenley had at first imagined he knew—he had had no choice but to deal with the man before the danger materialized. That Le Mazon had known very little with certainty seemed a reasonable assumption from the fact that he had not spoken to Colinet, but the story his wife had told was an indication that he had been actively engaged in trying to expand his knowledge.

Exenley, maybe with some such development in mind, had taken Latinam's cigarette-lighter from the dead man's pocket and planted it on Le Mazon—precautions about his own fingerprints had caused him to remove Latinam's as well, but he had expected that so flamboyant an article would be recognized at once. At first he had pretended to be doubtful of the suicide and murder theory, but when a careful question had brought out the fact that the police had found and put the interpretation he had hoped upon the lighter he had accepted it enthusiastically.

Gaston Le Mazon's wife, with her definite statement that her husband had had no thought of suicide but had in fact been anxious to clear himself, had brought that particular solution tumbling in ruins. But Exenley had still had another shot in the locker. There had still been Marfield.

It had not been until after the demolition of the case against Le Mazon that he had suggested that Marfield might be on the island. He had suggested it, of course, because he had known all along, but for his daughter's sake he had been hoping to say nothing; perhaps he might even have aided Marfield to get away when the excitement had died down.

The escaped convict, although an apparently obvious choice, had not been the killer. He had not shown the murderer's ruthlessness.

Tremaine was confident that it had been Marfield, seeing him spying upon Ruth Latinam, who had struck him down that night. And he did not doubt that in some such a similar manner Ivan Holt had received his injury.

If Marfield had been a murderer with his neck in peril there would have been more than bruises to show.

The whole pattern fell into place in Tremaine's mind whilst Exenley hung from the rock. Through blurred vision he saw the supporting arm begin to slip until the last fraction of time when there was space between the outstretched fingers and the crumbled edge of the cliff.

Colinet was already pounding heavily for the path leading to the beach, several of his men at his heels. His heart racing, Tremaine followed them.

Both men were dead when they reached them. The bullet, fired at close quarters, had gone through Marfield's heart; Exenley must have been killed the instant he had hit the jagged rocks among which they found him.

'Poor devil!' Geoffrey Bendall said, looking down at the crumpled body. 'What a ghastly thing to have happened!'

Tremaine thought of the last words Exenley had addressed to him.

'*There you are, Mordecai! There's your murderer! Marfield, after all! Everything neat and tidy. Couldn't wish for anything better!*'

Everything neat and tidy. No need to go digging up past history. That was what he had meant.

He had known that once he had turned the limelight on Marfield the game was up. He had known that it was essential to reach the man before he could talk.

Marfield on the run being accused of Latinam's murder was one thing; Marfield in the hands of the police and willing to tell all he knew would have been vastly different.

And Exenley had known that with Colinet's men concentrated upon the district he couldn't hope to get away with murder a third time . . .

Tremaine pushed back his pince-nez as he faced Bendall.

'Yes,' he said quietly. 'Yes, it was a tragic accident.'

He went back up the path with the Chief Officer, who was panting at the steepness of the climb.

'I suppose,' he remarked, probing, 'that although Marfield can't be brought to trial now he'll still go down in the record as the murderer?'

The big man paused a moment. He gave Tremaine a long, steady look, and then he nodded.

'That way there won't be any loose ends.'

Tremaine fell back a pace or two, pretending that the slope was defeating him. If Colinet was satisfied with that explanation there would clearly be no point in suggesting any other.

When they reached the top of the cliff he saw that the lights were on in the lounge of the hotel and that several people were standing on the terrace. As he drew nearer he saw Valerie Creed. She was very upset and her husband was trying to comfort her.

He was going towards her, wondering what he could say, when he saw the Chief Officer. The big man's eyes were on Valerie Creed, and for so purposeful a man the expression on his face was oddly gentle and understanding.

Slowly Mordecai Tremaine turned away. Colinet was shrewd. He kept in close touch with what took place on the island and there wasn't much he missed.

Maybe he did know, after all.

THE END

FRANCIS DUNCAN

Murder Has a Motive

When Mordecai Tremaine emerges from the little train station, murder is the last thing on his mind. But then again, he has never been able to resist anything in the nature of a mystery – and a mystery is precisely what awaits him in the village of Dalmering.

Rehearsals for the local amateur dramatic production are in full swing – but as Mordecai discovers all too soon, the real tragedy is unfolding offstage. The star of the show has been found dead, and the spotlight is soon on Mordecai, whose reputation in the field of crime-solving precedes him.

With a murderer waiting in the wings, it's up to Mordecai to derail the killer's performance . . . before it's curtains for another victim.

FRANCIS DUNCAN

Murder for Christmas

'Kept guessing to the end, I am left wondering why it has taken so long to discover Francis Duncan . . . With some 20 crime novels to his credit, a relaunch seems long overdue'
Daily Mail

Mordecai Tremaine, former tobacconist and perennial lover of romance novels, has been invited to spend Christmas in the sleepy village of Sherbroome at the country retreat of one Benedict Grame.

Arriving on Christmas Eve, he finds that the revelries are in full flow – but so too are tensions amongst the assortment of guests.

Midnight strikes and the party-goers discover that it's not just presents nestling under the tree . . . there's a dead body too. A dead body that bears a striking resemblance to Father Christmas.

With the snow falling and the suspicions flying, it's up to Mordecai to sniff out the culprit – and prevent someone else from getting murder for Christmas.

'The book nods towards Agatha Christie but retains a crackling atmosphere of dread and horror that will chill the heart however warm your fireside'
Metro

FRANCIS DUNCAN

So Pretty a Problem

Adrian Carthallow, *enfant terrible* of the art world, is no stranger to controversy. But this time it's not his paintings that have provoked a blaze of publicity – it's the fact that his career has been suddenly terminated by a bullet to the head. Not only that, but his wife has confessed to firing the fatal shot.

Inspector Penross of the town constabulary is, however, less than convinced by Helen Carthallow's story – but has no other explanation for the incident that occurred when the couple were alone in their clifftop house.

Luckily for the Inspector, amateur criminologist Mordecai Tremaine has an uncanny habit of being in the near neighbourhood whenever sudden death makes its appearance. Investigating the killing, Tremaine is quick to realise that however handsome a couple the Carthallows were, and however extravagant a life they led, beneath the surface there's a pretty devil's brew . . .

FRANCIS DUNCAN

In at the Death

Mordecai Tremaine and Chief Inspector Jonathan Boyce are never pleased to have a promising game of chess interrupted – though when murder is the disrupting force, they are persuaded to make an exception.

A quick stop at Scotland Yard to collect any detective's most trusted piece of equipment – the murder bag – the pair are spirited to Paddington Station to catch the train to the sleepy town of Bridgton.

No sooner have they arrived than it becomes clear that the town harbours more than its fair share of passions and motives . . . and one question echoes loudly throughout the cobbled streets: why did Dr Hardene, the local GP of impeccable reputation, bring a revolver with him on a routine visit to a patient?

Mordecai Tremaine's latest excursion into crime detection leaves him in doubt that, when it comes to murder, nothing can be assumed . . .

MORE VINTAGE MURDER MYSTERIES

EDMUND CRISPIN
Buried for Pleasure
The Case of the Gilded Fly
Swan Song

FRANCIS DUNCAN
Murder Has a Motive
Murder for Christmas
So Pretty a Problem
Behold a Fair Woman
In at the Death

A. A. MILNE
The Red House Mystery

GLADYS MITCHELL
Speedy Death
The Mystery of a Butcher's Shop
The Longer Bodies
The Saltmarsh Murders
Death at the Opera
The Devil at Saxon Wall
Dead Men's Morris
Come Away, Death
St Peter's Finger
Brazen Tongue
Hangman's Curfew
When Last I Died
Laurels Are Poison
Here Comes a Chopper
Death and the Maiden
Tom Brown's Body
Groaning Spinney
The Devil's Elbow
The Echoing Strangers
Watson's Choice
The Twenty-Third Man
Spotted Hemlock
My Bones Will Keep
Three Quick and Five Dead
Dance to Your Daddy
A Hearse on May-Day

Late, Late in the Evening
Fault in the Structure
Nest of Vipers

MARGERY ALLINGHAM
Mystery Mile
Police at the Funeral
Sweet Danger
Flowers for the Judge
The Case of the Late Pig
The Fashion in Shrouds
Traitor's Purse
Coroner's Pidgin
More Work for the Undertaker
The Tiger in the Smoke
The Beckoning Lady
Hide My Eyes
The China Governess
The Mind Readers
Cargo of Eagles

E. F. BENSON
The Blotting Book
The Luck of the Vails

NICHOLAS BLAKE
A Question of Proof
Thou Shell of Death
There's Trouble Brewing
The Beast Must Die
The Smiler With the Knife
Malice in Wonderland
The Case of the Abominable Snowman
Minute for Murder
Head of a Traveller
The Dreadful Hollow
The Whisper in the Gloom
End of Chapter
The Widow's Cruise
The Worm of Death
The Sad Variety
The Morning After Death

penguin.co.uk/vintage